Jacaranda

Larry Jeram-Croft

Front cover image: Mount Pelle Martinique

Also by Larry Jeram-Croft:

Fiction:

The 'Jon Hunt' series about the modern Royal Navy:

Sea Skimmer
The Caspian Monster
Cocaine
Arapaho
Bog Hammer
Glasnost
Retribution
Formidable
Conspiracy
Swan Song

The 'John Hunt' books about the Royal Navy's Fleet Air Arm in
the Second World War:

Better Lucky and Good
and the Pilot can't swim

The Winchester Chronicles:

Book one: The St Cross Mirror

The Caribbean: historical fiction and the 'Jacaranda' Trilogy.

Diamant

Jacaranda
The Guadeloupe Guillotine
Nautilus

Science Fiction:

Siren

Non Fiction:

The Royal Navy Lynx an Operational History
The Royal Navy Wasp an Operational and Retirement History
The Accidental Aviator

Chapter 1

Deep Caribbean blue; the sky, the sea and the hull of the lean, elegant yacht as she shouldered her way through the long lazy trade wind generated swell. Her bowsprit occasionally dipping into the translucent crests of the approaching waves, her long raked bow then lifting and flinging a bucket full of warm spray over the cockpit spray hood and the man sat half asleep at the wheel.

In the far distance, off the starboard bow, it was just possible to make out the grey loom of an island. According to the electronic navigation screen mounted above the wheel this was St Vincent one of the Windward Islands, slumbering in the sunny distance and like her cousins, lushly wooded and volcanic.

None of this registered on the consciousness of the man in the cockpit. His destination was the next island to the north still concealed by the clear horizon. St Lucia was his home now and after a long season of chartering he was heading back for a haul out and some quiet summer months of boat maintenance and preparation before the season started all over again in November. Not that such a treadmill was a problem for him. Compared to his previous life, he would not swap this new office of his for anything else. It was just that he was sagging with fatigue and all he really wanted was to get the boat alongside and sleep for twenty four hours.

Two very demanding American couples with as much money as energy had kept him and his sole crew on their toes for the last month. An unusually long charter starting from Rodney Bay in St Lucia and heading south through the island chain had ended up a long way away in Bonaire in the ABC islands only three days before. Here he finally waved farewell to his customers and gratefully pocketed a large sum of cash. Unfortunately, his girlfriend, who was also his crew, had decided to fly home and left him to sail the eighty foot boat back on his own. Nevertheless, he smiled inwardly to himself in the knowledge that not only did he now have enough money to keep the boat fully maintained and himself fed over the summer months but that he was completely debt free, both financially and emotionally. Debbie had been a great companion and really excellent at cooking and stewarding for the guests. She was even a handy yachtsman. Unfortunately, their relationship had evolved in the wrong direction as the season progressed. Yachts, even large ones, get smaller the longer one lives on board and by the end they both had to make every effort to be polite in front of the guests. He doubted he would see her again but he was not sad, this would allow him to concentrate solely for the next few months on the greatest love of his life, his wooden sailing masterpiece.

Jacaranda was a beautiful wooden built traditional looking eighty foot cutter. Her design was based upon the sleek lines and elegant curves of a 1930's racing yacht. Her one towering mast currently held a reefed mainsail while her foresail was fully deployed out along her bowsprit and sheeted free, making the best of the warm south easterly trade winds as she reached effortlessly at ten knots towards St Lucia. Although an old fashioned classic to the eye, in her build and fittings she was anything but. Only five years old, she was the result of detailed modern design effort and built to an exceptional standard. Her design was the result of a passion for the beauty of pre-war boats coupled with a desire for the convenience, reliability and safety of modern systems. Consequently, all her winches were hydraulically powered. She boasted the latest in navigation and communications systems. She generated enough electricity to keep two large freezers and a fridge cold and down below she was outfitted to luxurious standards. Despite her size, she could be sailed single handed as was currently the case. Her autopilot handled the chore of steering and the navigation system kept her on the right course. Jacaranda had started out as a rich man's whimsy, built to fulfil a desire for something with the beauty of days gone by but with all the advantages that modern technology could bring. She was never intended to be a working girl but the very nature of her quality and comfort had resulted in her being the perfect vehicle for top end exclusive Caribbean charter work. Despite only being able to sleep two couples, albeit in sybaritic luxury, she had proved a hit with a certain sort of rich and adventurous clientele and never been out of work since she arrived in the West Indies two years previously. Named after the Jacaranda tree, her hull was painted the same purple blue as the flower, with her name picked out in gold across the elegant transom. Her owner had picked the name after seeing a tree in full bloom on a previous visit to Grenada some years past. The colour suited her lines and the name when shortened, became the feminine to his own name of Jack which he felt to be somehow appropriate. More than one female had commented that the only girl Jack really loved was his boat, maybe there weren't wrong.

Despite all her labour saving systems and modern gizmos, Jack hated single handed sailing. It wasn't sailing the boat that was the problem. It was having to stay awake to keep a lookout that he hated. The track between Bonaire and St Lucia didn't cover any shipping lanes and anyway the Caribbean wasn't a busy sea. However, there was still the occasional merchantman to keep an eye out for as well as other yachts. At night there were often cruise liners going round in circles killing time before docking at another island for an eight hour stop to disembark their hordes of passengers. Mind you, they weren't exactly hard to spot as they were lit up like the blocks of flats they resembled. There was even the danger of collision with a whale. The Caribbean Sea was a sperm whale nursery and it was not unheard of for yachts to be sunk after hitting one. All this provided compelling reasons why someone had to keep their eyes open and with no one else around it all fell to him. Cat napping was the answer. Have a good look around, check the radar and then nod off for twenty minutes or so. If Ellen Mcarthur could do it sailing around the world, then so could he on a simple two day passage but it didn't mean he had to enjoy it.

Despite the spray hood erected over the cockpit, enough of the last blast of Caribbean spray had penetrated to jolt Jack back to full wakefulness. Guiltily, he looked around the clear horizon, checked the radar and assured himself that all was well.

'Bollocks, thanks for the wake up Jacky,' he mumbled to himself and then gave a guilty start as he realised he had actually dozed off for over an hour. Before his last nap, the sun had just started to show itself over the horizon and now it was at least a full width up in a clear blue sky. '*Time for caffeine*,' he thought and with one last quick check around headed below to put the kettle on.

He made his way down the main companionway into the small galley aft by the engine room. It was one of his favourite compartments as even when guests were on board they rarely ventured into its sanctuary leaving it to him and his crew. Consequently, it was far more personalised than the more public parts of the boat. He filled the kettle and set it to boil on the stove and then as he waited for the whistle from its spout, a fatigue headache nagging behind his eyes, he gazed gormlessly at his sharks. There was a complete row of them on the shelf above the stove. Most were of the 'cuddly' soft toy variety but a few were a bit more exotic. The habit had started years ago when he bought one after a diving holiday. It ended up sat on his computer at work and several more followed. For some reason, the girls in the office took a shine to them and they were often kidnapped, held to ransom or hidden in strange places. It became bit of a tradition to bring new ones back to him after holidays and the collection had grown alarmingly. They had all come with him when he left to live on the boat and had actually proved quite useful as they could be stuffed into various parts of the boat to stop things clunking about when the boat was rolling at anchor. They had all survived the years except for one. In its place was an IOU from one of his most likeable clients, a certain old American lady, who had taken such a shine to his purple Hammerhead that it now resided in a very large house in Arizona.

The kettle started to whistle and he set about making a large cup of strong coffee. As he took his first sip and felt the strong liquid start to wake him up, his eye was caught by his latest acquisition. A present from Debbie his departed girlfriend, this shark wasn't cuddly at all but made from some sort of bone and clearly very old. It was quite possibly scrimshaw work from the old whaling days and its most striking features were its two translucent green stone eyes. Debbie assured him it couldn't be valuable as she had paid only pennies for it from a street market in South America on a previous trip. The way she had presented it to him made him wonder if she was hinting about green eyed monsters and her jealousy of his real love, his boat. It was funny how the light could catch the eyes and they would appear to shine.

Suddenly, he noticed that the sun was shining through a window and onto the shark's eyes and that shouldn't be happening on the course they were on. As he realised this, the boat started to heel alarmingly and it was followed by a large bang from above as the boom jibbed across and slammed onto the opposite tack. There was an enormous sort of shudder, more felt than heard and then all seemed to settle down.

Grasping the opportunity and releasing his grip in the galley rail, he shot up into the cockpit expecting to see mayhem or the wash of a large merchantman or a receding giant wave or something for God's sake! What he saw was, well nothing. The sea hadn't changed, no boats were in sight anywhere and the wind hadn't changed direction or strength. Jacky had clearly jibbed and had now spun further round with the Genoa backed and fighting the pull of the mainsail which was now on other side. The boat had effectively 'hove to' with the two sails balancing each other and stopped in the water. It was probably the safest thing for her as he looked around trying to work out what on earth had happened. He moved to the compass and looked at the navigation system and suddenly a part of the jig saw fell into place. The little icon at the top right of the screen was showing that the system had lost its GPS signal, so it could no longer fix the boat's position. The navigation system had been locked into the autopilot and when the position was lost the boat didn't know where to steer to anymore. Jacky had gradually drifted off course until the wind had got around behind the mainsail and caused the heeling over and accidental jibe. It didn't explain the odd juddering he had felt but at least there seemed to be some sort of explanation which was a relief as it had been quite an inexplicable moment.

A little more settled, he took another quick look around and went back below to check the electronics. However, nothing appeared amiss. All the switches were in their correct positions, the batteries were fully charged and no circuit breakers had opened. Reaching below the chart table, he retrieved a spare hand held GPS, one of several on board in case the main system failed and switched it on. Within a few minutes, it was saying the same as the main system and couldn't lock onto any satellites. Going back to the galley he found his coffee still miraculously intact and nursing the still hot mug went back up top to think things through. Looking around again, he could still see nothing amiss. St Vincent was still in sight but so far away as to be indistinct. The visibility was not that good and that reminded him, after a quick glance at his watch, that it was time for a weather forecast. Not really necessary this close to home but the early morning weather net also gave an opportunity for local yachtsmen to pass on warnings and gossip and maybe someone else in the vicinity had experienced something odd. Going below back to the chart table he tuned in the HF Single Side Band radio to its normal morning frequency only to be met with a loud hissing noise and nothing else. Knowing that radio propagation could be very variable, he was not too surprised but with a slight suspicion at the back of his mind he decided to try a few more frequencies. Try as he might he could not raise one station anywhere on the dial. Once again, he checked all the circuit breakers and found nothing amiss. Glancing over to the bulkhead, he looked at the screen for the Iridium satellite telephone and that was showing no network either, so that had lost its satellites as well. What the hell was going on?

Irrespective of his electrical problems, there was one thing he was going to have to do and it had to be done quickly. With no electronic navigation systems available he was going to have to revert to good old fashioned pencil and paper. On any long passage he always kept a paper chart backup running but with a guilty start, he realised he hadn't plotted a position fix for some hours. Luckily, with Jacky hove to, she wouldn't have travelled very far at all since the incident and the chart plotter should still have a record of where she was when the GPS went down. Working from this, he plotted the position on the chart and then worked out a course to steer to Rodney Bay. It wouldn't be as accurate as using the GPS but the autopilot would happily steer any course given to it, even if it couldn't follow the navigation system and so little would be lost.

On return to the cockpit, he got the boat back on course using the simple expedient of starting the engines and motoring her head back through the wind. Her sails were already set on the course for St Lucia so with the autopilot engaged to steer the boat on the compass he stopped the engine and sat down to think.

So, no satellites, neither the telephone or the GPS and they were totally separate satellite constellations which was decidedly odd. No radio either. He picked up the cockpit VHF radio transmitter and put a call out on channel 16 the marine hailing and distress frequency and received no reply. However, this wasn't unusual as he was so far away from land. So, no help there. Looking up, the sky was unusually empty. You could nearly always pick up the contrail of a high flying airliner but there was nothing today. The more he thought about it the less he could fathom what the problem was and tired as he was, he soon found himself drifting and nodding back to a doze. After all, it was only about sixty miles to St Lucia and he could sort it all out then. It wasn't the first time he had had problems with the electronics and surely wouldn't be the last.

With a start, he realised he had drifted off again. He really must be knackered to be able to nod off so quickly after so exciting a morning. Looking forward and around the horizon, he suddenly realised that he was no longer alone. Dead ahead was the sharp white outline of a sail on the horizon and it looked like it was heading his way. It would be good to exchange a friendly wave with another mariner. He might even give them a call on the VHF when he was a bit closer and see if they were also having problems. However, as the minutes slipped past it was clear that this was not another normal yacht. It didn't take long to realise that she looked old fashioned; square rigged with several masts. This sort of rig was not unknown in the Caribbean. There were several sailing cruise ships around sporting various rigs but somehow this looked like none of them. For a start, she looked far too small and the closer she got the more scruffy she looked. In fact, the only vessel that Jack knew of that could resemble what he was seeing was a brig called the Unicorn. She did daily tourist trips from Rodney Bay down the St Lucian coast. She normally started her day with a cannon shot towards Pigeon Island in the north of the bay as a re-enactment of when the island was the lair of the notorious French pirate 'Jambe de Bois' or 'Peg Leg' in English. Anyway, it couldn't be Unicorn this far out and this early in the morning. He would just have to wait until they were closer.

With surprising speed, the two vessels approached each other. Jacaranda was doing a good ten knots and the other vessel, which was at least twice her size, was also making good speed, witnessed by the white foam being thrown up around her bows. Using his binoculars, Jack could make out that she was indeed an old fashioned brig. She was two masted. Her foremast carried a full set of square rigged sails with her rear mainmast carrying a large lateen sail with further square rigged sails above. Heading dead downwind, it seemed as if the other vessel was keen to make Jacaranda's acquaintance and was clearly sailing an intercept course. A friendly hail on the VHF radio garnered no response and as they got closer Jack was starting to get even more puzzled. Her sails, while clearly working well, were in pretty poor order heavily stained and frayed. As the distance closed, Jack could start making out her crew. There seemed an inordinate number of very scruffy bearded people crowded in her waist. Definitely not a load of tourists. Maybe they were making yet another film about Caribbean pirates? But if so where were the cameras and presumably there would more modern boats sailing with her?

As the strange vessel came within about half a mile there was a flurry of activity on her deck. Someone put the helm over and the crew were milling around various ropes and lines as she very quickly turned almost one hundred and eighty degrees and was suddenly paralleling Jacaranda's course about five hundred yards upwind with her sails neatly trimmed to match her speed. Very impressive seamanship if nothing else, especially as there was no sign of an engine exhaust anywhere on the filthy hull. A very faded yellow and red ensign flew from her stern and her name was completely unreadable. At this point, two things hit Jack. The first was the noise. All the crew were cheering and shouting in a strangely threatening manner. Some were brandishing what were clearly swords or cutlasses, some had pistols or muskets. The second thing was the smell. In fact, stench was a better word. It seemed to be a mixture of raw sewage and unwashed bodies. The sort of smell you got from a particularly ripe tramp in a doorway which had also been used as a latrine but multiplied a thousand fold. It was so strong that even travelling to him from 500 yards upwind it almost made him gag.

At this point, he didn't know what to think. If he didn't know better what he was seeing, hearing and smelling was an authentic Caribbean pirate ship of the eighteenth century. The state of the boat and its crew were one thing, one could imagine a party of crazy tourists wanting to sail around in authentic style as part of some silly adventure. But there was absolutely no way they would want to recreate that stench. In the twenty first century none of this was possible, so what the hell was going on?

Speculation had to take a back seat as the strange ship took in a couple of sails and started drifting back towards Jacaranda. The closer she got the more the noise and the smell increased but then suddenly the shouting stopped. A large bearded man near the stern shouted something across to Jack while brandishing a rather large rusty cutlass. Jack couldn't understand a word. It seemed to be some sort of Spanish or Portuguese but he couldn't make anything out. Looking over to what he presumed now to be the Captain of the brig, he cupped and hand to his ear in the universal gesture of not being able to hear. This only seemed to enrage the man on the other deck even more and he started violently gesturing and yelling. At this, the crew started up again in a chorus of enraged screaming.

The brig was getting seriously close to Jacaranda now and he could even see some of the crew preparing what appeared to be several small cannon on the upper deck. However, suddenly before Jack could react, everything changed as one of the crew pointed up to Jacaranda's mast and the flag flying from the crosstrees. This was a simple yellow square, the international flag representing the letter Q. Jack had put it up last night in case he forgot to later as it was always flown when entering a new island to inform the authorities that the boat had not cleared customs. However, its effect on the crew of the brig was not the same as it would be to a St Lucian customs officer. There now seemed to be some form of argument starting, with some members of the crew pointing at Jack and even one or two shouting up at the Captain. It was clearly a major disagreement of some sort.

By this time Jack had had enough and while the crew of the brig appeared distracted, he reached down to the switch by the wheel and started Jacarandas' two big diesels. As usual, they fired immediately with a reassuring rumble. He swiftly put the throttles into full reverse. Jacaranda seemed to suddenly stand still and the brig to shoot forward in opposition. Jack would never forget the sudden look of astonishment on the faces of the crew which suddenly changed to fear as he pulled away astern. However, he wasn't going to hang around anymore and he simply let the sails flap as he motored backwards away from the brig. When he was well clear, he turned into wind, tightened the sails in as far as possible and simply motor-sailed close to the wind. The square rigged brig was never going to be able to follow. Even at a distance, all appeared to be confusion on the brig and when eventually she tried to turn to pursue, it was clear she couldn't manage anything like Jacaranda's engine assisted course and she slowly drifted away downwind. At some point, a decision must have been made on board as she then bore away and slowly disappeared. Just before she turned away, there was a fusillade of cracks and jets of smoke appeared from her deck spouting towards Jacaranda but Jack didn't notice any effect. If they were really shooting at him the range by now was far too great to have any effect.

As she faded away astern Jack re-engaged the autopilot and sat down to think. He realised his hands were shaking and he recognised the symptoms of mild shock.

'What the fucking hell was that all about?' he said out loud to himself. But think as he might no rational explanation came to him. He found himself repeating to himself, 'that was not real, that can't have happened.' But another side of him seemed to answer, 'Oh yes it bloody well did!' Jack had been in the Royal Navy for nine years and had had his share of frightening experiences but nothing had scared him quite to the core as the last ten minutes. It wasn't that any damage had been done. It was more the sheer unreality of what had just happened. So totally out of context and that smell, it was going to stay with him forever.

Breaking the habit of a lifetime he went below to the galley but this time reached under the sink and pulled out his secretly stashed malt whisky bottle and poured himself a large one. He threw it down in one gulp and let the sudden warmth flood through his body. As his eye was caught once again by his shark collection, he suddenly felt that strange juddering through the soles of his feet. Swearing like a trooper, he shot back up to the cockpit, only to find nothing amiss. In fact, it was better than that, the GPS had a lock on its satellites again and he saw the contrail of four engine airliner passing overhead.

Jack felt an enormous sense of relief. Even though he was not sure what on earth had just happened. He headed north east towards St Lucia, Rodney Bay and a summer of sanity in the boatyard. Life was still good.

Chapter 2

The Honourable Charles Lonfort looked out over the blue Caribbean Sea. Over the last few days, the colour had slowly changed from forbidding Atlantic grey to the welcoming blue of his destination. Slim and of average height, even dressed in his seagoing gear of white shirt and trousers, with his short fair hair and imperious manner there was no doubt who was the Captain. He felt the sun through the back of his shirt as his ship corkscrewed easily down the quarter sea. Looking up at the two masts and the large spread of sail, his critical eye took it all in and although he didn't expect to see anything amiss, it didn't stop him checking every detail. Satisfied that all was well, he next looked down the deck at the eighteen 24 pound carronades secured safely on either side of the main deck. The deck itself gleamed whitely in the early morning sun, having been meticulously holystoned by the crew only hours before. The nettings were filled with the crew's hammocks and all looked ship shaped.

He turned to his First Lieutenant. 'Very good Thomas, all looks in good order,' he stated formally and then more informally, 'hopefully we will see land today or tomorrow. We certainly need to soon given the state of our provisions. The noon site should give us a good position now that we have clear skies.'

His First Lieutenant tipped his hat. 'Thank you Sir, it'll be good to get some shore time soon and top up the water barrels.' His formal words belied by his grin. Although the relationship between the Commander of one His Majesties warships and its First Lieutenant required a degree of formality it didn't stop people becoming close friends.

'Fine, I'll be down below for breakfast. I would ask you to join me but I have rather a lot to do this morning,' and with a rueful grin he added, 'and the Captain's larder has now run out, so it will be the same fare as everyone else.'

Charles turned to go below but not without one last look down the most important possession of his life, his first command, the

Cruizer class Brig Sloop HMS Andromeda. With only eighteen guns she was technically unrated and therefore he commanded her as 'Master and Commander.' In theory, he would revert to the rank of Lieutenant once he was no longer in command. In practice and unless he did something really silly, promotion to Post Captain would be his reward for a successful commission. However, as he told anyone who would listen, with eighteen 24 pound carronades, his ship had the greatest ratio of firepower to ship size of any within the Royal Navy. The down side was that the carronades didn't have anything like the range of traditional long cannon but that didn't really matter when she was used for the purpose she was destined for which was supporting trade in the West Indies.

Unfortunately, due to her shallow draft, another plus factor once on station, she was not able to carry large quantities of provisions. The Atlantic crossing had so far had used up much of what they had managed to cram on board before setting off from Portsmouth over six weeks ago. That crossing had been ordered as a matter of some urgency. Normally, a ship joining the West Indies station would plan to leave in the late summer or even later so that she could arrive after the worst of the summer hurricane season had abated. However, the news and orders that Andromeda carried could not be delayed by mere weather.

The Peace of Paris had been signed in April and the American Revolutionary war was over. Not only was Britain now at peace with her former colony but also with the rest of Europe including France, Spain and the Netherlands. The news had no doubt reached Andromeda's destination long before her arrival but formal notification had to be given. Subsequently, the reparation of the islands of the Bahamas, Grenada, Montserrat and St Kitts, all lost during the conflicts to the French, could be undertaken. However, that was not all. In an attempt to maintain trade, parliament had enacted the Navigation Acts which limited the British islands to trading with Britain alone. Everyone knew this was not going to be popular. Geography dictated that much of Caribbean trade was with the Americas. Informing the plantation owners of British possessions that they could no longer trade with their former partners was not going to be easy. Charles knew he was going to be working in a new and potentially unstable political situation. However, none of this got in the way of his primary orders to deliver all this information to his new Commander, Admiral Sir Richard Hughes. To this end, he was making best speed towards the British dockyard in English Harbour Antigua.

'Sail ho, one point on the starboard bow,' the cry from the lookout at the top of the foremast alerted all on deck. In theory, Charles knew he should carry on below and wait until the Officer on Watch informed him of the situation. In reality, he and everyone else knew that he would want to see the situation as soon as he could. After almost a month at sea without any external contact, even the passing of two ships would be welcome. Of course, had it been the previous year, it could also have meant a chance of action and prize money for all. Charles had to forcibly remind himself that every ship he came across at sea was now, at least technically, a friend.

It soon became clear that the ship ahead was a merchantman of some sort and sailing quite slowly in the same direction as Andromeda. Obviously, it would take some time to catch her up, so with no threat to the ship, Charles gave the deck back to Sailing Master who was on watch and headed below for a morning with his clerk.

Despite the fussing of his clerk and the mountain of paperwork, put off until the weather improved, Charles couldn't concentrate. Partly because he wondered what the strange sail meant but also because he was contemplating what the next few years would bring. The West Indies was not a popular station. The weather was normally benign and the islands welcoming but there was always the risk of yellow fever for which the only cure seemed to be to catch it and not die. For him and his crew, with only peace to look forward to, there wasn't even the prospect of much prize money unless one of the increasingly rare pirates was encountered. So it was with gratitude that Charles heard the knock of the duty Midshipman at his door announcing that the stranger was getting within hailing distance. Reaching for his threadbare sea going frock coat and hat he made his way back on deck.

The merchantman was half a mile away and Charles noted with approval that the Sailing Master had ensured that she would pass down Andromeda's leeward side. Even in peacetime, keeping the weather gauge was prudent.

It was clear that she was heavily laden as she wallowed along with the yellow and red flag of Spain at her stern. Turning to his First Lieutenant he asked, 'well, what do you make of her Tom?'

Putting down his telescope, Tom turned. 'Spanish, full up and almost certainly a slaver Sir.'

'How do you reckon that Tom?'

'Well Sir, her upper deck swivel guns are trained inboard on her hatches. She seems to have a very large crew for such a small ship and when the wind shifts there's that dreadful smell.'

Charles took his own glass out and confirmed the First Lieutenant's observations. He soon got a whiff of the smell. It was what you would expect, he supposed, if you trapped several hundred human beings below decks with no sanitary facilities for weeks on end. As if to deliberately confirm their conclusions three men appeared at the stern and threw a large black object overboard. Quite clearly a body, it drifted in the slavers wake for a few seconds before disappearing below the surface. Charles ground his teeth. Nothing he was seeing was illegal and anyway on a Spanish ship it was none of his business. That didn't stop him feeling nauseated. It was bad enough to buy human beings from Africa and force them to toil in the Caribbean plantations, even though it was hard to argue against when they were sold by their own race. But the inhuman treatment he had heard about and now witnessed was another thing. Luckily at the moment, there was another hail from the masthead.

'Land ho, dead ahead.'

'Ignore the blackbirder Tom, full sail please. I want to see where we are.'

Leaving the Spanish ship and her cargo of misery behind, Andromeda sailed hard towards the misty island on the horizon. It soon became clear that there was another land mass to the north and a consensus was quickly reached that they were heading into the channel between St Lucia and Martinique.

'Well done Sir,' said a smiling Tom to his Captain. 'You said you expected to be south of our intended track after that last blow and you were exactly right.'

Charles smiled back and then looked over to his Sailing Master. Mr Williams had been Sailing Master of several previous ships and Charles relied on him heavily, as was proper. However, as the trans-Atlantic crossing progressed they had both slowly diverged on their navigational conclusions.

Mr Williams approached with a rueful grin and tipped his hat to Charles. 'Yes, well done Sir, it seems you have the making of me now.'

'Not at all Mr Williams, you know how much I rely on you. It was still a matter of chance to large degree. So, how do we proceed from here?'

'Well Sir, I suggest we sail downwind past the islands as we don't want to sail up past several lee shores and then head north north west to Antigua. The wind is well in the east and as long as we stay clear of the island's wind shadows we should be in Antigua within two days.'

'Very good Mr Williams, please make it so,' and turning to Tom he observed, 'I suppose we could stop for water and provisions but our orders require us to press on. Oh and I would greatly obliged if you and the officers would dine with me tonight.'

'Yes Sir,' replied his First Lieutenant. 'We would be delighted and I'll pass word to the crew. I don't suppose they will mind another day on short rations especially as there'll be all we need on arrival.'

Charles acknowledged his salutes from the quarterdeck officers went below again, ruefully realising that the paperwork would not have done itself in his absence.

Two days later, HMS Andromeda ghosted into English Harbour Antigua on the last of the afternoon breeze. She slipped slowly past the cannons of the fort built onto the spit of land protecting the anchorage and at last dropped her anchor in the clear waters of the bay. Their steep sides were covered in mangroves and greenery. Just visible at the top of the main hill was the stone lookout station. Charles felt slightly overwhelmed by the scent and sounds of land after such a long time on the sterile ocean. Although they had gone past Martinique, Dominica and Guadeloupe on their northward passage, they were never close enough to do more than see the hills and occasional sugar plantation.

The only other ship at anchor was a large Frigate although there were several smaller ships in view at the head of the bay around the naval dockyard that was built there. The two ships had already exchanged signals and the Frigate had already hoisted Andromeda's number and the signal 'Captain repair on board.'

Charles looked at himself in the mirror as his steward fussed around his one decent uniform. He had certainly lost weight on the passage but his fair hair and boyish grin were still there. 'Hopefully, the ladies of Antigua will find some new blood welcoming,' he mused as his steward finally strapped on his sword and gave a grunt of approval.

Heading up on deck, Tom came over. 'HMS Boreas Sir, her Captains name is Nelson. He's senior naval officer for the Leeward Islands. It would seem that Admiral Hughes is not here as we expected.'

'Thank you Tom, I'm not sure how long I will be, so please get everything underway to re-provision and get her ready for sea again.'

'Aye, aye Sir,' responded Tom and he motioned to the boatswain to ready the Captain's gig and row the Captain across to the larger ship. Clutching the leather wallet of his orders, Charles descended the ship's side and sat formally in the stern as they crossed the short distance to HMS Boreas.

Climbing up the steep tumblehome of the larger ship's side Charles was greeted by the shrill call of the bosun's pipes and the sharp clack of the muskets presented by the ship's marine party. To his surprise, rather than being greeted by one of the ship's officers and taken to the Captain, he was met by the man himself.

Small, slim and with a shock of fair hair, Captain Nelson held out his hand with a welcoming grin. 'Good to see you Lonfort, it's always welcome to see new faces and hear from home.'

'Indeed Sir,' said Charles returning the smile and the handshake. 'I have a full pack of orders for you and the Admiral as well.'

'Time enough for that. Come let's share a glass and you can tell me of your voyage and any scandalous gossip from court.' Nelson led the way and they were soon ensconced in the ship's great cabin seated around a very welcome glass of Madeira.

Charles found himself warming to his new superior. He was clearly interested in him and his ship and not just for forms sake. They talked for some time before Nelson moved onto the more serious business of the orders and the future.

'I'll read them in detail but I am sure you know the general content. So, how about giving me a summary of what you know before I open them.'

Charles realised that this was probably a test. Nelson wanted to know how well informed his new subordinate was and also where his sympathies lay particularly regarding the new legislation regarding trade.

Choosing his words with care, he started with the easy issue. 'Well Sir, we are now in a position to formally take back the Leewards of St Kitts and Montserrat and the other islands of Grenada and the Bahamas as well but I am sure that's already just a formality. However, I have the Royal Warrants and Letters of Commission for the new Governors. I also have the full details of the Navigation Acts with me Sir and I don't think the plantations and merchants are going to like it much.'

'And why is that?' asked Nelson with a steady look.

Taking a mental gulp Charles pressed on. 'The Acts specifically forbid trade with the new country of America Sir. During the war, this was the case anyway but we all know how much illegal trade was conducted. Of course, we had rather a lot more on our plates than worrying about smuggling while hostilities were taking place. However, we are now going to have to enforce the law and I don't think we're going to be too well liked.'

'And your view on this?' queried Nelson.

'The law is the law Sir. Nobody said the navy had to be popular.'

'Good, you're exactly right and that is one of the reasons I requested more ships like yours. Your role now will be to help me enforce these laws and it's not going to be easy. I will look to you and your ship to be steadfast in this. Don't expect too many social invitations to the plantations once news of this gets about though and anyway I expect to keep you far too busy to worry about social life,' he added with a grin. 'Right, you will want to get back to your ship. Take her up to the dockyard tomorrow and get her prepared. Let me know when you're ready for sea again and we'll talk about tactics.'

Taking the hint, Charles took his leave and returned to the upper deck. He was surprised to see that it was now quite dark. He had been closeted with Nelson for several hours, although it only seemed like minutes. His boat was readied and he returned the short distance to Andromeda full of speculation about what the future would hold. However, in one thing his mind was at rest. His new superior seemed to be a good man and he felt sure he would enjoy working for him whatever transpired.

Standing on his own quarterdeck once again, feeling mellow from Nelson's Madeira and basking in the private satisfaction of having brought his ship and its crew safely across five thousand miles of ocean, Charles felt a great glow of happiness. Life was good.

Chapter 3

August in London, the jet stream hadn't moved from its winter track and a cold front associated with yet another Atlantic depression was sweeping across the country. The rain lashed in eddies around the tall buildings of the City. Everything was grey. The flowers in the parks seemed to have had all their colour washed out by the relentless downpour. Even the pigeons were hiding in the eaves of the buildings. Not that any of this affected the life of the great city. The traffic was freed and herded by the endless traffic lights and road works. People walked quickly. Some with umbrellas almost horizontal into the wind, some with just the collars of their coats turned up. No one made eye contact and all seemed to be in an urgent rush to be somewhere else. Even the Big Issue sellers, were hiding in their shop front alcoves making only half-hearted attempts to interest passers-by with the latest edition.

Paul Smythe came out of the tube station and was immediately hit in the face by a blast of rain as it gusted around the corner of the road junction he was about to cross. He tucked his copy of the Financial Times inside his expensive rain coat, turned up the collar and marched resolutely with the rest of the herd of people around him. Like them, his only goal was to get to the office and get to work.

Truth be known, he didn't even notice the weather or the press of people or the architecture or the traffic. He travelled this way every day of the week and had done so for years. On more than one occasion, when asked how his trip into the office had gone, he could honestly say he had absolutely no memory of the journey. One moment he was reading the paper over his first cup of coffee of the day in his kitchen, the next he was having his second cup as he read his e-mails at his desk.

He was hoping that today would be a good day and he defined that as meaning he would end up richer than he started. '*What better motivation could there be?*' he thought as he looked pityingly around at the throng of little people, all rushing to their menial jobs. In just nine years he had amassed a fortune by the simple expedient of being more hardnosed than others in a world where ruthlessness was the norm.

He pushed open the door to the bland office block that housed the company that owned his soul. He smiled briefly at the receptionist and headed for the lifts. Reaching his office, he hung his coat on the rack and looked at his desk. His cup of coffee was waiting for him and Marie his slim dark haired secretary sat behind hers with her early morning smile already fixed in place.

'Morning Marie,' he said automatically, smiling back. He and Marie had an arrangement. In the office, they were scrupulously professional. Some evenings when her husband was away they were unscrupulously unprofessional. She might be pushing forty but for pure animal sex, Marie took a lot of beating. Actually, that was probably an unfortunate phrase he thought and grinned inwardly to himself. Company rules were unwritten but strict and not shagging your subordinates was one of the top ones. Paul, therefore, took it as a personal challenge to break it and not get caught.

'The boss said for you to go straight up when you got in,' said Marie. 'Looks like today could be busy as he has told all the secretaries to cancel engagements and clear the floor.'

'Righty ho, let's hope the old bugger has finally decided the time is right,' he responded with an almost feral grin as he finished his coffee. With any luck, the intelligence he had recently provided was finally going to be put to good use.

Paul met his boss, Sir Nigel Dwyer in the boardroom. Nigel was best described as portly and seemed to always have a friendly grin on his bland homely face. However, Paul knew that looks were deceiving. He may look like a favourite old uncle but he also knew he should count all his fingers if he shook hands with the man. That bland countenance hid a sharp mind and a ruthlessness that even Paul was in awe of. In fact, Paul considered him very much his role model and had been honing his own brand of mercilessness ever since starting to work for him.

'Good morning Boss, from what my secretary tells me we're going to the bunkers today.'

'Something like that.' Sir Nigel responded. 'All the staff will be here in a few minutes. I am going to give them the outline but then you are going to take over. This is based on your intelligence and its time you ran one of these little forays yourself.'

A shiver ran down Paul's spine. He had worked here for almost ten years, starting like everyone else on the main floor and working slowly up through the organisation. To his knowledge, the boss had never let anyone else run the sort of financial raid they were planning today. To be allowed to do so was the culmination of years of hard work but it was also a real threat. It meant that Nigel trusted both his capabilities and the commercial intelligence he had accumulated. However, it also meant that the boss was testing him and also distancing himself from the action. Paul would take the credit if it went well but he also knew he was probably finished if it went wrong. Only once, since he had come to work here, had things gone wrong and he had successfully sorted that mess out without any one being the wiser. That wouldn't be possible today.

'Thank you Sir, so no pressure then,' he said returning the knowing grin with one of his own.

The staff trooped in and grabbed chairs or perched on the edge of the boardroom table. The company was very informal when working behind closed doors and clearly everyone had anticipated that today was going to be busy. So no suits were present and there were hardly even any ties. They were dressed for action.

Nigel called them to order and outlined the information that a well known merchant bank was in trouble. No one even dreamed of questioning how he got his information. A raid was going to be mounted and Paul was going to be running it. That got more than a few startled looks but they all knew not to question the boss.

Paul then took over and provided the hard information and plan of attack they needed to follow before the markets opened for trading and explained how he intended to run the day. He would stay on the floor and provide overall direction but he expected that they, the experts, would get on with the detailed work. He set out limits of authority within which they could work and made it clear they should come to him if those limits looked like they had to be exceeded. When the briefing was over and questions had been answered the grinning, noisy team filed out and headed for their workstations.

As they left, Paul imagined that this was what it was like be a general who had briefed his troops about a dangerous raid into enemy territory. And in his world of course that was exactly what it was; just as dangerous and just as rewarding.

As soon as the markets opened, Paul very quickly found the truth in another military phrase, 'no plan survives the first shot of the enemy.' However, improvisation and some good luck got them through the morning. By mid-afternoon, they had the markets on the run and as the bell rang for trading to cease, he flopped exhausted in his chair and asked his chief to summarise the day. As the figures were read out, the clapping started and by the time the final balance for the day was announced, his staff were standing and cheering him. His fatigue was forgotten in the adrenaline of the moment and from the corner of his eye, he saw Nigel enter the trading room. 'Well done everyone. That was a close run thing but you seem to have got it right. Your bonuses will reflect your efforts today.'

That got a further round of cheering and then someone suggested meeting in a well known bar for a celebratory drink or two. Nigel was happy to agree but called Paul over as the troops tidied their desks and filed out.

'Very well done Paul,' he said. 'I'm not sure I would have done it quite that way and there are going to be quite a few employees of that bank looking for work tomorrow. But you got the job done. I could ask for no more and your bonus will also be commensurate with your results. You go off with the guys and celebrate but come and see me tomorrow. I want to talk about your future.'

Thanking him in return, Paul quickly cleared his office, said goodnight to Marie who had held the fort for him with the outside world all day and set off to follow his team.

It was past midnight and the champagne and brandy had worked their magic. He had just masterminded his first major corporate raid and made a bomb. His boss wanted to talk about his future and that could only be good. Finally, Sarah the long legged blonde, known as the ice maiden in the office, as no one had managed to crack her, was smiling in invitation at him over the table. Meanwhile, under the table, her toes were expertly exploring the upper regions of his trousers. Life just didn't get any better than this.

Chapter 4

Even to someone acclimatised, the day was hot, humid and heavy. Being stuck ashore with the boat on shore didn't help. Any breeze there might have been was confined to the bay. Jack and his friend Lewis had finally given up working on Jacaranda and repaired to the marina bar for a 'Piton,' the local brew and to cool down. Dressed in only scruffy shorts and paint stained T- shirts, they resembled everyone else in the bar. This early in the season, the place had yet to fill up with its regular clientele of cruising and charter yachtsmen. It was only the diehards who were maintaining their boats in the yard that were present.

'Things have gone well these last few weeks Lewis. We should be able to get her back in the water soon once the antifouling is finished. I can't wait to get back afloat, even if the hurricane season isn't technically over for a few more weeks. You know, I already have almost a full season of bookings. Mind you, I am really going to have to get serious about finding some crew now.'

Lewis grinned and looked at his friend over his frosted glass and said in his best local accent. 'Yup boss and then I can go back to lazin' about an' catching de fish.'

'Oh yeah and making a fortune out of all those other cruisers especially when the Atlantic Rally arrives in a few weeks.'

Lewis acknowledged the remark with a grin. A native of St Lucia, he and Jack had become firm friends two years ago when Jack needed a local agent to help run and maintain the boat. Lewis now helped him exclusively while the boat was out of the water. But when Jacaranda was away he returned to his original occupation, offering his services to the plethora of cruising yachtsmen that used the facilities at Rodney Bay. A literal jack of all trades, he could sort out just about any yachting problem from a blocked head, to re rigging a mast and was in constant demand. Not only had they become close friends but Jack even lived with Lewis when not on the boat. Lewis's mother had an old sprawling house just two miles away. Far too big for the two of them, so Jack had moved in and now rented his own apartment at the rear of the house.

After this particularly hard days graft the beers were slipping down rather too well in the late afternoon sun and soon they were feeling that mellow 'just before sunset, really ought to do something but hey it's the Caribbean' mood.

Jack glanced over at Gloria the slim, cute barmaid and caught her eye. She grinned back at him with a conspiratorial glint in her eye and turned to get them some more beer. Lewis caught the exchange.

'Not her as well Jack? That's got to be half the female population of the island chasing you,' he said with both envy and admiration in his tone. 'Be careful man, you know Caribbean girls, as soon as they get a man and reach twenty five their backsides explode and you'll never get away.'

'Hey, who said anything about her getting me, anyway it's just platonic. You know, having my good looks and a bloody great yacht means you just have to bear the burden of all that female adulation. I know it's tough but someone has to do it.'

Lewis snorted with derision. While inwardly admitting Jack was probably right, he just wished he was as successful with the local girls. With his slim build, dark good looks and completely charming manner, he reckoned Jack could have just about any girl on the island. The strange thing was that apart from that girl Debbie last season, Jack had kept clear of any relationships. Lewis had tried to pry out whether there was a special girl somewhere else but Jack had a really annoying knack of dodging questions about his private life.

Anyway, with the beer getting under Jack's guard, Lewis looked speculatively over at him and asked for the umpteenth time. 'Come on Jacky boy, you're off again soon, you gonna tell me what really happened on that last trip back in the summer?'

Lewis had been on the jetty to meet Jacaranda as Jack brought her ino the marina all those months ago. He could see he was very tired but also sensed that something had happened. Jack seemed strangely agitated but refused to say a word about what, if anything, had occurred. Despite repeated probing, Lewis had completely failed to prise anything out of him.

'Lewis, I told you nothing happened. I was just tired and emotional.'

Lewis acknowledged the standard reply with a frown. 'OK man but how do you explain that scar on the mast and the hole in the sail?' Lewis had seen the damage to the top of the mast when they had taken it down for maintenance. It looked like something had struck it a glancing blow and so he had checked the top of the mainsail and sure enough, there was a corresponding hole through the material of the sail. It didn't make sense. If he didn't know better he would have said it was done by a bullet. But surely a bullet would have produced more damage, rather than just glance off a wooden mast? When he showed it to Jack, his reaction was unusual. He turned white, stared at it for some time with a strange look on his face and then just blanked out, denying its existence, merely telling Lewis to get it fixed.

Jack contemplated the question again. Maybe it was the combination of the beer and his mood but he knew he owed his friend some explanation. 'Look Lewis, yes, something happened but you wouldn't believe me if I told you. Dammit, I don't believe it even now. If it hadn't been for that bloody scar on the mast I would have been able to deny it to myself. Let's drink up. Your mum has supper on and we'll talk after.'

With that promise made, Jack and Lewis finished their beers and then had their usual fight over whose round it was and as usual Jack lost. He went over to Gloria to pay up. She gave him a wide smile as he found some change and he grinned back.

Jack and Lewis kept two rather tatty old motorbikes for transport and set off for home. Just for once it didn't end up with a race. Partly because the traffic was unusually heavy but also because Jack had had rather more beer than normal and despite the liberal Caribbean attitude to drinking and driving, he just for once felt the need for some caution. Cutting through the snarled up traffic and avoiding the near suicidal driving of the locally run mini busses, they turned off the main road and made their way up the narrow drive to the house. Built in old colonial style, with an airy veranda, it was a throwback to more affluent days. Backed by palm trees and surrounded by the standard Caribbean garden, which mainly consisted of old oil drums, a car long past its sell by date and various vegetable patches, it still managed to maintain an air of peaceful grandeur. From the outside, it looked slightly run down and it could certainly do with a coat of paint but Lewis kept it maintained and his mother kept it scrupulously clean. She had inherited it from an uncle many years past after her husband had passed away. Scattering a few chickens, they put their bikes in a shed and made their way indoors.

'See you for supper in half an hour,' said Jack as he made his way to his rooms. This was not a psychic prediction. Martha kept strict dinner hours and if you weren't there you didn't get fed. He was lucky enough to have his own bathroom and the shower made a welcome end to the working day. As he let the cool water run over him and wash the grime from various nooks and crannies, he contemplated what he was going to tell Lewis and his mother. And it would have to be both of them. Just telling Lewis would only delay his mother knowing by twenty four hours at the most and at least this way she would get all the facts first hand. Lewis was an excellent engineer and good friend but he had a great penchant for embellishing a tale. His mother was a delightful lady but she ruled the roost with no arguing and as long as Jack lived under her roof he was her surrogate son and was expected to follow her rules. But if he told them everything what would they say? The real problem was that if he tried to make anything up it would probably seem just as improbable and Martha could see through an untruth in a second flat.

With no solution in mind, he quickly dressed. Feeling refreshed and slightly more sober, he headed for the kitchen to greet his Caribbean family.

Martha was at the stove with her back to him but as usual, her radar picked him up as soon as he entered the room.

'Evenin' Jack, sit yourself down, supper's on its way.'

Jack was slightly in awe of Martha. Unlike many older Caribbean women she had kept her youthful figure. It was even hard to tell her age. With jet black hair and an unlined complexion she could have been anything from forty to sixty. She was also well educated and knew much about the island's history. She was also a phenomenal cook.

'Fish stew again I'm afraid,' she said glancing over her shoulder as Jack headed towards the booze cabinet. 'They had some fresh Mahi Mahi at the market, so it should be a good one.'

Not that it was served every day but most people would get fed up with regular servings of fish stew Jack reflected but Martha made it differently every time depending on what had been caught that day and it was always great. Grasping the rum bottle he poured three generous helpings and added lime juice and water.

At that moment Lewis bounced in, grabbed a glass and announced, 'Hey Martha, Jack says he gonna tell us what happened when he sailed in this summer.'

Martha glanced over her shoulder and gave Jack a thoughtful look and then turned reprovingly to Lewis, 'I'm sure Jack would have told me in his own good time boy and anyway you well know that we don't have serious talk at the table, so just button it for a while.'

Managing to look slightly sheepish but maintaining a grin at the same time, Lewis handed Martha the glass and then took his own from Jack.

They sat down to eat and sure enough the stew was fantastic; fresh Caribbean fish with local vegetables, fiery chilli sauce and bread. *'What more could one ask? You could take this to the best Michelin starred restaurant in London or Paris and blow them away,'* thought Jack. Except the real secret was that the fish was so fresh. It would never be the same once frozen and transported across the Atlantic.

Table talk was limited to progress on the boat and the latest hurricane predictions. There had been very few this summer and it looked like the islands were going to get away with no damage at all, unlike the previous year, when hurricane Omar had done a u-turn half way to Panama and shot back up towards the north. The wind had not been bad but the savage westerly swell had done some serious damage to the normally safe west facing coasts, especially in the French islands to the north. However, despite the dire predictions of the global warming alarmists, hurricane activity seemed to have been on the wane for some years now. Some still grabbed the headlines like Katrina in New Orleans but overall the number and severity seemed to be slowly tailing off year on year.

Supper finished, the two men did their duty at the washing up bowl while Martha put the kettle on and brewed some strong black coffee. She also refreshed the rum glasses and they all then retired to three scruffy but eminently comfortable cane chairs on the veranda. The last of the sunset was dying away. The sky was a dark burned orange and the Cicadas and tree frogs were starting their nightly chorus. From their vantage, they looked out over the other houses, towards the sweep of Rodney Bay, with Pigeon Island sticking out on their right and the lights of Castries, the capital, reflected on the hills to their left. A warm breeze wafted in carrying the night scents of flowers and the sea. Not for the first time, Jack wondered how much this house was really worth. The view alone was a million dollars. Jack knew that Martha would never sell and he could hardly blame her.

Nobody said anything as they drank in the view. Over the summer months this was their regular evening routine and normally followed by an early night. After a time in the Caribbean, the body clock seemed to naturally adjust to the steady rhythm of the tropics, early to bed and early to rise timed to the setting and rising of the sun. Not that they always retired early. Many was the time that their discussions had ranged far and wide. Jack's experiences with the navy and latterly in the City of London and Martha's enquiring mind, supported by Lewis's local knowledge, often resulted in long discussions. However, tonight Martha and Lewis kept quiet, letting Jack collect his thoughts.

Deciding to take the bull by the horns, Jack drew a mental breath and started to describe the facts of his last voyage and what he had experienced and seen. Martha and Lewis listened in silence and let Jack talk it all out. The loss of satellites and radio, the strange ship and its behaviour and the sudden return to normality. He explained about the smell from the other ship and their reaction to his yellow flag. How he had used his engines to outmanoeuvre them and get clear away. He gave his theory about the scar on the mast and hole in the sail which could have been caused by a stray bullet just before the other ship had turned away. He also explained how tired he was and how it couldn't have really happened and why, until he had seen the mast damage, he had been three quarters of the way to rationalising it all as a fatigue induced dream.

Eventually, he stopped and looked at his two companions. 'So that's it. I told you it was unbelievable and ridiculous. I thought about trying to make something up but you'll just have to take it from me that something really weird happened.'

Lewis looked puzzled but not surprised which was odd. In fact, Jack couldn't fathom their reaction. However, before he could speak, Martha broke the silence, forthright as usual.

'Well Jack, I guess there are several options. It could have been a coincidence caused by some electronic failures and you being so sleepy that you didn't really see what you thought you did. But you are quite specific on some things and I am guessing that you don't know the true meaning of some of them, so you could hardly have dreamed them. Maybe we should put belief on hold for a second and check up on a few facts. Now, what was the colour of the ensign on that boat and did it have any markings on it?'

'It was yellow with two horizontal red stripes but it was so faded I couldn't make out anything more than that. I thought I knew all the national ensigns but I've not seen that one before'

'Martha got up and went to the bookshelf and brought out an old faded book. 'Like this?' she queried, pointing to an illustration.

'Yes, that's it and it's the Spanish civil ensign of the eighteen hundreds,' he replied in a puzzled voice, reading the legend under the drawing.

'You say you were flying flag 'Q' on the spreaders presumably for customs when you arrived. But do you know the history and meaning of that flag?'

'Well,' replied Jack. 'I know it means you are requesting customs clearance and I have heard the word 'pratique' used but have no idea what that actually means.'

Lewis broke in. 'Yeah well 'pratique' is actually the granting of a licence to the ship to say there is no disease on board. Some yank skipper told me that last year. I also know that it all originated from the original quarantine flag which was yellow and that meant you did have fever on board. Round here that would only mean yellow fever. Those guys saw it and thought you were infected and with only one crew in sight on a boat that size that probably confirmed it.'

Martha cut back in. 'Now Jack, that smell, do you think that a crew the size of the one you saw could make it and didn't you say that when they got close they were moving some small cannon around? Presumably, they were originally facing inboard?'

Jack thought for a while. He was never going to forget that smell. 'No, I don't think even the disreputable crew I saw could have generated such a smell and thinking about it yes, those little cannon were pointing inboard at the decks when she bore down on me but what are you getting at?'

Martha looked at Lewis, took a deep breath and said, 'look, whether it's possible or not, you've described an eighteenth century sailing brig down the smallest detail. You've described a unique smell that could only have been made by hundreds of people confined for a long time and that coupled with the inboard facing cannon could only mean one thing. She was carrying slaves. No, let me finish,' she said as Jack was about to interject. 'She was flying an ensign that hasn't been used for centuries and the crew's reaction to your yellow flag would require a collective knowledge of history that no modern crew would have and anyway why would a modern crew care? Yellow fever is hardly a problem these days.'

'Don't ask me how but you saw an eighteenth century Spanish slaving ship.'

'OK,' said Jack, half in relief as at least no one was laughing at him. 'But if they were slavers why did they act so threatening?'

'Well, no one in those days was that single minded. I guess that seeing such an unmanned clean looking boat, a touch of piracy crossed their minds. I'd loved to have seen their faces when you shot astern mind you.'

Jack was puzzled. 'You know, you're both talking as if this did actually happen and not treating me like some crazed idiot. How come you're accepting this and not recommending a trip to a psychiatrist?'

Martha and Lewis exchanged a strange look and she turned to Jack. 'Before I answer that Jack can you show me exactly where this occurred? I have an old chart here somewhere.' Rummaging around in the desk at the back of the room, she came up with an old sailing passage chart of the West Indies.

Jack got up and studied the chart. 'Here,' he said pointing to a position about forty miles south west of Rodney Bay. 'I can give you an exact latitude and longitude if we go to the boat. It's still in the chartplotter.'

Martha frowned. 'No, that's not necessary Jack. It was around there that my husband went missing all those years ago. Like you, he had been a long way out west and was returning to St Lucia. We had an old wartime High Frequency radio set and he called in saying he had a good catch and where he was. That was the last we heard. He never showed up. The authorities were pretty limited in what they could do but some of the other boats went out and nothing was ever found.'

Lewis broke in. 'Jack, we keep it pretty quiet as we don't want all that silly publicity that goes with all the Bermuda triangle crap but all the locals know that if you go out to the west, sometimes people don't come back or see things they can't explain. There's one of the guys down at the fishing dock who swears blind that he was off Martinique some years ago and saw the volcano above St

Pierre smoking away and that's been dormant since it blew its top hundreds of years ago.'

'So, Jack,' said Martha. 'You can see why we're not as sceptical as you might have expected. I guess the question is what are you going to do about it?'

Jack couldn't answer that question immediately and the discussion carried on through the dark hours. He learned a great deal more about strange local occurrences. They talked more about his experience in detail. There was a great relief in sharing something like this and in some ways a load was taken from his mind. However, Jack was not the sort of person to file such a thing in the 'unexplained, so forget it and move on box.' Before they all went to bed he decided he needed to understand more and co-opted the two of them to help gather as much information as they could. He really wanted to see if there was any pattern to the events. As usual, Lewis was full of enthusiasm but to his surprise, even Martha agreed to help. After all these years, he knew she had never accepted the loss of her husband. Maybe helping him look into this would give her some form of closure.

As he went to bed that night he felt far more composed. However, his mind was racing with all sorts theories. He had never been one to believe in ghosts, crop circles or UFOs but he now found himself in exactly that position. As sleep overwhelmed him, he promised to find a rational explanation if there was one to find. As soon as Jacaranda was ready of course.

Chapter 5

HMS Andromeda snubbed gently against her single anchor cable in the sweeping bay of Basse Terre, the capital of St Christopher or St Kitts as she was more generally known. A few cables away HMS Boreas was also at her anchor in the clear blue water. A third ship, a merchantman, flying the ensign of the new United States of America but with the Union flag hoisted above it was also in the anchorage.

The two warships had only recently been reunited. Nelson had sent Andromeda off to Jamaica to report to Admiral Sir Richard Hughes with his despatches as soon as she had been refurbished and reprovisioned. Hughes had then ordered her back to the Leeward Islands to become part of Nelson's squadron and help 'enforce' the peace. Calling back into English Harbour, Charles learned that Nelson was wasting no time in carrying out his duties and had already sailed on his first patrol. However, he had caught up with his superior in St Kitts knowing that his first duty would be to hand over the Letters of Commission to her new Governor.

The two Captains stood on the quarterdeck of HMS Boreas conversing quietly in the gentle morning sun.

'So, all is well with Sir Richard, that is good news and his orders to me are as expected,' confided Nelson to his subordinate. 'We will have a council of war in a few day's time but we have an unavoidable social obligation first. Now that St Kitts and Nevis are formally back in our hands, the new Governor is holding a ball to celebrate the occasion. You, me and all our officers are invited. I'm sorry but there is no way out of it.'

Clearly, the two men had differing views over the necessity of social interaction. As the second son of an Earl, Charles was well versed in social etiquette and moved easily in such circles. A celebratory ball in such a little island was hardly going to measure up to the grandeur of court life in London but it would make a very welcome break to the tedium of naval routine. Besides, he had been hearing stories of the quality of female company in the islands and their desire for new distractions. Truth be known, he was delighted at the prospect. However, he managed to hide his delight and gravely agreed with his superior.

'Aye, aye Sir, I'm sure it will be a great occasion,' he said formally. 'Bye the bye, might I ask about the presence of the merchantman over yonder?' The American had been lying with Boreas as Andromeda arrived and speculation was rife as to her presence. Charles could only assume she was the first victim of the Navigation Acts but had yet to have confirmation.

'Caught her red handed, so to say,' replied Nelson. 'She was about to leave Basse Terre as we arrived and clearly heavily laden. I sent over a boarding party and found that she was full of St Kitts sugar. Can't find out who supplied it and her Master denies all knowledge of anything illegal. Says he knows nothing of the Acts and that they don't apply to her but to me they are quite clear. So she is going nowhere. He says he is going to sue me. We shall see. I'm afraid we might not be quite so popular with the natives because of it but it can't be helped.'

'I understand Sir and I'm afraid Sir Charles did not appear that happy with the Acts either. May I ask whether his despatches make his views clear?'

Nelson grimaced. 'He chooses his words carefully. He is clearly a diplomat. Well Lonfort, I am not and my duty is clear. No trade with Americas and be sure you follow my lead.'

Two evenings later, Charles was sweating copiously inside his full frock coat, his armpits were sore and so was his crotch where the material was digging in tightly. His dress sword was banging uncomfortably on his hip. The air was filled with tobacco smoke and noise. He was loving every minute of it. What a welcome break from the routines of naval duty. He looked down at Lizzy, the slim young blonde girl on his arm and suggested that they join the throng on the dance floor. She demurely agreed and they were quickly in the thick of it.

'Captain Lonfort, is it true you father is the Earl of Hinchfield?' she asked with an almost predatory glint in her eye.

'I'm afraid you must find us all rather provincial out here in the islands.'

'Yes my dear, the Earl is my father, although I am his second son and so condemned to a life of penury and service. Unlike my older brother who will of course inherit one day and no I do not find you at all provincial. Beauty is not limited by geography,' he added gallantly. She blushed prettily. They both knew that his remark about penury was wide of the mark. Even the second son of one of the richest men in England was going to be a damn good prospect and despite feigning ignorance, Lizzy almost certainly knew all there was to be known about him and his family. And Charles knew that she knew. Not that it mattered. This was a social game to be played out with strict unwritten rules. Lizzy herself was the second daughter of the new Governor and no doubt had her sights on Charles for one main reason. He of course also had his reasons, not the least that she was by far the most attractive girl in the room and who knows what could transpire later in the tropical evening.

'Oh look, even Captain Nelson is enjoying himself,' remarked Lizzy, looking over Charles's shoulder and indeed there he was dancing with enthusiasm with a tall girl of almost his own age.

'Who is she?' enquired Charles surprised that his superior was joining in with such gusto after his less than enthusiastic remarks the other day.

'Ah, that is Fanny Nisbet. She is a friend of mine and has a plantation over on Nevis but all the landowners from both islands are here tonight.'

'Surely she can't have her own plantation?' It would be most unusual, even unheard of for a female to be running her own estate.

Lizzy looked up at Charles. 'You know ladies can do more than embroidery and have babies,' she said with a note of asperity. 'However, you are right. She was recently widowed and has just come out of mourning. She is running the estate until her brother can come out and take over. By all accounts, she is doing a good job, which no doubt annoys some of the other men around here.'

Charles looked around at the men in the room. He probably wouldn't be too popular with them at the best of times, having snared the prettiest and most eligible girl in the room almost within minutes of his arrival. However, that was not the real reason for the almost naked dislike he saw in several eyes as they made contact with his. The Navigation Acts were likely to have a strong and negative effect on trade in the islands and many were not shy about making their feelings known. Charles had already been approached by local owners trying to sound him out. To their chagrin, he had been steadfast in espousing Nelson's firm line on the matter. The presence of the arrested American ship in the harbour attested to that policy in a very forthright way.

The dance ended and Charles was just about to suggest that he and Lizzy retire to the seclusion and coolness of the veranda when a young man approached and asked Lizzy for the next dance. He gave Charles a sharp glance as if challenging him to object and not wanting to cause offence, he released her arm. She gave him a knowing smile and was whisked away into the press.

Walking over to the table loaded with food and a rum punch that he was going to have to treat with circumspection, he joined Thomas Deerly his First Lieutenant who was in conversation with Nelson.

'Sir, Tom, it seems to be going well even if we are not the most popular people here.'

Tom looked at Charles. 'I suppose you would consider it to be going well if you were dancing with the prettiest girl in the room,' there was a note of amused envy in his voice.

'Fair point, although I noticed that Captain Nelson seemed to be enjoying himself as well,' he said looking speculatively over at his superior.

Nelson took the jibe well. 'Yes Charles, I do seem to be having a rather better time than I imagined I would. Remarkable lady you know. She's been running her plantation on Nevis now for over six months. She even sacked her overseer and has been doing the day to day work herself.'

Charles was just about to make an unfortunate remark about hoping that the sugar in the American ship was not from her plantation when there was an interruption. The dull thud of a cannon shot carried up from the harbour down below. The orchestra wheezed to a stop and the three of them followed by the rest of the throng made their way to the garden that overlooked the harbour. The moon was almost full and it was immediately clear that the American ship had somehow managed to cut her anchor cable and was heading out of the harbour. The cannon shot had come from Andromeda where someone had eventually seen what was going on but far too late to do anything about it.

'Dammit,' swore Nelson. 'That man gave me his word. I'll know not to trust a bloody colonial the next time.'

'Is there nothing we can do?' enquired Charles knowing full well that it was highly unlikely either of the two British ships could be made ready in time before the American was well over the horizon. However, he didn't hear the answer as any conversation was drowned out by the cheers of the assembled plantation owners and merchants as they realised what was going on in the bay.

Tight lipped, Nelson turned to the other naval officers and ordered them all back to the ships. 'If that is how it is to be, we will have to take even firmer steps. Lonfort, repair to Fort Brimstone tomorrow morning and we will have that council of war.'

Charles saw Lizzy briefly through the crowd as he took his leave. At least she gave him a sympathetic smile as she waved her fan at him in parting. Not everything in the evening had been lost.

The next morning, Charles was early at Fort Brimstone. He had heard much about the place and was eager to look around before the others arrived. One hundred years in the making and a task originally claimed to be impossible by the French, the British had made a fortress known locally as the Gibraltar of the West Indies. Standing on Brimstone hill, a remarkable outcrop of rock overlooking the coast north of Basse Terre, the ramparts held a complete garrison of troops and an array of large guns on all four sides. From the ramparts, to the north, Charles could see the dome shaped islands of St Eustace and Saba and looking south he could just make out the edge of Nevis. Montserrat would be another twenty leagues further on. This high up, the air was cool and clear and he was enjoying the refreshing breeze when one of the troopers came up and saluted.

'Commanders compliments Sir and Captain Nelson and the Governor are on the way up. He requests you join them in the officer's mess.'

Acknowledging the troopers salute, Charles made his way back down the steps. On the way, he noticed some graffiti on the stone walls. Not unusual in itself except that it was written in French. Two years ago the fort had been besieged by the French under Admiral de Grasse. Even Admiral Hood could not dislodge him and when the island of Nevis had surrendered the cannons from the British forts there were added to the French inventory. Brimstone had held out for over a month but eventually had simply run out of ammunition. The fort surrendered but in an unusual display of gallantry, the French had allowed the British to march out with arms held high and flags flying. Within a year, the fort was back in British hands, restored under the Treaty of Paris that ended the war. However, it was clear that the military were not going to be caught out again and everywhere Charles looked there were parties of soldiers and slaves working on increasing the fortifications.

He reached the room where the meeting was to take place before the others arrived and was offered a cup of strong black coffee by a black slave steward. The Fort Commander was the first to arrive followed by Nelson and Governor.

Nelson beckoned Charles over. 'I don't think you had a chance to meet last night. Sir, may I present Commander Lonfort, Captain of HMS Andromeda.'

Sir David Babbage looked haughtily over at Charles. A tall florid man, Charles wondered how he had managed to sire such a small and pretty daughter.

'Humph, Lonfort,' he grunted putting out a huge paw of a hand for Charles to shake. 'Seems you managed to acquaint yourself with my daughter for all that.' However, the gruff tone belied a friendly grin on the Governor's face. Having one's daughter show interest in a member of an old and rich aristocratic family was clearly no bad thing.

'Right, let's to business,' boomed the Governor and they all took seats around the highly polished oak table.

From the outset, it was clear that the meeting was not going to be easy. Colonel Henry Spittlewood, the Fort Commander, had no axe to grind as his job was relatively easy and he didn't need to get mired in politics. But there was clearly a gulf between the Governor, who also owned land on the island and Nelson. The Governor was of a mind that the navy's primary job was to protect the islands against military threats and there was still piracy to deal with. The Navigation Acts were about trade and therefore not what the navy was there for. It was clear that Nelson didn't agree. By this time Charles had sufficient experience to feel he had the measure of the man. He already respected Nelson for his style of leadership and his quick natural intelligence. But in one matter Nelson appeared to be totally inflexible. When it came to duty, he only saw things in black and white. In wartime, this would clearly be a formidable quality but in this time of peace Charles felt that there was room for pragmatism in interpreting the new trade rules. Still, it was his duty to obey and if his commander said it was so, then it was so.

After two hours the meeting broke up. The only outcome being that the two antagonists agreed to differ. Privately, Charles suspected that the Governor had now decided that underhand measures would be needed to circumvent the navy. The Leeward Islands covered a large area of sea and with only a few ships to patrol the area it would be difficult to stop all illegal activity and the Governor knew it.

Discussions aside, they all repaired to lunch and later with an invitation to Charles to call at Government House whenever he was available, an invitation pointedly not offered to Nelson, the Governor took his leave.

Nelson then took Charles aside and handed him an envelope.

'Your orders Lonfort,' said a grim faced Nelson. 'Proceed to patrol the southern islands as far as St Lucia. You may stop and search any American vessel you suspect of trading with British possessions. If you arrest any ship I expect you to place a prize crew on board. I don't want a repetition of what happened last night.'

Chapter 6

Paul woke the next day with a throbbing head, dry mouth and a feeling of great well being. Sarah stretched lazily next to him under the sheets. They were both naked. Their clothes were strewn all over the bedroom as well as on the way up the stairs. What a night, what a day. He looked at his watch and reluctantly gave Sarah a pat on her glorious backside. Much as he was tempted to make it more lingering he still needed to be in the office on time. The boss would not expect him to be late.

'Shower's over there my dear, I'll use the one in the main bathroom.' So saying, he made his way out of the door casting one lingering glance over girl emerging from the bed sheets. To his surprise, as he was letting the first of the needles of water wake him up, he felt a cold blast of air as the door opened and a long legged naked body slipped in next to him.

'Stuff the boss,' said a husky voice in his ear as a hand reached down to confirm that the body was willing even if the brain was initially reluctant.

Somehow, they still made it on time. Sarah, looking every inch the office ice maiden, Paul, his normal groomed self. They had had to resort to using a taxi, something Paul never usually did and having arranged to be dropped off around the corner they both managed to arrive several minutes apart. Not surprisingly, the subterfuge was a complete waste of time. As he arrived in his office, Marie gave him a knowing smile and within a few minutes certain male heads pushed around the door with various ribald but mainly envious remarks. Feigning indifference didn't really work and anyway it was quite flattering, especially after the financial success of the day before. He only hoped that Sarah would take it in good spirit. She had worked on the floor for several years and should be used to the mainly male, testosterone fuelled, banter that went on.

Anyway, that was play and now it was time for work again.

'Marie, has Nigel arrived and did he put anything in the diary for today?'

'Yes Paul, he asked if you could go up once you have caught up with the backlog from yesterday. So I've booked you in for ten thirty that should be plenty of time. I've dealt with all the routine stuff and what's left on your desk shouldn't take too long.'

'Marie, what would I do without you?' he smiled.

Looking him straight in the eye she said, 'seems you've already worked that out,' and then with a laugh as she saw the flash of guilt across his face. 'Don't worry. We both know what we do is just for fun. It's about time you found another girl after Melissa left you.'

Hearing that name brought on a mental wince. Paul's last relationship had ended with some quite spectacular acrimony and as usual, the office got to hear about it almost at the same time that he did. Who knows, maybe he could keep a girl for a bit longer this time round.

However, this was not helping the work backlog so he settled down to his electronic in tray and the few hard copy letters he needed to deal with and sure enough, well before ten thirty, he was putting the last one to bed. Looking at his watch to ensure he would arrive just slightly before his deadline, he looked over at Marie. 'Righty ho Marie, I'm off to see the head honcho. I've no idea how long I'm going to be, so hold any calls. You never know I might even get a lunch out him!'

Marie smiled back. 'Now that would be something.' It was a standing joke in the office that the boss never took staff out to lunch. Clients or potential victims yes, all the time but never his employees.

So it was with more than some surprise when that was exactly what the boss did. After meeting in his office, they spent the morning dissecting the main lessons learned from the previous day before moving on to discuss future plans and strategies. It was with mounting excitement that Paul realised he was being trusted with his boss's innermost thoughts. Indeed further in than anyone else had probably ever been allowed before. There was very little rank structure in the company. Nigel was in charge and there were five senior managers of which Paul was one. Below that were just the troops. In reality, they all danced to his tune. The senior guys were really only there to look after the more important day to day stuff and allow the worker bees to get on with the number crunching. So, it was unprecedented for anyone to be given such access to the companies longer term strategy. However much excitement he felt, Paul kept his feelings under control. After all, this could be yet another of the man's bloody tests. Management by mental manipulation was not a technique found in most management manuals but it had been honed by Nigel over the years into a very effective tool.

With discussions over, he looked over at Paul. 'That's enough shop, let's go to that new French restaurant they've opened down the road. I've been wanting to check it out for some time now.'

And there it was. The Holy Grail of office speculation, the lunch invite from the boss. Inside, Paul was ecstatic, outside he accepted the invitation with a straight face. They collected coats and quietly walked without talking down the streets thronged with other lunch going, City people. Nigel muttered a few hellos to acquaintances as they passed and they soon found themselves seated on the second floor in a relatively secluded part of the restaurant but with a panoramic view over the river. He ordered them both an aperitif while they waited for their orders to arrive.

He smiled over at Paul. 'Paul, I'm impressed, you and I both know I've never taken an employee out to lunch before. Mind you, I've never let them run a raid like yesterday before either. Indeed, I even hear on the grapevine that you cracked a certain female challenge last night.' Seeing the look on Paul's face he quickly continued. 'Yes, I am human you know and I can tap into the office grapevine as well as anyone but well done on all accounts. You really can relax, please this isn't a test. I know I keep my staff at arm's length. It's always been my way. I never mix my private life and business but I need to speak to you on a personal level now.'

Paul smiled back. The first hit of the alcohol in his glass was warming through and he finally felt he could lower his guard. Not all the way maybe, he would never do that but certainly far more than he had ever done in front of his boss before.

'Sir, firstly, thank you very much for taking me on in the first place and secondly for the faith you have put in me over the years and particularly over the last few days.'

'Now look Paul, you can stop calling me Sir. You know, the passing of time is a bugger and for some years I have been wondering about my exit strategy. Nothing lasts forever. I built the company and I could just as easily break it up. God knows I have made enough money out of it over the years. But and you may not believe this, I actually care for the edifice itself and the staff. That may seem unlikely after all the people I have probably put out of work over the years but that was business. I am going to retire soon, while I still have my health. Did you know that many business people only last six months after stopping work? Well, it's not going to happen to me and I am not going to solve the problem by working until I die. So, if I retire, I want the company to continue. I need a successor and you are it. Feel up to the challenge?'

There it was, straight and true. Paul felt an enormous sense of elation but he also felt slightly sick. Everything he had worked for over the years, everything he had dreamed of suddenly was there for the taking. But it was one thing to dream of this day, quite another to face up to it in reality.

'Are you alright? Just for once I seem to have rendered you speechless,' said Nigel with a grin.

'No, no, I'm sure you know what this means to me and yes of course I would like to accept. I'm sure you know it's what I would want. I'm just overwhelmed that's all. Thank you very much for the chance. Yes, I would like the job.' Paul realised he was burbling and shut up.

'Right, that's my little bombshell done with. We can talk details later. Now let's concentrate on the menu for a bit. It looks extremely good. I hear the chef is excellent and apparently the cellar is pretty good too.'

It ended up being one of those lunches that took much longer than intended. The food was indeed spectacular and when Nigel spent money on wine, he spent lavishly and expected only the best. Paul soon realised he could really relax. He was seeing a side of his boss he never expected to see. He was surprised to find that not only did he have a human side to his character but he was also a great raconteur with a large library of funny and quite rude jokes. This was not the disciplined, humourless and ruthless man he had known all those years and he found it quite easy to respond in kind. Nigel had a large family and intended to spend more time with his grandchildren. They also discovered a mutual love of sailing and Paul found, much to his surprise, that he kept a yacht in a Solent marina and had plans to take her abroad for extended cruising.

'I got the idea from that crook who worked for us for a couple of years. It was about the only good thing that came out of employing him.'

Paul kept quiet at that remark, conscious that Nigel was well aware that he was responsible for 'the crook' being employed in the first place. Luckily, it didn't seem to be held against him. Despite the pleasant atmosphere, it was hard not to let the discussions revert to shop at some stage and by the end of the afternoon, it had been agreed that the post of Managing Director would be formally established for Paul and that Nigel would become Chairman. Depending on business he intended to slowly ease himself out of the harness and hand over all responsibility within a year. Finally, the bill arrived and they were ready to leave.

'Don't worry about going back to the office. I told our secretaries not to expect us back,' said a slightly swaying and very mellow Nigel. 'Have a good weekend and I'll see you Monday and we can get things moving.'

Paul thanked him once again and for the second time in one day called a taxi. Despite his euphoria, the last two days coupled with the lunchtime booze were really catching up with him and when he got home he was snoring in front of the television within minutes of sitting down.

Chapter 7

Jacaranda was in her element, back at sea. The previous weeks had been hectic as Jack sought to launch her ahead of schedule. Now her antifouling was applied, her mast re-stepped and most of her systems were working. During the last ten days sailing, a small list of minor snags had arisen, all of which could be easily fixed on return to Rodney Bay. Then she would be ready for the new chartering season.

With all sails fully set, she was shouldering herself through a gentle offshore swell cruising back down from Anse D'Arlet, Martinique their last brief overnight stop. It was a glorious morning, with light trade winds and clear blue skies. It was typical of the weather at the end of the Hurricane season. Soon the Caribbean 'winter' would set in with stronger trade winds and squalls being the norm, quite often to the surprise of the paying guests but as Jack pointed out, even the rain was warm. They had left early and been accompanied by a school of dolphins as they rounded the southern part of the island and had even briefly sighted a pod of sperm whales heading in the opposite direction. Jack was very content. The boat was working well and his first paying customers were due to arrive in two weeks. The only small cloud on the horizon was that he still hadn't managed to get any crew. However, there was time and he had a few enquiries from the various web sites he used. Lewis had volunteered to cover if needed. Jack was very grateful to his friend but pointed out that he would not look quite right in a skimpy bikini and as he couldn't cook to save his life, Jack would be pretty busy.

He was also reflecting on the previous ten days.

He had accelerated Jacaranda's launching schedule after his night of confession with Lewis and his mother. Having unburdened himself, he consequently felt the need to investigate what was going on. Once started on a subject, he could be very single minded. A trait he knew sometimes attracted criticism but he really needed to get some answers. Lewis had mentioned that other locals had experienced similar incidents and this spurred him on to making enquiries on the island. At first, he was met with the blank looks and reticence only a Caribbean islander can manage but by taking Lewis along to smooth the way he was soon taken into the confidence of the local maritime community. Once it was accepted that he had had a genuine encounter, he seemed to be accepted into a sort of exclusive club and doors opened. There was indeed an old fisherman who had been fishing north of Martinique and when returning home, had claimed to see the volcano over St Pierre smoking heavily and seemingly much larger than its present size. As it had erupted several centuries ago Jack was at least able to put a latest date on the event. He was also told several stories of strange sightings, mainly of old fashioned sailing vessels but nothing as detailed as his own. One thing led to another and he was offered several second hand stories of weird occurrences from other islands. So, with sufficient time before charters started, he decided the best way to get real information was to go to the source himself. He therefore used the excuse of an early shakedown cruise for Jacky to visit some of the other islands and get information first hand.

Initially, they had headed south as far as the Grenadines stopping at Bequia and Union Island before heading back up to St Vincent. Everywhere he went, he was told similar tales. Some were clearly caused by lurid imaginations, probably fuelled by rum or smoking strange substances. When going to sea for several days in a small boat, all sorts of things could be mistaken for the paranormal. However, there were a disquieting number of incidents where boats simply never returned. Caribbean fishermen were not noted for the quality of the maintenance of their craft and no doubt some of these were due to simple bad luck but too many losses had happened in calm weather and for no apparent reason. There also remained a hard core number of sightings of vessels that had sufficient detail in them to defy logic. Most modern fishing boats were of the narrow, high bowed, pirogue design and all sported at least one if not two large outboards so it was not surprising that most people used their horsepower to keep out of the way of something they didn't like the look of. Finally, while talking to an old guy in Wallilabou in St Vincent, they heard of a much more detailed sighting near the Saintes, the French owned islands north of Dominica. Apparently, from a very well regarded Frenchman who had lived in the islands for many years. As this was the first European they had been referred to, they decided on an overnight sail up there even though it was much further than they had originally intended.

Anchoring off the Bourg, the main town in the biggest of the islands, for once proved to be easy. The Saintes are stunningly beautiful and during the cruising season very popular. Squeezing a boat as big as Jacky into the anchorage could often prove difficult. However, for now, there were only a handful of diehards clustered around the dingy dock.

Jack and Lewis went ashore in the tender together and went to the town hall, the 'Marie', as they needed to clear customs and hoped they would be able to track down their contact at the same time. Sure enough, the helpful customs officer knew of Monsieur Blanchard and gave them directions to a large house overlooking the bay a short walk out of the picturesque little town. The door was answered by a large Caribbean lady who at first seemed inclined to deny anyone's presence in the house but as they were talking, a small dark haired man enquired as to who was calling and shooed her away.

Pierre Blanchard was in his seventies but to look at him you would have thought he was much younger. Tough and wiry, he gave Jack and Lewis an appraising look as they explained their business. As soon as Jack mentioned that he was the owner of Jacaranda, which could clearly be seen swinging gently to her anchor in the bay, his attitude softened and they were invited in.

'I have sailed these islands nearly all my life and always appreciate the beauty of a classic yacht,' he said with an appreciative smile. 'Now please, sit and tell me more.'

Jack immediately decided that the only way to deal with the canny looking Frenchman was to take him fully into his confidence and so recounted a full description of his encounter and the results of their enquiries to date.

As Jack wound up, Pierre gave them both another hard look. 'Well my friends, I take it you have spoken to that old scoundrel Marco in St Vincent. I knew I should have kept my mouth closed but he and I have been good friends for many years and like you, I had to tell someone. However, unlike you, I was happy to let it lie.' And then with a sigh, 'maybe you are right, maybe it is time to find out what is really going on. Please join me in a drink and I will tell you my story but please, please, do not use my name. This is all off the record. An old man like me does not want any publicity or accusations of being a crank. You, of course, can run that risk if you wish.'

So saying, he opened a bottle of red wine and poured them all a large glass. 'Thirty two years ago like you, I ran a small charter company but my boat was only fifty feet. I had been sailing in the US Virgin islands and had dropped off my party in St Johns and was returning here. It was late in the season and the wind was from the south and so I was forced to tack. I had stood well out to sea and because I was on my own, I had fallen asleep a little too long. I had actually gone too far and was therefore heading back here from the west. Just like you Jack it was early morning and I saw something very strange as I approached home. At first, I thought it was some racing regatta as there were sails in sight from the north of Dominica right up past the Saintes. Then I realised they were two separate groups heading towards each other. Within half an hour, there were clouds of white smoke and I then heard large explosions. To this day I have trouble believing it but I think I actually saw the battle of Dominica taking place.'

Seeing Jack's blank look he continued. 'You British call it the battle of the Saintes and I suppose that is your right, as your admirals Rodney and Hood actually won the day but as you know, we French like to have our own take on history,' he said with a wry grin.

'Right,' said Jack smiling back. 'Now I know. The fort overlooking the end of the harbour has a museum which tells the story. I often take my customers there. I've always thought it was an example of how you French manage to turn defeat into a victory with the telling! But what happened after you saw the fleets join battle?'

'You must understand that the ships were still a good way off and even if I didn't really appreciate what I was actually seeing, to me it didn't seem a good idea to get too close. I wasn't able to do what you did and use my engine as I had been having trouble starting it. In those days we didn't have electric starters and hand swinging it was really a two man job. So, I decided to head further south and clear around them. It was fascinating to watch and I think I must have been too focused on what was going on because a big wave hit me and I slipped on the wet cockpit floor. I hit my head but do not think I was knocked out. When I sat back up, they were gone, the sea was empty. But to this day, I do believe I saw your Admiral Rodney and our Admiral de Grasse start to fight it out on the twelfth of April seventeen eighty two. I told Marco all this some years ago after too much rum and I was surprised when he didn't call me a fool. But after what you told me of your story, you are the only others I have told.'

'I know exactly how you feel,' responded Jack. 'When you have experienced something so completely out of the ordinary, it's hard enough to acknowledge it to yourself, let alone tell it to others. I can only thank you for being so open with us.'

'So, what will you do now? You clearly have a large amount of information and I guess maybe even enough to write a book or something.'

'That's a very good question. You know I don't actually have a clue. This started out as a way of proving to myself that I wasn't the only lunatic in the asylum and that clearly isn't the case. I really need to sit down and collate everything we have been told and try to see if there is any common denominator. But to answer your question, no I don't intend to publicise it in any way. There is enough rubbish and mis-information around about the Caribbean already and I don't want to encourage the lunatic fringe with these sorts of stories. But look, I would like to keep in touch if that's alright? Most of the people I have spoken to have agreed and I have their contact details. I will certainly do nothing without contacting everyone and will respect everybody's privacy whatever happens.'

Pierre readily agreed and furnished Jack with an e-mail address and cell phone number. In the mood for returning hospitality, Jack then invited Pierre back to Jacaranda for a few more drinks and to show off his pride and joy to someone who would clearly appreciate her. They talked well into the night discussing Pierre's experience in more detail, as well as the more general results of Jack and Lewis's investigations. The next morning, with a slightly throbbing head, probably due to the amount of rum consumed, Lewis ran Pierre ashore and Jacaranda then set course south for St Lucia.

Back to the present and the boat was now half way across the passage between Martinique and home. In the distance, Lewis made out the sleek grey shape of what appeared to be a warship heading towards the same island.

'Hey Jack, is that one of yours?' enquired Lewis.

Following his gaze, Jack looked at the distant shape and with a pang of regret answered his friend. 'Bloody hell, you're right. That's a Type 23 grey war canoe of her Majesty's Royal Navy. Must be the current West Indies guard ship. Yes, it is one of 'mine' as you put it. The same sort that I used to fly from.'

Just as he said this, there was a loud growling sound from behind and suddenly a small grey helicopter shot past them well below mast height and at enormous speed. It then climbed almost vertically and corkscrewed around and came back at them. It pulled its nose up steeply to slow down and turned sharply back into wind. The crew in the cockpit were clearly reading the name of the boat before giving a friendly wave and shooting off back towards the distant Frigate.

'Hey Jack, isn't that what you used to do? It looks really good fun. Why did you stop?' asked a grinning Lewis.

'Long story mate, far too boring to burden you with.'

'Nah man, come on, you've dropped the odd hint but never told me what really happened?'

With a sigh, Jack knew that Lewis was not going to let it lie, so he told his story. 'Alright, alright, I joined the RN after my degree and did a short service commission as a pilot. God knows why as my degree was in economics but maybe I needed some excitement after that,' he said wryly. 'But I loved every minute and did my nine years. I was contemplating staying on and making a full time career and then the Second Gulf War came along. You know, many of us were really unhappy with that. My Squadron boss had served in the Falklands and the first Gulf War. He was totally certain that we did the right thing on both occasions but this time it was clearly contrived. I was actually due for release just before it all started but they invoked my reserve status and made me stay on. I was the Flight Commander of a ship just like that one. I did my duty and got the hell out of it as soon as I could afterwards. It pains me to say it but I have never been so ashamed of my country as after that, especially when our excuse to invade in the first place was proved to be a lie. There was no way I could look myself in the mirror if I had stayed in. As you know, I then went to work in the City of London, made a packet and got this boat. So I guess it all turned out OK in the end. Just don't let me within two feet of Tony Blair or George Bush because I might do something they would regret!'

'Yeah but flying like that must be so much fun.'

'You've no idea. It can be exhilarating and terrifying and quite often at the same time. You should try landing a Lynx helicopter on the deck of that thing at night with a big swell and no moon but I loved every minute of it. That ship is probably heading into Castries for a formal visit. They will hold a cocktail party on board one night and stay about five days or until their livers give out. Mind you, when they're at sea they get pretty busy. They helped out after the Montserrat eruption big time and do a lot of anti-drug stuff. I did a similar trip many years ago and that's how I originally came to know the Caribbean. It was a tough job but someone had to do it,' he added with a big grin. 'But hey, that's the past, let's get home now and sort out all these snags and also look at all these stories we've got in a bit more detail. Not long now and my day job has to start.'

Just then the VHF radio crackled into life 'Sailing Vessel Jacaranda, this warship Suffolk on channel 16 do you read?'

Jack picked up the cockpit microphone. 'Suffolk, this is Jacaranda. Let's go to Channel 8, over.'

Changing frequencies from channel 16, Jack then called, 'Suffolk, this is Jacaranda. What can I do for you today.'

'Jacaranda, that wouldn't be the boat skippered by a certain incompetent ass called Lieutenant Vincent RN retired would it be now?' called a very familiar voice tinged with a slight Irish accent.

'Robbie you old bugger, what on earth are you doing on that grey steamer?' replied a smiling Jack who had immediately recognised the voice of his old Observer. You couldn't spend several years of your life sat next another person and sharing the responsibility for safely flying around the sky without instantly knowing their voice over the radio.

'Believe it or not me old bucket, their lordships in their wisdom, have seen fit to allow me to be in command and before you say anything, no we have not rammed any rocks or got lost yet. Anyway, we are heading into Castries for an official visit and the Cock and Arse party is in two nights from now. You, of course, are cordially invited but my Number One has stipulated you have to bring some local totty particularly for the wardroom party afterwards. So, you up to it me old mucker?'

'You got it, I'll see what I can rustle up on the female front but why do I think it's not your First Lieutenant who wants the crumpet? Just remember that as the CO you have to behave yourself on official occasions. Bet you find that difficult, poacher and gamekeeper and all that.'

'Right you are Jack. We'd better stop hogging the radio. See you on Saturday night about 1930. That's assuming you have anything more formal to wear than shorts and a T shirt. Suffolk back to 16.'

'That's amazing,' said Jack to Lewis with a grin. 'Robbie O'Brien and I go back right to flying training days and now he's in command of a Frigate. Maybe I should have stayed in. Bloody hell, if he made it I'm damn sure I could have. He was notorious for being the worst behaved naval officer in the Fleet Air Arm on a run ashore, bloody good Observer though.'

'Yeah but then you wouldn't be commanding your own super yacht,' responded Lewis.

'Good point, well made old chum let's go home.'

Chapter 8

Andromeda was cruising slowly down the coast of St Lucia the southernmost part of her patrol area. Soon, she would turn north and head back towards Antigua some three hundred miles to the north. Charles was daydreaming. Despite standing formally on his quarterdeck in his sea going frock coat and hat and looking every inch the naval Captain, inside he was miles away, dreaming of Lizzy back in St Kitts. Her cute dimpled smile, tiny waist and long blonde hair kept coming back to haunt him at the most inopportune moments. Despite Nelson's orders to start his first patrol, it had taken Andromeda almost two weeks to get ready for extended cruising and Charles had taken time out to take the Governor up on his invitation to call. Despite some half-hearted chaperoning by Lizzy's mother, they had managed to spend quite a few hours together walking in the residence's garden and down by the sea. Charles was worldly wise enough to know that the whole family were happy with the assignations but didn't see why that should stop him enjoying the lively company of a beautiful girl. Although he knew his own family would not be happy, should things go further. After all, she was nowhere near his social level. He was half way to thinking that maybe that didn't matter after all. He also knew that at least some of the attraction was the result of weeks and weeks at sea and a lack of social engagement except for his all male crew. He wondered whether Nelson was falling into the same trap. Rumour had it that he and Mrs Nisbet had been seeing each other regularly since the Governor's ball. A shout from the masthead broke his reverie.

'Sail Ho! Fine on the starboard bow.'

'Right Mr Bevan, up you go,' he said to the Midshipman on watch. Charles expected all his young officers to be able to take on any task that his sailors could do. Climbing to the masthead being one of the more demanding.

With the fearlessness of his whole fifteen years, Mr Bevan was soon sat next to the sailor at the foremast head and looking through his telescope at the distant speck.

'Small lateen sail Sir, almost certainly another fisherman, heading our way.'

A groan spread around the quarterdeck. Tom the First Lieutenant expressed the consensus of the whole crew. 'That's all we seem to see, six weeks patrolling and nothing but fishermen. What about all these stories of pirates and the blockade runners we should be intercepting?'

'I'm afraid I agree,' responded Charles, now back in the real world. 'Anyway, run up towards him and if nothing else we can buy some fish and see if he has any intelligence for us.'

Within half an hour, Andromeda rendezvoused with the boat which was indeed a local fishing boat and successful negotiations were made for enough fish to give the whole crew a good dinner. Charles invited the boat's skipper on board, a wizened old man of indeterminate race and questioned him as to whether he had seen anything unusual. This was a technique that might eventually prove useful. Every boat they stopped, they had given the skipper a small sum of money, even if they had nothing to report with the instruction to keep their eyes open. It was clear that this was getting around the local fishing communities and Charles felt he was effectively building up quite a good spying network to help him know what was going on over a much larger area of sea than he could cover on his own.

This particular fisherman, initially seemed quite reluctant to say anything but after the cash reward was in the open, his attitude changed. He reported that he had seen several large merchantmen in recent weeks but all had been flying French colours and all were heading to or from Martinique. It was getting quite frustrating. Charles knew the British islands had to be getting supplies and money from the Americas and therefore had to be paying in the only currency they had which was sugar. But luck seemed to be on their side and every time Andromeda got the slightest sniff of an intervention it simply melted away in the Caribbean sunshine.

Maybe the same fishermen who were taking his cash were also taking it from his adversaries. Not that there was anything he could do about it. Just before the fisherman left, he pulled Charles aside, clearly wanting to add something else. With a slightly apologetic air, he explained that when going back home to St Lucia on his last voyage he had seen a most unusual sight. It had been a clear day and when looking up he had seen what looked like four straight clouds streaming across the sky heading to the west. This was accompanied by a very distant roaring noise which he could not account for. He gave Charles a curious look and wondered if he knew what it could have been.

Nonplussed, Charles responded that he had no idea. Although this wasn't the first time that local skippers had reported odd incidents. One they had spoken to some weeks ago was adamant that he had seen a pirogue shaped boat moving at great speed with no sign of a mast or sail anywhere. Charles didn't know what to make of these odd reports and as he couldn't explain them he put them down to the fact that most fishermen had as much rum on board as bait.

With the fishing boat falling away astern, Tom came up to Charles and asked what the man had wanted to confide.

'Another strange one,' he grimaced. 'This time it was something in the sky. A dragon or somesuch. I do wonder what these locals get up to on their boats apart from fishing and drinking rum. They certainly seem to have vivid imaginations.' He paused, 'but you know there is so little we really know about the world. Do you know of Sir Joseph Banks, Tom?'

'The name is familiar but no more Sir.'

'Sir Joseph is a naturalist and now the President of the Royal Society but some years ago he travelled in Endeavour with Cook on his first voyage. He is a close friend of my father and has spent many an evening entertaining the family with stories of his journey. He travelled to places where no European has set foot, yet humankind was well established amongst beasts and trees that bear no resemblance to those we know. There is so much out there that we have yet to find. And it's not just in the natural world. Maybe these strange stories the locals are telling us are a manifestation of something we have yet to discover.'

Tom looked uncertain. 'But surely the classics give us all the knowledge we need? That's certainly what school taught us.'

'Hmm, maybe but look how much we have learned for ourselves over the last few centuries. The work of Newton and others in the scientific world for example. You know, none of that was propounded by Aristotle and Homer. Even our doctor knows as much if not more than those ancient Greeks. I often wonder whether we should have shrugged off their influence years ago and made more effort to find our own way. Look at our carronades,' he said, giving the nearest one an affectionate pat. 'Think what effect they would have had a hundred years ago. Tom, can you imagine what life will be like hundreds of years from now if we keep discovering new things?'

Tom had the look of a subordinate who was humouring his senior officer and Charles could see it.

'Right, so that's not going to stop us finding out how all this illegal trade is happening, as clearly it must be. Let's have all officers in my cabin in an hour for lunch and we will put our heads together and see if we can come up with something new.'

And so it was that an hour later the great cabin was full. Charles and Tom were joined by John Stone the Second Lieutenant and Mr Williams the Sailing Master. Also in attendance were the two midshipmen, Jason Wright and the irrepressible John Bevan. This was the first time the youngster had been party to one of Charles's councils of war and he was very conscious that he needed to keep in the background.

Charles looked at his officers. 'Gentlemen, we have a dilemma. We are pretty certain that American ships are trading with the islands but don't seem to be able to apprehend anyone. So, let us put ourselves in the mind of a Captain trying to run our little blockade and try to think as he would. Does anyone have any ideas?'

Mr Williams responded immediately. 'One obvious tactic would be to use the windward side of an island but I think that now the trade winds have fully set in that would be just too dangerous. So that leaves the leeward coasts and ports but there are just so many places one could anchor, especially if the transaction could be completed overnight.'

'Yes, I agree with that,' interjected Tom. 'But they still have to sail in and out of the coast and if they trade cargoes at night we would have seen something in daylight. We have cruised regularly up and down and seen nothing.'

'What are you suggesting?' asked Charles. 'That they somehow camouflage themselves by day?'

'No but they might be hiding somewhere. Trading by day and then sailing in and out in the dark. Someone with good local knowledge should be capable of that. Our presence is well known, especially if the locals are taking money from both sides. The question is where? We look carefully at the whole coast as we pass by. It doesn't make sense.'

A small voice piped up from the back. 'How about Marigot Bay Sir?'

Charles looked over at his young Midshipman. 'Well Mr Bevan, tell us what you mean.'

Looking slightly abashed but determined, the youngster continued. 'Sir, my father served here some years ago and he told me that Marigot Bay used to be a hide out for pirates because it is so hard to see from seaward. Maybe they are hiding there.' His voice trailed off as the First Lieutenant turned his stare on him.

'Mr Bevan, we look at the bay every time we go past and as you know, we have seen nothing.'

'Yes Sir,' continued the determined voice. 'But we don't go in and look. We just sail past. My father said the pirates would tie tree branches to their masts to make them look like palm trees and it was almost impossible to make them out against the background.'

'So, you're suggesting that the Americans might be using the same trick,' interjected Charles before Tom could dampen the young man's enthusiasm any further. 'Well, it might be worth investigating. Unless anyone else has any other bright ideas?'

Despite some further debate, no one else was able to come up with anything better, so Charles decided to follow it up.

'Now, we can't just go charging in. If the bay is empty, we will alert the locals that we are on to them and if a ship is inside they could have time to dump their cargo, so we must be more circumspect. Mr Bevan this is your idea, so this is what we will do. There is an open sandy bay just south of Marigot here called Anse Cochon.' He pointed to the chart laid out on the table. 'We will anchor there and you will take a shore party of three men with you and walk overland and spy out the bay. You can have two days no more. The locals will be suspicious if we linger too long. That will give us time to cruise down to Vieux Fort and Castries and return. Be waiting for us and we will then see if your idea has any value.'

Mr Bevan beamed from ear to ear. For the first time, the Captain was trusting him with an independent task. Perhaps someone older might be more worried about snakes, yellow fever or antagonistic locals but at fifteen you were immortal and this was his chance to see his first action off the ship.

Charles, well aware of the effect his words, was nevertheless pleased for the lad and hoped that giving the youngster some independence and command would do him good. He knew his father who was a retired naval Captain and had taken on the boy at his request. Just as importantly, he thought that the lad had come up with a sound idea and it was worth taking further.

Two days later, Midshipman Bevan, the ship's gnarled old experienced, Coxswain John Cummins and two able seamen were lying in a thicket on the southern hill overlooking Marigot Bay. As soon as the bay was in sight it was clear why it was such a good hiding place. In fact 'Bay' was totally the wrong description. It was more like a small narrow estuary leading into a landlocked lagoon surrounded by mangroves. A spit of sand covered with palm trees almost enclosed the entrance and from seaward it would actually be impossible to see a ship in the lagoon except for its masts were they tall enough. Unfortunately, the lagoon was empty except for a few birds and jumping fish. The only sign of human intervention was a small wooden jetty that could just be seen sticking out into the lagoon from the southern shore.

Mr Bevan was hot and thirsty. It had taken almost a day to get to their vantage point. They had been landed with a large ship's party ostensibly looking to refill water casks and had slipped away into the undergrowth, hopefully out of sight of any watchers. The short overland trip proved more difficult than anticipated. Partly because of the terrain which was thickly wooded but also because there were plenty of locals about which they did their best to avoid.

'Well Cummins, it seems to be rather too quiet,' observed the young man, idly scratching at insect bites on his neck.

'Aye Sir but look at the right of the lagoon. That small jetty has seen some recent use. Some of that timber is fresh and we have heard a lot of voices from behind that bluff.' If the experienced Cummins resented calling a fifteen year old boy 'Sir' he didn't show it.

'Indeed, something is definitely going on there. We need to find out what. We'll slowly make our way inland and see if we can see what they're up to.'

So saying, they part crawled, part walked, further inland until they could overlook the southern part of the bay in its entirety. Immediately, it was clear that something was indeed going on. A party of slaves were coming down a track into a large area at the head of the jetty and depositing barrels which were beginning to pile up in ordered rows.

'Molasses Sir, I've seen that sort of barrel many a time. They must be getting ready for a shipment within the next few days.'

'How long do you reckon?' Bevan asked. 'It seems to me they've not been long at it.'

'Aye Sir, I reckon it will take a while to stockpile enough for a ship to embark but they won't want to leave it here longer than they have to. I reckon the ship will be in soon to load up.'

'I hope you're right because that will be perfect for us. We should be back in Andromeda tomorrow night and that will give us time to arrange a little surprise. Assuming this is illegal of course.'

'Well Sir, if it was all above board why not use the docks at Soufriere or Castries like everyone else?'

'Good point. Well, let's keep an eye on the activity here and head back tomorrow for our rendezvous.'

Night fell and they split into two watches. Sometime after midnight, the Midshipman was awakened by an urgent voice.

'Sir, something is coming into the anchorage.'

Sure enough, by the light of a very small sickle moon, a ghostly shape slowly appeared to seaward. Accompanied by the quiet splash of oars from two cutters attached by ropes to the bow, a two masted trading ship was slowly making her way past the spit of land and into the shelter of the lagoon.

'They must be really confident of not being found even by daylight,' muttered Cummins.

'Indeed,' responded Bevan. 'I suspect they have done this before and have got away with it. They may be getting overconfident.'

They kept watch through the night and saw how, as soon as the ship was anchored, a line was taken ashore and the stern pulled close to the mangroves thus moving the ship well behind the enclosing sand spit. As soon as that was done, crew went ashore and started cutting palm fronds which were then taken up to the top of the masts and arrayed just like the top of a palm tree. By now anyone out to sea would only have seen a forest of palms and there would be no sign of a ship.

'Very clever and just how my father described it to me. I am guessing that if they have gone to all this trouble, they will be staying a few days. We must get back to our ship and tell the Captain.'

Later the next evening, after another furtive scramble cross country, the young man was back in the great cabin telling his story to the assembled officers.

'Well done Mr Bevan. Clearly, my faith in you has been rewarded,' Charles said to a beaming Midshipman.

Even Tom offered a congratulatory smile to the young man.

'Now we know how at least one island is playing this game. We need to decide what we should do. This is not a military cutting out expedition, so it's not a case of going in all guns blazing. Mister Bevan, was there any sign of the nationality of the ship? We would look pretty foolish if she were British after all.'

'No Sir, she flew no flags that we could see but it was very still in the anchorage and we could hear some voices. It seemed to us that the accents weren't English.'

'Hmm,' Charles looked thoughtful. 'And they are clearly at pains not to be seen. So, whatever they're up to, it must be unlawful. At the end of the day gentlemen, this is a British island and we are a British ship. So, let us go and sample the delights of Marigot Bay.'

The next morning HMS Andromeda sailed serenely in. At first, she had stood off to appear as if she was just sailing past on her way northward. At the last moment, she had turned close into the wind and used the remaining light airs to ghost into the entrance and use her last momentum to clear the sand spit and anchor in the lagoon.

On the other ship, they looked close to panic for a few minutes. The crew started to rush around closing hatches until a portly gentleman in a frock coat came on deck and shouted for order. The crew activity subsided and they all looked expectantly over at Andromeda. On shore, all activity had also ceased, although it was quite clear that most of the cargo had already been embarked.

Charles smiled inwardly to himself. It looked like perfect surprise. 'Tom, take one of the boats ashore, find out who is in charge and tell him that if we find that he is trading with an American he will not be seeing his produce again or any payment for it. I will go over to the ship and have a talk with that fine fellow on her quarterdeck.'

'Aye, aye Sir,' said a smiling First Lieutenant as he called for his boat's crew.

Charles climbed up the side of the other ship and was greeted with a stony silence from the crew. He went up to the portly gentleman at the stern.

'Captain Charles Lonfort at your service Sir and might I ask who you are and what ship this is?'

'No you may not Sir,' blustered the other ships Master. 'By what right do you board me in this fashion?'

'I could say by right of the fact that I am the Captain of a Royal Naval warship. This is a British island. You Sir, are not flying any national flag and are clearly at pains not to be seen,' replied Charles looking up to the palm fronds on the mastheads. 'If that is not enough, you could always try this,' and he took out a handkerchief and waved it above his head.

There was a growling rumbling noise and on Andromeda the muzzles of nine, twenty four pound carronades appeared through the now open gun ports. Behind them could be seen the grinning faces of the gun crews.

The face of the other Captain turned a sickly green. Clearly faced with an impossible situation, he realised he was discovered and was going to have to come clean.

'Captain Jonathon Williams Sir, of the American ship Artemis.'

'And your business here in this British island?'

Completely deflated now, the American Captain admitted that he had been buying molasses from ashore but denied all knowledge of any trade restrictions. He even tried to make counter accusations of piracy but when Charles pointed out that the deliberate attempts to camouflage the ship and remain hidden were hardly the actions of an innocent man who thought he was trading legally, he caved in completely. The only information he was not prepared to give was the name of his shore side supplier. Charles could hardly force him and anyway was not too concerned as this would be a matter for the island's Governor. Depending on what Tom discovered ashore, he would write a report and send it overland and let the island authorities deal with it. His job was to intercept and stop the sea borne element of the trade and this he had done. Now that the use of the bay was common knowledge it was going to be much harder for others to do the same thing.

The next day, the two ships sailed in company out of Marigot Bay. Despite renewed recriminations from the American, Charles simply kept him under his guns and made it clear that any repetition of the actions of the other American in St Kitts would be met with a warning shot followed by more accurate gunfire if that is what he wanted. Andromeda was a happy ship. They may not agree necessarily with the reason for arresting the foreigner but they had done their job and done it well. Charles knew that Nelson would be pleased. He also wondered if he had just made his job much harder. He suspected that the next time would not be so easy.

Chapter 9

The magnificent stag was standing half way up the valley looking down over the bracken covered glen and his harem of does. The day was cold but clear after the rains of the previous days. It was late in the year and late in the day. The setting sun was producing a startling sunset to illuminate the superb animal.

'Right, I'll give you Monarch of the fucking Glen,' muttered Paul under his breath as he took sight through the telescopic sight on his rifle. Paul was not where he wanted to be. He was cold, wet and bloody miserable. They had been stalking this herd of deer all day. Every time they had got near, something had spooked them and they were forced to keep following. They had waded burns and got soaked. Pushed through heavy bracken and got even colder and wetter. Climbed steep ridges, the sort where when you eventually got to the skyline, it was only to find another sodding, fucking skyline hiding behind it. At one point the stalker had shouted for them all to get down and he had ended up face down in a bloody bog. Eventually, they had managed to get downwind of the stag. Unfortunately, that had meant being below him and it presented the most difficult of shots, uphill against a strong light. Paul wasn't going to let any of that stop him. The sooner the bloody animal was dead or had run away the sooner he could get off this sodding, fucking hill and have a hot bath.

'Take the shot Sir,' muttered Craig the stalker who had been leading Paul and the rest of the party all day.

Paul ignored him, concentrating on controlling his breathing and keeping the crosshairs centred on the correct spot on the neck. He gently squeezed the trigger and the rifle kicked back hard into his shoulder. The report was shockingly loud but the deer would feel the bullet before it heard the shot.

The stag jerked slightly, crumpled onto its forelegs and gently keeled over.

They all stood up and cheered. 'Well done Paul,' said Alasdair McDonald, laird of the estate, owner of all they could survey and the only reason Paul was on the side of this God forsaken hill in the first place.

Maintaining the same smile he had fixed in place all day, Paul accepted the congratulations of the hunting party. Inside he was not happy with Nigel who had sent him up here to the back end of beyond in the first place.

However, Alasdair was a major investor in the company and every year he had a party at his lodge in the Highlands. Someone had to attend and this year Nigel had despatched Paul to carry out what would normally have been his duty. Not unreasonable under the circumstances but very definitely not Paul's cup of tea. It wasn't even that the very Scottish sounding Alasdair was even Scottish. He was in fact from Hampshire and had purchased his estate and the title years ago. Paul hated people who embraced the life of a country gentleman when late in life. For the last week he had stood up to his waist in freezing water in his waders in the almost vain attempt to catch a salmon and when he succeeded, he then had to throw the bloody thing back. He had a sore shoulder from shooting stupid shot guns at stupid bloody birds that he didn't even get to eat. The only good thing was that this was the last day. Soon, he could get on the plane and head back to the office and sanity.

As they tramped down the hill towards the waiting Land Rovers that had driven round to pick them up, the stalker came up to Paul and spoke to him quietly.

'Well done Sir, I got the feeling that you weren't really into today's activities but that was one of the best shots I've seen in many a year and much better than the laird has ever managed.'

Slightly mollified, Paul smiled back. 'Thanks for the compliment Craig. I learned to shoot in the army years back and I love guns. They are a bit of a passion of mine. Your perception does you justice. I can think of a million things I'd rather be doing but as you have probably guessed this is business for me. And thank you for all your help this week. You managed to make me look less of the amateur that we both know I am.'

Craig smiled, satisfied that he had done all he could to ensure at least one good tip would be coming his way before the party all trooped back to London.

They returned to the lodge quickly compared to the time it had taken to stalk the stag, driving down rutted farm tracks and directly across the heather where necessary. Paul started to mellow out, partly due to the universal praise for his shooting but also because the hip flasks had been passed around freely and at least in Scotland there was no shortage of a decent malt whiskey. The magnificent building came into view down a long drive. A classic Scottish castle looking like it was straight out of a TV series. In fact it had been used in several. They all disembarked in front of the main front doors with instructions to meet at seven thirty for dinner.

Paul made his way up the oak staircase past innumerable sets of antlers and oil paintings of serious looking Scotsmen in kilts who were almost certainly no relatives of the current owner. He found his room on the second floor and gave a muttered prayer of thanks to the gods of the hot bath as he entered.

Sarah was waiting for him, sitting by the open fireplace with a dreamy grin on her face. 'Hello darling, have you murdered any more wildlife today?'

'Er, well yes, I actually shot this rather large Bambi but my excuse is that we were then able to stop playing silly buggers and come home. How about you? What did the WAGs get up to today?'

'We went to the distillery and sampled lots and lots of shcotch,' hiccupped Sarah. 'And it was really great.' She got to her feet and sidled up to Paul looking into his eyes. 'You need a bath and I am the person to give you the scrub you need.'

Paul looked at his new girlfriend with wry amusement but also what was becoming a great deal of fondness. Both of them were driven people, needing success in their lives and not too concerned at how they achieved it. They say opposites attract but in this case the converse seemed to be the case. There was no doubt they were both of a like mind, in the boardroom and in bed.

The bathroom was through the large open door and the big old fashioned bath was plenty big enough for two. What started out as a back scrub soon turned into a lot more and they were soon lying back exhausted at opposite ends of the bath with their toes next to each other's ears. Sarah's breasts and pink nipples seeming to float just clear of the surface of the bathwater like two little alps.

'Oh thank God, it's our last night and then back to the office. I just can't wait to get away from all this huntin', shootin' and fishin' crap,' groaned Paul.

'At least it's given us a bit of a break,' responded Sarah through the steam. 'And Oh goody, I expect we can look forward to a nice meal of offal stuffed into a sheep's gut.'

'I bloody well hope not again,' grimaced Paul. 'I wouldn't mind if the bloody man was Scottish but he comes from Southampton for God's sake. Just because he has a Scottish surname doesn't mean he has to like all this crap. You know, I hear we are going to have a piper tonight after dinner. Can you please tell me what is the difference between the sound they make and someone castrating a cat? Because I'm buggered if I know.'

Sarah giggled. 'Poor darling, how do you manage to keep sucking up to the man if you hate all this so much?'

'Ah,' grinned Paul. 'Simple, one word answer, money, lots and lots of money and I don't care what side of the border it comes from. Hey, I guess that makes me a prostitute. What's your excuse?'

'Oh the same as you darling, so that makes us both prostitutes. Let's do a bit more prostituting before dinner,' responded Sarah as her hand slipped around under water. 'Oops thought that was the soap,' she giggled.

Dinner was over and it was all that Paul had feared. Luckily, there was also venison and salmon on the menu, so he was able to discreetly avoid the haggis. The piper had actually been quite good, mainly because he played on the battlements and was therefore far enough away not to be overpowering. After dinner, they all retired to the massive library. '*It was just the sort of place where the Inspector would come and accuse someone in the room of murdering Colonel Mustard with the lead pipe,'* thought Paul. He was also pretty sure that no one had ever opened, let alone read, any of the multitude of books covering the walls. It was like living in some sort of time warp but at least there was some business to be done and that was as contemporary as could be.

All the other guests had already gone to bed and Paul and Alasdair were enjoying a late night scotch by the fireplace. Despite joining in convivially with everyone, Paul had been very careful with his alcoholic intake and was close to being sober. Alasdair was a tall and big boned man and despite prodigious consumption, he also seemed quite alert.

'So Paul, Sir Nigel is letting you take over the reins? If you are as good a business man as you are a shot, then the company is in good hands.'

'Thank you,' replied Paul looking into the dancing flames of the fire. 'I left the army years ago which is where I learned to shoot but since then I've worked very hard for that man and I am very proud of the trust he has put in me.'

'Yes, we've done good business over the years. He has taken my hard earned cash and made me a considerable amount more. The big question is, are you going to continue with his investment policies or how can I put this, are you going to become all ethical on me?'

Paul smiled. Ruthlessness was a key part of his boss's success and sentiment for the people he dealt with was not part of his 'policy'.

Paul chose his words carefully. 'I think you'll find that I've learned well from Sir Nigel. You would definitely not do well in his organisation without following his business approach.'

'Good point. It seems we are of a like mind, so let's talk about future ideas.'

They talked into the night. Paul was impressed by Alasdair's business insight. He hoped Alasdair was impressed by his own abilities. By the time they went to bed they had settled on several issues and Alasdair agreed to visit the London office in a few weeks time.

The next morning they all climbed into Alasdair's helicopter for the short flight to Edinburgh airport and their various destinations onwards.

Two days later, Paul and Nigel were in the board room talking about Paul's 'Scottish week'.

'So, how did you enjoy tramping around the heather freezing your bollocks off and murdering the wildlife?' Nigel asked with a grin. 'I'll bet it was right up your street, what with you being ex army and all that.'

Paul responded ruefully. 'The whiskey and open fires were good but you can stuff the country lifestyle up your 'you know what'. I've decided I am not a country mouse. Give me the City any day. Mind you, I have this weird vision of you in plus fours striding across the heather and it just doesn't seem to ring true.'

'Ahah,' Nigel grinned in return. 'Must have slipped my mind but I told the old fraud that he could stuff his hunting shooting and fishing up his 'you know what' the first time I visited his Disneyland castle and he didn't seem to mind. You should have done the same. No, I usually had a great time with the ladies while the men were out playing.'

'Well thanks for telling me,' Paul responded. 'Remind me not to trust your social advice in the future.'

'Anyway, to business, did you get anything out of him? He may be a country snob but he has lots of cash and a good business brain.'

'Er well, there was this,' replied Paul, holding out a piece of paper. 'He must have liked something about me because he gave me a cheque for twelve million which, I believe, is far more than you ever screwed out of the bastard.'

Nigel sat back smiling and looked thoughtfully at Paul. 'Bloody well done. Seems you do have the touch and what exactly do we have to do with this cash?'

They talked all morning about Alasdair's investment ideas and how to maximise such a large injection of money. Any company could invest it in various ways but Paul had a few innovative ideas that he had sold Alasdair and now needed to convince his boss. By the end of the morning, they had agreed a way forward and would present their ideas at the meeting with Alasdair in the near future.

Just as the meeting was about to finish, Nigel brought up one more issue.

'Paul, one further thing, taking over as boss of the company isn't all weekends in the country and playing with other people's money I'm afraid. That little raid we mounted the other day has come to the notice of the Financial Services Authority. Now you and I know that although we came close to the line we didn't cross it but it seems some of our rivals have been making a bit of a fuss. It's not the first time we have been put under the microscope but the last time was ages ago before you joined us. They have asked to come in and do a full audit, starting sometime early next year. Your chore I'm afraid, we normally just give them office space and computer access to the records and leave them to it but you are going to have to run it from our side.'

Paul felt like ice water had been poured down his spine. 'How long back do they go?' he asked trying desperately to keep a normal voice, even though he was pretty sure he knew the answer.

'Normally a couple of years but they seem to be bloody minded this time and are asking for the full seven.'

Paul felt the onset of panic which he fought down and somehow managed to maintain a calm demeanour while he thought furiously. *'No, he had covered his tracks too well there was no risk. He was sure no one could dig out the results of his actions all those years ago.'*

'Fine Nigel, well we have several months, so I'll get us ready. I can't see any problems,' he managed to get out in a reasonably normal voice. 'Just leave it with me.'

Chapter 10

HMS Suffolk looked much larger when alongside the jetty than when seen at sea. The lean grey ship loomed over the visitors as they made their way up the steep gangplank to the flight deck at the stern. The muted growl of diesel generators could just be heard over the laughter and music from the party that was taking place under the blue and white striped awning that was spread over the area where the ship's helicopter would normally come into land

A smartly suited Jack reached the top of the gangway and he had to resist the urge to turn and salute the white ensign hanging limply from the flag staff at the rear of the ship. '*Old habits die hard*' he thought to himself as a shout came up from the crowd and Commander Robbie O'Brien made his way through and welcomed Jack like the long lost brother he almost was.

Greetings over, Jack turned to the ladies waiting behind him. Gathering them around, he introduced them to the Commanding Officer of HMS Suffolk, sternly warning them all that he was a very untrustworthy individual as were all his officers. It didn't seem to matter, within a heartbeat the girls had all been whisked off by smiling hosts.

'Well done mate, where did you scare up that lot of lovelies from then?' asked a grinning Robbie.

'Never underestimate local knowledge and the attraction of owning a bloody great yacht,' responded an equally grinning Jack. 'And I'll be watching out to make sure your lads are not ignoring the local bigwigs and monopolising the females,' he added with a grin. They both smiled at this. It was something they had both been accused of many times at similar parties in the past.

'So, how are you anyway Jack? Nice to see you actually managed to find a suit to wear and where is that lovely girl you were with when last we met?'

A shadow crossed Jack's face. 'Long gone mate but that's another story. How long are you going to stand there and not offer me a bloody drink? I could die of thirst standing here.'

The two friends merged into the throng. Having obtained a naval 'Horses Neck' or a large brandy and ginger ale for Jack, Robbie excused himself saying he really did have to talk to the bigwigs for a while and arranged to meet up after the party to catch up properly.

So, it was some hours later, that Jack and Robbie were sat in the Captain's cabin below the bridge of the ship sharing a drink and reminiscing over past times. Talk ranged from when they had flown together to what they had both been up to after they parted.

Robbie explained, 'you know I got promoted to Commander right out of the blue. Not what I was expecting to be honest and then they gave me a staff job in bloody Whitehall. But then they offered me this command. As you said on the radio the other day, sort of Poacher turned Gamekeeper really.'

For his part, Jack said, 'yeah well, you know how disillusioned I got. My old mate Paul Smythe heard I was kicking my heels and got me this job in the City. To be frank, with my degree and military background, the work was actually quite easy and bloody rewarding. You know it was weird, I couldn't seem to do anything wrong and all those stories you hear about ridiculous City bonuses are all true. That's how I got the boat. She was a project started by this old chap who died after the hull was finished. I was sailing down the Hamble River on a friend's boat and saw her in a yard. It was strange to see such an old fashioned boat with such a modern underwater profile. She even has two rudders like a modern ocean racer for God's sake. Anyway, I enquired and found she was for sale at a knockdown price and that was it, I was in love. Not going to say how much she cost to get finished but she was all mine within a year.'

'But why did you leave such a good job?' asked Ronnie with a frown. 'Surely, you could have made a fortune.'

'That's another long story,' responded Jack evasively. 'Suffice to say it's not a sustainable lifestyle. At least not for me anyway and now I'm sailing around my office, which beats the crap out of a desk in an office block in the City any day!'

'So you've been chartering here for several years now? I'm not sure I could continue to be nice to all those strangers. I reckon I'd last ten minutes before telling some damn yank what I thought of him.'

'Yes, that can be a problem but in the main the people who can afford my outrageous prices are sailors as well and generally turn out to be pretty good types. You get the odd pain in the ass but you always know they will be off the boat in a few days and anyway their money is always good.'

Robbie gave Jack a thoughtful look. 'Don't suppose you get to see anything unusual while you're swanning about on the blue stuff do you?'

Jack immediately reacted to his old friend's words with suspicion but didn't betray his feelings. 'Like when you have too much rum you mean?'

'No look, when we were flying together how many UFO's did we see?'

'I think I can safely say that in six years and almost two thousand hours in the air, the answer is the square root of fuck all. As well you know. Why the silly question?'

'I'm not really supposed to tell you this but when you climb to the dizzy heights of command of a warship you get to be told lots of things that most scum of the earth proles like you aren't meant to know about. UFOs, the Bermuda triangle and other things have some basis in fact and I am required to keep an eye out for them especially in this area.'

Jack had a nasty feeling he knew where this was going. 'Oh, what other things? I get the feeling you're not telling me everything.'

Robbie bit his lip. 'Look mate, I can't tell you everything but I will say as much as I can. Your help could be really useful here. Have you heard of the Philadelphia experiment?'

'Vaguely, wasn't it some conspiracy theory about some US navy destroyer in the war and didn't they make a film out of it?'

'Yes and that's how it was covered up. Let the loonies run around shouting conspiracy and most people then ignore it. During the war, both sides did experiments with magnetic fields. On the allies side, we had Einstein's Unified Field theory to try out. The Yanks really did make a warship disappear but the side effects were dreadful for the crew and even now, there appears to be no solution. However, we the Brits, also tried a few things but we were more circumspect. We did it away from prying eyes out here or to be exact about fifteen miles to the west. We made our ship disappear but she never came back and since then we've been getting the occasional very odd story surfacing that appears to link in with the experiment. The government are taking this really seriously at the moment. Not the least because it might allow us to get one over the Yanks for a change. So, I could really do with some eyes and ears out here. Unless of course you've already come across anything?'

Jack managed to remain looking nonplussed. The last thing he needed was to share his findings with his old friend at this moment. His first charter was coming up in a few weeks and he had promised all his sources that he would not take anything further without their various permissions. Talking to Her Majesties Government, in the form of Robbie would just complicate things too much.

'Bloody hell, how much have you had to drink? This is not like the old drunken Irishman I came to know and love. Anyway, sorry to disappoint you but all I've seen are whales, dolphins and quite a few cute bikini fish, the female variety that is. I'll keep a look out mate but don't hold your breath.'

Robbie actually looked relieved at this denial and quickly moved the conversation on to other topics. At one point they went down to the wardroom after an invitation from the First Lieutenant where the 'post cocktail party', party was in full swing. Jack was amused but not surprised to see that all the girls he had invited were there enjoying themselves. However, it soon became clear that having the Captain around was putting a bit of a damper on the officer's further intentions for the evening, so they withdrew after an appropriate time.

Seated back in his cabin Robbie blew out his lips and complained. 'They talk about the loneliness of command but no one mentioned that I can't chat up totty in my own ship any more. Bloody hell Jack.'

'What you need me old mucker is a run ashore. Presumably, you have a sober Officer of the Day to watch over this steamer. So how about I use my local knowledge to give you the best hangover of your trip so far?'

Robbie took no convincing at all and soon the two old friends were touring certain establishment known to Jack as good places to enjoy oneself.

Five o'clock the next morning, a taxi drew up at the jetty and the Commanding Officer of HMS Suffolk made his stately way up the gangway. He bade a bleary, cheery, good night to the Quartermaster on duty, found his cabin and fell into bed with a smile on his face.

Jack took the same taxi home and went to bed ruefully remembering what a dangerous man his old friend was. Hollow legs, an eye for a pretty girl and the ability to get more bouncy the more he drank, made him a hard act to keep up with. Still, it had been bloody good fun.

The next morning or was it afternoon? Jack felt slightly differently. On going down to the kitchen he made straight for the coffee pot that Martha kept on the brew. She came in just as he was starting a second cup.

Before she could say anything Jack got in first. 'Yes I know but you don't get to meet an old friend who invites you onto his ship every day and anyway the good thing about a hangover is that you know you are going to get better.'

'Pardon me but did I say anything?' queried Martha raising an eyebrow. 'Anyway, Lewis asked me to say that if you surfaced any time today he's down on Jacky and to remind you that you said you wanted to put all your results on the chart today.'

'Oh, yes you're right,' said Jack looking at his watch for the first time. 'Bloody hell, I'd better get down there right away.'

Jack enjoyed the blast down to the marina on his old bike and slalomed her down the jetty avoiding all the hoses and other yachting paraphernalia until he arrived at Jacaranda who was moored right at the far end. On going down to the saloon, he found Lewis poring over an oversize chart of the area spread out on the large table.

Lewis looked up with a grin. 'Ah, must have been a good night with the navy then?'

'Yeah, yeah and if you're good I might even tell you about it some time. I see you've managed to get that large scale chart then. One thing I will tell you about last night is that my old mate who is in command, asked if we had seen anything odd. Seems they might even know what is causing all this and are keeping an eye out for strange goings-on around here.'

Lewis frowned. 'Hope you didn't tell him anything. We promised a lot of guys we would keep quiet.'

'I'm well ahead of you, no I just looked blank and inferred he was the daft one and he let it drop. But you know, it's really good in some ways, as it proves that we are not the only ones interested in what is going on. It's sort of reassuring really. Anyway, let's get on with it.'

Two hours and several more coffees later they had plotted all their information on the chart noting location, time and date when known, speed and direction and anything else relevant.

Jack sat back and looked at the chart. 'Well one thing seems clear, even allowing for error, every incident seems to be on a line about fifteen miles to the west and it curves with the island chain and everyone seems to have been heading east back towards the islands when whatever happened to them occurred. It's a shame that we can't get any accurate dating. We know the date of the eruption in St Pierre but that is only an upper limit to one sighting but why do I still get a feeling that the same time bracket is involved in all these incidents?'

Lewis broke in. 'Yes but have you noted anything more about the dates when people reported things?'

Jack looked again, at first not seeing anything significant, as just about every month of the year was mentioned and then he saw it. 'Yes, there seems to be a cycle. Nothing for the previous six years and look another six year gap. We seem to have a cycle with a year's activity and then six years of quiet. Oh and look, it seems to run from mid-year to mid-year. So that means we have until next summer and then it should all go quiet again, bloody strange.' Looking again he also observed. 'There also seems to be a concentration of sightings around Martinique and St Lucia they seem to tail off by the Grenadines to the south and Guadeloupe to the north.

'Well, that could be because that's as far as we sailed but you're right, the Martinique to St Lucia passage seems the busiest area. There may be something else,' said Lewis with a frown on his face. 'Look at the size of the boats involved. Apart from our French friend they are all small boats less than twenty five feet and even he was relatively small. If this is universal, why haven't any cruise liners reported something? After all, they go out to the west overnight and come back in probably more often than any other shipping around here. I'm surprised that a boat as big as Jacaranda got caught up. She is over twice the size of any others. Jack, were you doing anything odd when it happened?'

'Not really, I'd just come down to make a cup of coffee. I was looking at the sharks and waiting for the kettle to boil.'

'Hang on,' said Lewis, who shot off to the galley and returned with the bone shark that Debbie had given to Jack. 'You know this has always seemed out of place. It reminds me of some of the religious stuff some of the islanders use when they think no one's looking.'

Jack took the shark and looked hard at it. 'Could be I guess. I was looking at it at the time and the sun reflecting in its eyes was what first alerted me to the fact that the boat was turning. But how would we find out if it has any significance? I'm not actually intending to go out and try a re-run you know.'

'I'll ask mother, she knows a bit about the local religions and see if she can recognise it,' responded Lewis. 'Can I borrow it for a while?'

Jack nodded absentmindedly and sat back with his hands behind his head. 'Lewis, where are we? Look, we know something is happening and it seems to affect people coming back towards the islands either experiencing a trip back a couple of hundred years or seeing something of that age. I don't know, maybe the past is also coming forward somehow. We seem to have got some hard information that it happens for about a year every six years and mainly involves small boats. But the real question is what are we going to do about it now we know all this? And the most important question of all, is what time is it now?'

Lewis looked blank.

'I'll tell you old chum. Its beer o'clock and I need a hair of the dog. I've been sat down here for far too long. Let's go to the bar and carry on there.'

So they did and relaxing on the veranda with a cold beer they carried on speculating. However, in the end they couldn't come up with any more than they had already surmised.

Jack drew a line under it. 'We've found out a lot and at least I know I'm not going soft in the head but what can we do about it? Lewis, let's just let it lie for now. We can keep our eyes out until the summer and then it should all stop for six years if we're right. Oi, Lewis, are you listening?'

Lewis wasn't, he was looking over Jack's shoulder and smiling. A timid female voice broke in.

'Hello Jack, I hear you are looking for crew?'

The familiar voice sent a shiver down Jack's spine and he spun around to see two very pretty female faces looking expectantly at him.

The first girl had curly blonde hair and a bright oval face. She was dressed in a tight T shirt that showed off a curvy figure with long legs ending in a very tight pair of denim shorts. Her name was Melissa. The second girl was shorter and more petite. Lustrous black hair was tied behind her neck in a pony tail. She was also dressed in T shirt and shorts. Where Melissa could be described as attractive, the other girl was just stunning. A small up turned nose and elfin chin were almost her finest features but the best were her deep brown eyes that seemed to be always smiling. They were smiling tentatively now. Her name was Emma and Jack had known her since he was three. At least that was what their respective parents claimed. When introduced, Jack had apparently hit her over the head with a toy brick and instead of crying she had retaliated with her doll. They had been inseparable. They went to the same schools, the same parties, when teenage years overcame them, they became lovers. When universities beckoned they had separated but never lost touch. They had met again and been together for several years until Jack had left England in Jacaranda. Jack thought he had got over her but seeing her again, he realised he could never really love anyone else and it drove a spike right through his heart.

To Lewis's stunned surprise, Jack stood up knocking his chair over in the process, not looking at both girls as he pushed past them.

'You have got to be bloody joking,' he almost snarled as he half ran back down the jetty to his boat.

Lewis saw the look of pain that crossed the dark haired girl's face, which crumpled as she tried to stifle a sob.

The blonde girl turned to Lewis. 'Are you his friend? We weren't expecting that.'

Lewis gestured to the empty seats. 'Yes, I help him out with his boat during the off season. I've known him for several years and I've never known him to be so rude to any girl. Let me get you a drink.'

Initially, the girls declined but probably realising that he was their best method of approach they soon relented. They talked for a while. Lewis learned that their offer was real. They had come out to St Lucia on holiday but were also hoping to find Jack. They had seen the advert he had placed on the marina office notice board and so knew where and when to find him. Lewis tried to probe, to find out why Jack had acted so strangely but neither girl was prepared to tell him, though it was clear that neither were too surprised by his reaction. That said, the dark haired girl Emma, was clearly very disappointed.

'Look, I don't know what to say. He rents part of the house that I live in when he's not on the boat but knowing him he will stay on the boat tonight. We can go down there and try to talk to him if you like.'

Melissa looked at Emma. 'Come on love, let's give it one more try. You know you've never talked to him properly about it. Maybe we can get Lewis to get him to at least listen to you.'

Emma nodded and so they set off down towards the boat. Despite the circumstances, they were both impressed when they saw Jacaranda at the end of the jetty. Far bigger than any of the surrounding yachts, she looked stunning with her newly varnished woodwork and elegant lines.

'My God, I'd forgotten what a beautiful boat she is,' whispered Melissa. 'No wonder he ran away with her.'

Lewis heard the remark and gave her a questioning look but she didn't respond.

'Right girls, just hang on here while I go and talk to him. I'll call you on board once I've got him to agree.'

Lewis came down the saloon stairs to see Jack helping himself to a large whiskey from his private stash.

He turned as he saw him. 'Lewis my old friend, don't take this the wrong way but please will you fuck off.'

'No, no I don't think I will thank you very much. What the hell were you playing at up there? I've never seen you act so rudely to anyone. You really upset those two girls and that's not like you.'

Jack sat down with a sigh and took a large gulp. 'Alright, that was part of my murky past catching up with me and it's something I don't want to talk about.'

'Well, I think you should. I stayed talking to the girls and apart from making good crew, if their qualifications are what they claim, you owe them an apology.'

'Oh, I know what their qualifications are. I bloody well should do as I taught them in the first place. They have had over two years to talk to me, why should I have to listen now?'

Lewis looked puzzled. 'Listen mate, I have absolutely no idea what you are on about but they are both on the dock at the moment and I promised to get you to talk to them. Come on man, what harm can it do?'

Jack realised that Lewis was once again quite determined and he owed his friend an explanation. As much as he denied it to himself, deep down, he really wanted to hear Emma's side of the story. With a sigh, he agreed. 'Alright, let them come down.'

Lewis stuck his head out of the companionway and the girls came into the saloon. Jack gestured to a seat but didn't offer any drinks. Lewis went to the fridge and pointedly got out some beers for them all and looked expectantly over at Jack.

Jack exhaled. 'Alright, I owe Lewis an explanation and I will have my say but then I really think you girls should leave.'

At least let us say our piece once you've finished.' interjected Melissa.

'You mean Emma's piece don't you?' Responded Jack, not making eye contact with anyone. 'Right, this is how it went. I left the navy after the Second Gulf war as you all know and went to work in the City for a company run by Sir Nigel Dwyer. I was recruited by my old friend Paul Smythe who, incidentally, was Melissa's boy friend at the time.

'Not any more he bloody well isn't.'

'Whatever. Emma and I had also just got back together again. I did really well. The company was very predatory and I guess my military background was a help but in the three years I was there, I made enough money to build this boat and buy a house in Notting Hill which is in Emma's and my name. I assume you are still living there?'

Emma still looking miserable just nodded.

'One day, two and half years ago, I came in to work on a Monday as usual. My desk had been cleared and I couldn't log onto my computer. There was a yellow post-it note on the screen telling me to report to the boss at once. I went up to his office and he ripped me to shreds. He accused me of financial irresponsibility bordering on criminality and of losing large sums of money. To this day, I don't have clue what he was talking about. He was so angry, he wouldn't let me get a word in edgewise. Eventually, I also lost my temper and accused him of operating a kangaroo court and acting like Hitler. He ordered me off the premises. At that point, I suddenly realised I didn't give a flying fuck about him, his company or the lifestyle it had given me and I told him so. If Paul hadn't come in then, I think I might have taken a swing at the fat bastard. So I walked out. As I left, he told never to try and work in the City again and I told him what he could do with the City of London, except it would never have fitted.'

Lewis broke in. 'So, were you formally accused of anything?'

'No, I wasn't and that seemed a bit odd to me but all my business contacts were suddenly unavailable and it was clear that the word was out. And you know what, I didn't care. I really didn't. I had this stupendous boat and she was all mine. I still had a little money in the bank. I had my house and girlfriend. It was one of those cathartic breaks and suddenly there was no reason in world not to do what I had always said I would and sod off to the sun. However, there was one problem. I quickly found out that I had also lost my girlfriend.' Jack looked accusingly at Emma for the first time.

'Oh Jack, you knew I was in South Africa on a photographic assignment,' she replied in a small voice.

'Yes and does that mean you couldn't pick up mobile phone texts, that you couldn't read e-mails from your hotel? I left voicemails. I even wrote a real letter for God's sake.'

Emma replied with a frantic note in her voice. 'Jack please believe me. I never got any of them. We were out in the bush for three weeks more than planned because one of the Land Cruisers was washed away in a flash flood and my phone was in it. The company should have informed families at home but as we were not married maybe they forgot. By the time I replaced it, all voicemails and texts had been timed out. When we eventually got back to the hotel there were no e-mails from you and I got frantic trying to get in contact. I got hold of Melissa and she put me onto Paul who said there had been some trouble at work and no one knew where you were.'

'What about the letter I wrote?'

'I got one letter from you which said you were leaving for somewhere warm and how upset you were. Maybe if I had got the earlier texts and e-mails it would have made sense but all it seemed to do was blame me for your problems and for not getting in touch. I really didn't know what to do. Paul was very supportive and told me that you had been fired but wouldn't say any more. He seemed to think you had had some form of breakdown and didn't want to see anyone including me.'

Jack looked shocked. 'It was never like that but I suppose I can see why it might look that way but why wait so long before getting in touch now?'

Melissa broke in. 'Jack, we found you quite quickly, as soon as you put up your web site for chartering Jacaranda but you were half way round the world and we really didn't know what was in your mind.'

'You mean you actually thought I had gone off my head?' He asked looking at Emma.

'Jack, I didn't know what to think. Paul strongly suggested that I give you some time to yourself but eventually Melissa convinced me we had waited long enough. So, we decided to come out and see you. Did we do the wrong thing?'

'Oh God,' said Jack putting his head in his hands. 'No, you didn't. Excuse me a second please.' He got up and went up the stairs to the cockpit and sat down by the wheel. He felt tears welling in his eyes, just as he felt a pair of arms go around his neck and pair of small breasts push into this back. A familiar scent filled his nostrils and a voice whispered in his ear.

'I know that whatever happened in London was nothing to do with you. I know I have missed you every second we've been apart. I know that now I've found you again, I am never letting you go.'

Tears poured down his cheeks. 'Oh Christ Emma, I am so sorry,' and he turned and grabbed her, hugging her hard and suddenly they were both crying and kissing each other at the same time. 'Welcome back.'

Lewis could hear what was going on above and turned smiling to Melissa. 'Were you serious about that offer to crew? Because otherwise Jack is going to dress me up in a bikini and frankly you would look a lot better than me.'

Melissa smiled back. 'Oh yes, very serious.'

Chapter 11

Captain Nelson was delighted with the capture of the American trader but also extremely grateful for the intelligence on how some ships were managing to break the blockade. Once again, he and Charles were walking together on the quarterdeck of HMS Boreas in the sunshine of English harbour.

Nelson was thinking out loud. 'The idea of hiding in some inlet will only work on some of the islands. There are plenty of hiding places here in Antigua and I can use my cutters to keep up an intensive patrol. However, islands like Dominica, Montserrat and St Kitts really only have a straight coastline with no harbours to hide in, so I suppose they may be doing something different.'

'Yes Sir, I've been thinking about Dominica. I wonder whether they might be using the islands of the Saintes just to the north. They could slip out at dusk and be in Portsmouth in a few hours. As the Saintes belong to Guadeloupe and are French, there would be little we could do once a ship was in their waters. We may have signed a peace with France but there is no love lost and all these plantation owners stick together. Let's not forget that most of the population of Dominica is French as well.'

Nelson pondered for a moment. 'What are you proposing?'

'Well Sir, if we are known to be in the vicinity everything will stop until we depart but why don't I reverse the technique and camouflage Andromeda? It would be quite easy to make her look like a merchantman. If we catch anyone, they can hardly complain. We will be in the British waters of a British island.'

'I commend your zeal Lonfort but what are you going to do about your crew? You've the Yellow Jack on board have you not?'

Charles looked sad. 'Yes Sir and the first case was young Mr Bevan. The lad who I have to credit with the intelligence that gained our recent arrest. He and one of the sailors with him are ashore in the hospital but since then about a quarter of my crew are showing signs. Frankly, I'd rather be at sea in clean air. I'm sure it's healthier than swinging around our anchor in these landlocked bays.'

'Most people recover from it you know and the lad is young and strong but I agree with your proposal. It's not as if you need a full fighting ship's company to arrest merchantmen. Yes, you can give it a try. I will have orders prepared presently.'

So for the next two days, Andromeda was transformed from a fighting warship into a slovenly looking trader. Charles flinched when the beautiful guilding on her hull was painted over with coarse black paint. It had cost him a fortune all those months ago in Portsmouth and he could only hope the paint could be scraped off later. Her oldest set of sails, the ones they had used on the Atlantic crossing, were bent on with a few extra patches sewn on for good measure. Her rigging was slackened off and the decks stopped receiving their morning holystoning. The biggest problem were the carronades, as these were on the upper deck and in plain sight. In the end, they were covered with tarpaulins and old crates but care was taken so these could be removed in short order and the weapons made ready.

By the time he was ready to sail, these were minor problems. He was fast losing his crew to the fever. Although, as Nelson had pointed out most people recovered in a few days, the unfortunate few developed a second phase which could easily lead to death, of which there had now been two. Fortunately, Mr Bevan was not one and he had convinced the naval doctor that he was fit to return. But all this meant that he either had to sail straight away with barely half his crew fit or he would have to wait an unaccountable time until all those who were going to recover, actually did. Not being one to sit around and wait, he prevailed on Nelson to let him loose despite his problems. With the crew he had, he could still sail the ship and man some of the guns which was all he needed.

The next day, the trading merchantmen 'Albion' made sail and headed south in as slovenly a manner as Charles could prevail upon his professional seamen to convey. As soon as they could, they headed east out into the Atlantic. Charles wanted to make landfall at the northern tip of Dominica as if they had just completed an ocean crossing. He also wanted sufficient rigging damage to be apparent so that he could drop anchor in the great bay of Portsmouth and stay some time without arousing suspicion.

Two days later, they did just that. Rounding into the bay, they saw it was empty except for a few fishing boats pulled up on the shore. The small settlement of Portsmouth was clustered around the mouth of the little Indian River in the middle. To the north, on the Cabrit peninsular, towered the walls of the British fort. They slipped into the northern part of the anchorage and dropped anchor, giving every indication of a ship tired and worn out after a long passage. As soon as he felt it reasonable, Charles took his smaller ship's boat with a couple of crew and was rowed ashore the jetty below the fort. Underneath his boat cloak, he had put his uniform back on. He needed the Fort Commander to know who was even if no one else did.

As soon as he got ashore he was hit by the humidity and sounds of the half tamed jungle. Walking up the narrow path from the jetty he swatted away at clouds of mosquitoes but wasn't able to stop several taking stinging bites out of him. Eventually, reaching the gate to the fort, he was challenged by the sentry. Wanting to keep the secret as long as possible, he stayed in character and explained he was the Master of the merchantman in the bay and would like to pay his respects to the fort's senior officer. He was told to wait while a runner was despatched and soon enough he found himself in the office of a large sweating, red faced, red nosed officer who had clearly been at the lunchtime claret.

Major Brett Huntingdon was unhappy with having his lunch interrupted even though it was mid-afternoon. He was even more annoyed when Charles revealed himself and described his mission.

'Your Nelson can play high and mighty with these damned Acts,' exclaimed the choleric officer. 'But some of us have to live on these islands and its not popular you know, not popular.'

Charles quizzed the man as to whether anything untoward had been seen in the bay but it soon became clear that even if there had he wasn't going to be told. The man's sympathies clearly lay with the plantation owners and Charles would be lucky to get any support from the fort at all. Taking his leave, he tried to impress on the officer the need to maintain his ships cover, even to the extent of making it clear what should happen should the ruse be revealed. But he didn't get a feeling of much confidence in even that.

Back on board, Charles gathered his remaining officers together and they discussed the way ahead. In the end, they concluded that desultory attempts to fix the 'damaged' rigging and get the ship ready could reasonably take up to six days. They would also send parties ashore for water and food but Charles insisted that everyone going ashore was vetted and briefed to ensure they knew how to behave in character. One wrong word ashore would easily give the game away. Any boats that approached the ship were to be encouraged and local produce welcomed on board, just as would be expected of a ship that had been at sea for some time. In addition, Charles wanted a permanent lookout at the masthead. This was to fulfil two functions, the first to look out sea for any approaching ships but the second was to watch the fort to see if there was any activity with the island. Being stuck out an isthmus it was quite easy to see the approaches to the fort and hence monitor any communications. And that was it. Having taken all precautions, all they could do now was sit tight and wait.

Three days later they were all starting to show signs of strain. The need to appear scruffy and unprofessional was galling to every competent seaman on board. It was hot and the need to keep most of the crew below decks meant that the men were uncomfortable most of the time. Even with her sickness reduced crew, there were still far too many men on board for a merchantman. The only good thing was that the incidences of yellow fever seemed to be abating. There had only been a few new cases since sailing and these all seemed to be on the mend. Charles felt vindicated in his discussion with Nelson about getting the ship away to sea. The bay in Portsmouth was so large and open that it didn't have the festering feeling of some of the enclosed Antiguan anchorages.

At dusk, on the fourth night, their luck changed. Just as the great orange ball of the sun was slipping below the horizon and the few clouds in the sky were turning the same glorious colour, the lookout clambered down the rigging and reported quietly that a strange sail was in sight coming from the north. Within half an hour they could all see the newcomer as she slipped slowly into the bay with the last of the light and anchored as close to the shore by the settlement as she could.

'If I didn't know better I would say that is our old American friend from St Kitts,' muttered Tom to Charles as they heard her anchor rumble into the calm blue waters of the bay.

'Yes, I think you're right,' agreed Charles. 'We could probably re-arrest her on sight if that's the case but I think we'll make sure. If our theories are correct, she will start her loading straight away. The moon sets at about three in the morning, so let's plan to go across as soon as it's properly dark. They will probably try to complete all their work by then and sail with the dawn. With any luck, we'll catch her fully loaded with contraband and no excuses will prevail. Tom, you can lead the boarding party. Take both boats and twelve men per boat that should be plenty.'

Half past two in the morning and the American had been loading all night with help from boats from shore but now she lay quietly at anchor. The boarding parties prepared below decks. They had covered their faces with lamp soot and sharpened boarding cutlasses. Charles only allowed the officers to carry firearms, after all this was an anti-smuggling operation, not a wartime cutting out party. As soon as the moon disappeared behind the horizon, they slipped quietly down the ship's side facing away from the merchantman. Then with oars muffled with rags and grease, they slowly pulled across the half a mile to the American who could just be made out against the starlight but was also still showing a few lights.

Charles watched anxiously from the quarterdeck. The boats quickly vanished into the night and even when straining hard he had not been able to hear much apart from the occasional muted splash of an oar. He hated letting others take the risks and would much rather be in one of the boats but he knew his place. Anyway, it was time his First Lieutenant was given the opportunity to show his mettle.

Just as he estimated that his boats were half way across, there was a single solitary musket shot from the fort. In the silence of the night, it sounded unnaturally loud. Suddenly, he could see a flurry of activity on the deck of the other ship. With dismay, he saw that once again the American was prepared to leave a valuable anchor on the seabed to make good his escape. He prayed that his boats would make it in time but it soon became clear that it was going to be unlikely. There had been a good offshore breeze all night and the lights of the other ship were already accelerating out towards open sea. No sooner than said, the lights were extinguished and Charles completely lost sight of his quarry.

'All hands on deck. Get ready to make sail as soon as the boats return,' Charles ordered the Sailing Master. 'And if there's any problem weighing anchor, cut the damned hawser.'

'Aye, Aye Sir,' responded Mr Williams immediately, striding down the ship and calling all remaining hands on deck to make ready. The time for subterfuge was over.

Shortly afterwards, the two boats returned. Not wasting time hoisting them inboard, they were tied on to be towed astern.

'Someone in that fort will have a lot answer for,' snarled an enraged Tom. 'I can't believe for one moment that was accidental.'

'You're right,' agreed a grim looking Charles. 'But I suspect we'll never be able to prove it. We'll have to leave the problem with our Commander and no doubt he will have something to say to the good Major. However, that doesn't help us presently. I am not going to let her get away again and this time we are not stuck up a hill dressed in our best coats. I estimate he will still be in sight at sunrise wherever he goes and then we have a chase on our hands.'

'But what if he heads into French waters?'

'Well, we are not a warship unless we want to be,' replied Charles with a feral smile. 'So, we will maintain our pretence and see what transpires.'

In the event, there was no need to deal with the problem of French collusion as it was quite clear at sunrise that the American was heading out to sea.

'My guess is, that he thinks he can outrun us and is heading back to the Americas,' observed Tom to Charles as they watched their quarry through their telescopes several miles ahead.

'Yes, well I think it's now time to become a warship again and show that scoundrel what we can do. Set as much sail as she will carry Tom and let's get her flying. Oh and have our ensign broken out. Let him know who is after him.'

All morning the two ships headed away from land flying before the wind. Sure enough, as soon as Andromeda was let free, with all sails set, she slowly started creeping up on her heavily laden quarry.

'I'll bet her Master wishes he had turned for the Saintes now. He clearly didn't allow for the effect of the weight of his cargo,' observed Mr Williams. 'He should be in range of our bow chasers within the half hour.'

Charles was just about to agree when a wave of nausea swept over him and piercing pain struck his forehead. He had to suddenly clutch onto the shrouds to save himself from falling to the deck.

'Sir, are you alright?' called an anxious Mr Williams and he turned to the duty Midshipman, 'get the First Lieutenant at once.'

Charles waved him away but a dread feeling inside told him that maybe it was now his turn to suffer the fever. The timing couldn't have been worse. At all costs, he intended to remain on deck until his quarry was secured.

He told this to Tom as he arrived by his side. 'Yes Tom it could be the fever but I'll not go below until we have him. You can then take us home if necessary.'

'Aye Sir but shall I call for the surgeon just in case?'

Swallowing another bout of sickness, Charles agreed but made it clear his intention to remain on deck.

'Sir, Sir, we may have another problem, look astern,' shouted the Sailing Master waving frantically at what was slowly bearing down on the two ships.

Behind Andromeda was a black mass of cloud. They were all used to the sudden squalls of the Caribbean that could strike at almost any time. However, this looked much worse than normal. The whole horizon was dark and flashes of lightning could be seen. Two waterspouts were clearly visible lancing down from the darkest clouds, giving a clear indication of the savagery that was about to smite them.

The wind was already starting to rise and the rigging was starting to groan from the increased strain.

'Get the sails off her,' ordered Charles. 'We'll have to ride this out and just hope we don't lose our quarry when it's passed through.'

'Or collide with her', observed Mr Williams. 'We are in the lap of the gods now.'

Even with a depleted crew, the sails were reefed in good order, unlike the American, who had also seen the danger and was having trouble shortening sail. At one point she was saved the trouble, as all her topsails blew out one after the other turning into rags in an instant and streaming from the yards in the rising gale.

'Oh my God,' exclaimed Tom as the squall line approached. A white wall of water was all that could be seen. Suddenly, visibility dropped to almost nothing and heavy rain thundered onto them all. For a few seconds, the wind seemed to drop and then it returned with a savage howl but ninety degrees from its previous direction. Andromeda broached. She heeled savagely to port as the wind struck her. Within seconds, her gun deck was awash.

Charles had been standing on the starboard side when suddenly the deck was almost vertical and a great wave of water washed towards him. He reached out for something to cling to but couldn't find any purchase. In an instant, he was over the side and struggling for his life in the foam and waves. With horror, he surfaced and on looking up saw the stern of the ship passing almost over him. The wind was so loud, no one could hear his screams and within seconds the ship was lost to sight.

Luckily, Tom had seen what happened and without thinking, clawed his way to the stern of the ship. Grabbing a boarding axe, he hacked desperately at the painter of one of the boats they were towing astern. With a sudden crack the line parted and the boat disappeared into the rain.

Pulling himself hand over hand back to the deck he looked at the Sailing Master and shouted, 'there's nothing else we can do for the Captain. We must look to ourselves now and may God have mercy on all our souls.'

Charles was choking. The spray was being blown into his mouth by the vicious wind and the weight of his clothes was pulling him down. Desperately, he reached down and managed to pull off his boots and then shuck off his heavy jacket. Unlike most seamen of his age, Charles was a good swimmer, a legacy of boy's summers swimming in the lakes of his father's estate. This was different though, the wind was savage and the waves were breaking over him. He knew he couldn't last long, that it was only a matter of minutes before he succumbed. Looking ahead, he caught a flash of white that looked different to the breaking wave tops. Suddenly, with a surge of hope, he realised he was seeing one of his ship's boats. Someone must have seen him go over the side and had had the sense to cut one free for him. If only he could reach it. Desperately, he started swimming but it wasn't easy as the wind was blowing it away from him. One minute it had disappeared from sight as he fell into a trough, the next it was in sight, way below him as he crested a wave. Choking on sea water, he slowly made ground and with a last desperate effort, he managed to grab hold of the painter trailing behind it in the water. He pulled himself into the bow of the boat and managed to get his arms over the side. Holding on with grim determination, he slowly regained his breath before making one last effort to haul himself on board. He fell into the bilge in a heap, gasping for breath but relieved he hadn't turned the boat over in the process.

Now he was out of the wind and immediate danger from drowning he knew he should take stock of his situation and start to look out for his survival. Just then another shivering attack shook him and he vomited violently into the bilge. Despite his good intentions, he clutched onto a seat and slowly lapsed into unconsciousness.

Sometime later, he had no way of telling how long, he slowly came to. He was still shivering but thinking more clearly. He heaved himself up and looked about. The large squalls had gone and the sea had returned to its normal self. Scanning out to the horizon all around, the vain hope of seeing a sail was dashed. The sea was empty and he realised he was on his own. Andromeda might have survived and even now be looking for him but he couldn't count on it. No, his best chance would be to try and find land himself and that would mean rigging the small mast and sailing to the east as soon as he could. He struggled to raise the mast and then haul up the heavy canvas sail but it wasn't too long before it filled and pulling in hard on the sheets he found he could make a course of about south east. He knew this should take him down towards St Lucia but he also knew the permanent west running equatorial current was going to push him back. He had a pretty good idea of how far out they were when the storm struck and soon realised that it was going to be several days at least before he sighted land. Apart from some oars, the mast, sail and steering compass, he had no other equipment and certainly no water. This would be hard at the best of times but shivering and sickness were fast draining his strength.

Night came soon but he was able to steer by the stars when it became too dark to see the compass. He was drifting in and out of consciousness. Luckily, the boat was able to steer herself reasonably well once the sail was adjusted and the tiller lashed in the right position. The next day was worse. He was tormented by thirst and racked by fever. Hallucinations came and went. At one point he was sure that Lizzy was sat next to him describing the finer points of flower arranging, then suddenly she was Nelson berating him for losing his ship. Late in the afternoon, he thought he could see the grey indistinct shape of an island in the far distance but sunset overtook him before he could be sure. He fought on through the dark hours again and was awake to see the sun rise from behind a land mass rather than the sea but he was fast losing any will to keep going. Soon after, he lapsed into unconsciousness.

His final memory was of a beautiful blonde mermaid or was she an angel? She was leaning over him and promising he would be alright.

Chapter 12

Paul was on the horns of a dilemma. Everything he had worked for, all the late nights, all the worry, everything he had built up could come crashing down around his ears. The last thing he had expected was a full external audit, especially one going back so long. At the time, he had assured the boss that the worst that had happened was that an employee had made a big mistake, an incompetent professional misjudgement. There was never any argument that anything illegal had occurred. Indeed, that was the case but what he hadn't told Nigel was that it was Paul himself who had made the error and that was because he had covered it up. An opportunity had come along and Paul decided to take a risk without consulting his boss. In retrospect, it was a stupid thing to do, especially as the information came from an established competitor. Paul had been too keen to impress and fallen for the oldest trick in the book.

Luckily, despite the panic that had overtaken him, he had remained calm enough to see a way out of it. It was a Friday afternoon and most of the office had left for the weekend. Paul looked through his friend's desk and found what he expected. He knew that Jack was notoriously paranoid about forgetting passwords even though he rarely did and sure enough inside his top desk drawer was his day book. Inside the back cover were written several strings of letters and numbers. Within minutes, Paul had managed to access Jack's company trading account and with the skill of someone who had worked the system for years, had managed to transfer his trading data to Jack's account. Once done, he had informed Sir Nigel and blamed the loss on his friend. Jack left the company on Monday, taking all the blame and Paul had breathed a sigh of relief. He supposed he ought to feel guilty about what he had done but somehow just getting away with it was a rush in itself and Jack shouldn't have been so stupid as to leave his passwords about. They may have been friends for years but deep down Paul knew he had got Jack his job to show that, just for once, he could do better than his friend. As bloody usual, Jack proved very effective even in an area he should have struggled with and anyway this was work and Paul had learned ruthlessness at the feet of a master.

However, Paul never anticipated a full audit. He needed to be sure that his tracks were well covered. His first port of call was the IT department. The computer geeks were parked around their terminals and on the excuse of taking over management of the company, he spent a whole day going through the system with them. As part of his new executive authority, he had overriding password access to all accounts but he didn't want to use it as it would leave a record of his presence which might be queried. However, by using the pretence of needing to understand the system better, he got his head of IT to do some random access of the system and this included previous employees records. The IT guru gave him one slight palpitation when he reminded Paul of employee's private accounts. Paul had never been able to find Jack's password for his. However, it was not part of the auditor's normal agenda to look at these accounts, so by the end of the day, he was able to breathe a quiet sigh of relief. Everything he had seen had assured him that his little bit of creative accounting would not be detectable.

That evening, lying in bed with Sarah after a particularly energetic session of love making, she turned on one elbow and looked him in the eye. 'Paul you've been working really hard recently. Why don't we take a break?'

He lay back contemplating the ceiling. 'You know that would be so nice but I'm not sure the boss would appreciate me disappearing right now.'

'Don't be too sure of that. He popped by my desk the other day and hinted that I ought to take you away. He said you were working too hard and needed a holiday. You know he's actually quite a sweety once you drill through that tough City exterior.'

'Oh, don't tell me you are starting to fancy him now.'

That got him a sharp dig in the ribs. 'No, I am not and don't try to change the subject.'

'OK, what are you suggesting?'

She took a breath, 'er, well on the basis of my conversation with him and knowing your tastes, I've actually booked something. I hope you don't mind. We've got two weeks away from next Saturday. Somewhere hot and sunny.'

Paul looked pleased but puzzled. 'Sounds great and actually I could really use some down time. So, where are we going?'

Sarah gave him an impish smile. 'Not telling you, I want it to be a surprise. You'll just have to trust me.'

Paul reached under the covers. 'Alright then but I will need extra payment for my trust.'

Sarah giggled. 'I'd better surprise you more often then.'

Chapter 13

'Perfection, heaven, living the dream and all that bollocks.' Jack was sitting in the cockpit with Emma sharing a can of beer. It was lunchtime and he and the girls were sailing Jacaranda back to St Lucia. They had just completed a wonderful fortnight with two British couples who were excellent sailors and really nice people. They had just dropped them off in Antigua. So nice that Jack was looking forward to giving his liver a major rest for a while and seriously catching up on some sleep.

'Yup, that's what Brian's wife kept saying, without the 'bollocks' bit that is,' continued Jack sitting back and looking up at the deep blue sky. 'And you know what? She was absolutely right. Is this the life or is this the life?'

Emma smiled and put her head on his shoulder. 'Well I'm not arguing.'

At that moment, Melissa came up the hatch, wearing nothing more than a skimpy pair of bikini bottoms and a smile. Jack could not help but admire her glorious figure and full breasts which were swaying provocatively as she climbed into the cockpit. Melissa was notoriously uninhibited. It was all he could do to keep her decent when guests were on board. Now they were on their own, she was making the most of it. Not that Jack could complain. He was a human male after all.

'I hope that you've put plenty of sun block on those two. I would hate to see such a magnificent pair get all blistered,' quipped Jack, while at the same time receiving a sharp kick on his ankle from Emma.

Melissa gave Jack a haughty look. 'You may remember that I'm a qualified nurse and I am quite aware of the risk of second degree burns,' and then with a grin, 'you can always put some more sunscreen on if you like but I suspect that Emma would kill me if I let you.'

'Melissa, you are my oldest friend but if you let Jack touch your tits, you're going over the side,' responded Emma with the sort of grin that only two friends could share.

Jack broke in. 'What you need my girl is some male company. I'll see if we can arrange a charter with a single rich yank who likes blondes.'

Melissa snorted. 'I've had enough of bloody men to last a lifetime thank you. It's rather nice to have a rest and let you two lovebirds get on with it.'

Jack, suddenly curious, asked, 'come on Melissa, you said when you came down that you had a bust up with Paul, so what really happened? I always thought you two made a good couple.'

'So did I but you know what a one track mind he has. After a while, it became clear that I was just an ornament. He would trundle me out at parties and proudly introduce me to his friends but in private we became further and further apart. It just got worse after you had your little run in with Sir Nigel. Eventually, he became bloody impossible and I walked out. Best thing I ever did to be quite honest.'

Emma joined in. 'Yes but he was really supportive with me. Especially when we couldn't find you Jack.'

'I wouldn't be surprised if he was trying to get into your knickers dear. You know, I think he has always fancied you a bit.' Melissa answered waspishly.

'Oh come on,' said Jack. 'How long have we all known each other? The three of us here all went to school together and we've all known Paul since university days. He may be a single minded money grabber but he's not that sort of chap.'

'If you had to live with him for a while you might have a different viewpoint.'

Jack was about to reply when there was a sudden screeching sound from the back of the boat.

'FISH' he shouted and jumped up and ran back over the rear deck to the rod he kept permanently rigged at sea. It was bent over and line was screaming off the reel.

They all quickly fell into what was now becoming a well rehearsed routine. As Jack grabbed the rod, Emma started the two engines, motored Jacaranda into wind, slowed her down and engaged the auto pilot so that she just had steerage way. The sails were flapping but not doing any harm. Melissa opened a cockpit locker and got out a large gaff, an old washing up liquid bottle full of rum and a leather belt.

'Christ girls, this is a big one,' said an excited Jack. Even with the boat slowed down, the pull on the line was enormous. 'Melissa, quick get the bollock protector.'

Melissa reached around Jack's waist and did up the leather belt which had a socket in the front for the bottom of the rod. While maintaining the tension on the line, Jack put the rod in its place and immediately he was able to exercise more control.

'What do you think it is?' called Emma from the cockpit.

'No idea, not seen anything jump yet,' answered Jack laughing with excitement. 'But whatever it is, it's huge because even now we are moving slowly it's still pulling the bloody rod over double. The problem with fishing off the back of a yacht,' he grunted as he pumped some line back onto the reel. 'Is that it's not designed for fishing but I'm buggered if I am going to lose whatever this is, like we did the other day with that bloody great Marlin off Martinique.'

For fifteen minutes Jack fought the fish. Every time he got it close to the boat it got spooked and turned away, stripping fifty metres of line off the reel. He didn't dare tighten the brake any harder for fear of breaking the line. So it was a straight fight for who got tired first. Suddenly, it leapt out of the water in a spray of blue and gold and they could see what it was.

'Bloody hell, that's the biggest Mahi Mahi I've ever seen,' shouted Jack. 'It must be over forty pounds. I'm not letting him get away. The fish was now tiring fast and Jack was able to get it closer to the boat every time it leapt up into the air. Soon it was alongside being towed through the clear water. The beautiful blue and gold markings could clearly be seen.

'God, that's a handsome fish,' said Jack carefully putting on his sailing gloves and pulling it further along the boat, using one hand on the wire trace. Melissa reached over with the gaff and managed to hook it and together they hauled it up over the side where it started thrashing enthusiastically on the deck. Melissa passed Jack the washing up liquid bottle and he sprayed rum into the mouth and gills and it immediately stopped moving.

'I can't stand French rum but its bloody good at killing fish,' said an exultant Jack. 'Quickly now, get it into the cool box before it bleeds all over my lovely decks.' Jacaranda may not have been a fishing boat but Jack had a specially made cool box on deck for just this eventuality.

'Whooh, that was fun,' he exclaimed, feeling the adrenalin course through him. 'That should fill the freezer once it's cleaned and filleted. I might even have to give some away. Martha always likes Mahi Mahi. Well girls, guess what's for supper tonight?'

Getting no reply he looked around he saw that Emma wasn't listening. She was staring ahead with a frown on her face. Following her gaze, he could see something in the water dead ahead at about five hundred yards.

'Jack, what is that?' asked Emma in a puzzled voice.

'Hang on,' he replied and he shot down below to retrieve a pair of binoculars. Looking through them, he could see what looked like an old fashioned wooden boat painted white and half awash. There was a small mast with a sail flapping in the wind and what looked like some old rags at the back. Suddenly, he realised the rags were covering a man's body. It was slumped over the tiller and not moving.

'Bloody hell, there's someone in that thing. Quick let's get the sails down.'

First, he and Melissa furled the Genoa and then dropped the mainsail into its bag while Emma kept Jacaranda headed into the wind. As soon as the sails were stowed, she opened the throttles and headed towards the stationary boat. The three of them had sailed together for many years and Jack knew he needed to say little to either of them in this sort of situation.

They soon drew alongside the little boat with Emma expertly manoeuvring Jacaranda across and up wind of the boat. Jack tied a couple of fenders over the side and when close enough he reached over with a boat hook and managed to snag a line from the boat's bow which he tied onto a deck cleat.

It was immediately apparent that the man in the boat was either dead or in a bad way. His exposed skin was red and blistered by the sun but he also had a pallid yellow tinge. Jack jumped down into the boat and saw that he was breathing in a fast shallow fashion.

'Melissa, can you get down here?' called Jack. 'I think we need your medical expertise and bring some water.'

Melissa managed to jump down as the two boats rolled together and pushed past Jack. She opened the bottle of water and dribbled a little into the casualty's mouth. For a second his eyes opened and he focused on Melissa. He smiled and said something before closing his eyes and lapsing into unconsciousness.

'What do you think?' asked Jack.

'He's quite young and fit by the looks of it and has obviously been exposed in this boat without water for some time but there may be something more. I'm not going to be able to find out anything until we get him on board and how on earth are we going to do that?'

When fitting out Jacaranda Jack had not skimped on safety equipment. 'Melissa, jump back on board. In the main cockpit locker is a man overboard rescue sling. It's in a bright orange bag, you can't miss it. Chuck it down to me and the get the spare spinnaker halliard ready on one of the main winches. We should be able to pull him up quite easily.'

As soon as he had the sling, Jack put the main strop underneath the man's shoulders and a smaller one under his knees. Attaching the shackle at the end of the halliard, he then signalled Emma to operate the winch while he and Melissa guided the inert body up the side and over the guard rails. They then half carried, half pulled the body back to the cockpit.

'Bugger me and I thought that fish was heavy,' gasped Jack as they finally got him settled on one of the cockpit cushions. 'Well Melissa, he's all yours.'

Melissa started to examine the man while Jack untied the painter from the side of Jacaranda and let the little boat drift astern. He then tied it up so it could be towed back in behind them. Looking at the rope in his hands prompted him to look very carefully at the boat. He reached down and retrieved something from the stern thwart, a deep suspicion forming in his mind.

'Jack, this chap needs hospitalisation,' called Melissa. 'Can you get on the radio and arrange for us to be met by an ambulance please?'

'We're too far out at the moment I'm afraid. We need to be much closer before I can get reception.'

'OK, I don't suppose you have any intravenous drips in that massive first aid kit you carry have you?'

'Actually, I do. It's only saline, is that alright?'

'Great, go and get it. This guy is seriously dehydrated we need to get some fluid into him.'

Within half an hour they had the casualty as settled as possible. Jack decided it was just too difficult to try and get him down into the saloon but they managed to rig up some shade in the cockpit and with the help of the drip his breathing started to ease, although he remained deeply unconscious.

Melissa looked thoughtful, 'You know if I didn't know better I would say he either has jaundice or yellow fever, which in some ways is much the same thing. If that's the case, there's not much more we can do except try and get some paracetamol into him and hope his constitution is good.'

Jack looked worried. 'I thought yellow fever had been eradicated?'

'Only if you are inoculated. The bloody mosquitoes that spread it are still about.'

At this, Jack looked even more concerned. He went over to the chart plotter. Jacaranda was motoring back towards Rodney Bay as fast as she would go. He would rather have sailed her, it was usually faster but the wind was in the wrong direction and the heeling of the boat would not be good for the comfort of the patient.

'Ladies, we have about three hours before we get within VHF range and four hours before we can get alongside and I think I need to tell you something. But before I say anything, do you notice anything odd about this guy and the boat we are towing?'

The girls looked puzzled but followed Jack's gaze.

Emma was the first to break the silence. 'Well, the boat looks in pretty good condition but it's a very old clinker design and the sails seem to be made of old fashioned canvas.'

'Yes and look at this,' said Jack, showing them the brass compass he had rescued from the boat. 'It doesn't have degrees on it, just thirty two equal marks. I've counted them.'

Emma and Melissa looked at him puzzled.

'Now, look at this guy. Look at his trousers, no zips, just a front that buttons up in a way I've not seen before. No underpants and his shirt is made of some very cheap or badly woven material. He's clearly never worn a watch, there's no strap mark. I've got a feeling about him but look, I need to explain something first.'

Jack told his story. It took quite a while. He told them about the incident the previous summer. He pointed to the top of the mast where the bullet scar was still just visible if you knew where to look. He then went on to explain how he and Lewis had compiled data on reported sightings and showed them the map where they had plotted them all. He went on to say why he hadn't broached the subject with the girls before, not being sure how he could without being considered a raving lunatic. Emma was one of the smartest people he knew and he also knew she didn't suffer UFO believers or tree huggers gladly. Dammit, nor did he until last summer. The last thing he wanted to do was scare her, having only just got her back.

Both girls listened but were clearly very sceptical. Realising he needed something more to convince them, he recounted how his old friend commanding HMS Suffolk had asked him about unexplained local occurrences. He went below and fetched the bone shark, explaining how Martha had confirmed that it was some sort of local religious icon used as a catalyst to make spells stronger.

'So, that's it and I think this guy is also part of it,' he finished lamely.

Melissa looked less unconvinced of the two. 'So, what you're saying is that he's from the past, is that it? Bloody hell, I am really having trouble believing this.'

'Yes, look, how else do you explain a compass marked in points rather than degrees. It's clearly from the eighteen hundreds. We have a boat whose design is of the same era and a shipwrecked sailor who is dressed from the same period.'

'I guess we can ask him when he wakes up can't we?'

'If I'm right and he finds himself in a modern hospital what do you think his reaction is going to be?'

Emma spoke thoughtfully. 'If you're right, he will think he's insane and then everyone else will think he's insane. Is that what you're suggesting? But look at the state of him he has to get medical attention.'

Surprised and grateful that Emma was at least accepting the possibility that he was right, Jack turned to Melissa. 'Melissa you're a nurse. You've already said that apart from fluids and some paracetamol he will have to fight through this himself. The sunburn can be treated anywhere. Look, if I can get him to somewhere secluded, with good facilities, we can at least wait until he comes to and find out if I am right. And if I am, at least we have a chance of talking to him in a way he will understand because culture shock will be enormous. This guy will have come at least two hundred years into his future. If I am wrong, we can get him to hospital.'

Melissa nodded. 'OK, I'm assuming you're talking of taking him to your flat at Martha's house. From what you've said, Lewis and Martha are as barking mad as you are but I'll go along with this right up until he is conscious and then all bets are off. What do you think Emma?'

'Oh God, I don't know, there is so much to think about.' Looking at Jack she said, 'I've known you for a very long time. I've always trusted you and if you truly believe what you have told us and you certainly have some convincing evidence, then yes I will also go along with you but only until he wakes up, alright?'

Jack let out a great sight of relief. Truth be known, he wasn't totally sure himself and would be more than happy to find out the guy was just some local with a fetish for an old fashioned way of life. There were people like that in several of the islands. He certainly didn't want this sort of complication in his life. But what the hell was he going to do with the man if he was right? However, one thing was certain, if he was from the past Jack wasn't going to risk what could happen to him if they delivered him to the authorities.

Melissa was looking carefully at their casualty. 'And anyway he is a bloody good looking time traveller. I wonder what his name is?'

Jack grinned at her. 'By the way, what did he say to you that moment he was conscious?'

Melissa looked embarrassed for a second and blushed. 'He said and I quote, 'I must be in heaven, you are the most beautiful naked angel I have ever seen,' then he passed out again'

Jack and Emma grinned. 'I said you needed another man in your life, looks like you've got one now.'

Chapter 14

Charles was at home in his bedroom and his mother was looking after him, he had fallen off his horse and hit his head. No that wasn't right he could hear voices talking but it didn't matter, he was safe at home. He drifted off to sleep and then slowly awoke, he felt terribly weak, the bed sheets were damp and the room didn't look right. This wasn't his bedroom at home, he must be on his ship, what was she called? Andromeda that's right but this couldn't be his cabin. The ceiling was painted white not the rough oak planks of his ship.

A face appeared in his vision. It was an angel he knew her from somewhere but couldn't remember where.

'Shh, you've been ill but you are getting better now. Try to drink some of this.'

Strong hands lifted his head and a cold liquid was poured into his mouth. He coughed and spilt some down his chin but managed to get some down his parched throat, it felt wonderful.

'Can you tell me your name?' asked the angel gently. 'We really need to know.'

He tried to talk but it came out a croak, so he whispered. She came closer and he told her beautiful ear. 'The Honourable Charles Lonfort, Commanding Officer of HMS Andromeda under the command of Captain Nelson.'

He fell back, the effort of talking draining him and slowly slipped back into oblivion.

Melissa looked down at him and satisfied that he was sleeping deeply, crept out of the room.

'Oh really, you're all like a bunch of school kids,' she said with exasperation to everyone waiting just outside the door. All four were there, Jack, Emma, Lewis and Martha.

'Never mind that, did he say anything?' asked Jack eagerly.

'He tried but had to whisper it in the end. His throat is very sore.'

'For God's sake girl, what did he say?'

'As near as I could make out, it was Charles Longwood or something similar, Commanding Officer HMS Andromeda.'

'Wow,' said Lewis. 'I thought the ship here is HMS Suffolk?'

'Was there more Melissa?' asked Jack, ignoring Lewis. 'Come on, I can tell by the look on your face that he said something else.'

'Yes,' she admitted. 'He also said he was under the command of Captain Nelson.'

'See, I told you,' said an exultant Jack. 'Oh my God this is real,' he added as the realisation hit him.

Martha cut in. 'I think we all need to go and sit down and think about this. Jack, you can go on your laptop and see if we can locate the ship or this character on the net or google or something.'

'You all go down, I'll stay with him,' responded Melissa. 'He may be a man from the past but someone still has to look after him.'

Emma looked at her friend. 'Thank you Melissa, we couldn't have done this without you.' Then she added with a smile, 'mind you, you do seem to be enjoying it. He is good looking isn't he.'

'Just sod off and do some investigating and I'll do my job.' Melissa replied with another grin.

It hadn't been easy getting the man ashore. As soon as Jack could raise the marina on the VHF, he had asked them to get Lewis to contact him. By then, they were in cell phone range and Lewis had been able to telephone Jack. He spent some time explaining the problem and then Lewis had talked to his mother. By the time Jacaranda was motoring into the lagoon, they had a plan of sorts. Martha had agreed they could use the house and she and Lewis would meet them at the fuelling jetty with her old Toyota. Normally, when coming in from another island Jack, as the ships Master, would have to clear them in through customs and immigration before anyone was allowed ashore. It was a tiresome procedure that all the islands used and which cynics felt was purely to give the locals paid work. However, he was counting on the fact that the fuelling jetty was out of sight of the customs office. He and the boat were well known to them all with his regular charters, so there was no reason for them to assume anything other than a normal homecoming.

As soon as they were tied up, Martha drew up as close as she could with the pickup and while Emma talked to and distracted the lad who dispensed the fuel, the others managed to lift the casualty off Jacaranda using a jury rigged stretcher that Jack had cobbled together using the oars from their tender and an old tarpaulin. As soon as the pickup disappeared through the marina gates, Jack made his way to the customs office. He needn't have worried, the cricket was on the television above the customs officer's desk and the West Indies were giving England their usual thrashing. A pleasant chat with all the staff, with the usual ribbing about the quality of English cricket and the forms were filled in and stamped. Jack breathed a sigh of relief as he left but wondered what the hell they were going to do if the man turned out to be a normal contemporary shipwrecked mariner. Mentally shrugging to himself, he concluded that he would have to cross that bridge when he came to it. He then went back to Jacky and motored her across the lagoon to her normal berth before retrieving his motorbike and heading off to Martha's house.

The next three days were fraught with worry. Had they done the right thing? What were they going to do if the casualty got worse? Melissa was tireless and without her Jack knew they would have had to have called on local help. Much of the time he was delirious and last night had been the worst. Then, at about two in the morning, the fever had seemed to break and his breathing had eased. He settled into a deep sleep. Even then, Jack had to insist that Melissa go to bed and get some rest herself.

At the same time, they had another problem to solve. If the patient was really from the past then they were going to have to remove every trace of the twenty first century from the room. They all agreed that coming to in a strange place was going to be hard enough but even common place modern technology would probably scare the man rigid until it was explained.

While Melissa tended her patient, Lewis and Jack scoured the room for technology. What they thought would be relatively easy turned out to be harder than they envisaged. They removed all the light fittings, covered up the electric wall sockets and switches. Luckily, the bed was made of wood and the floor was bare boards with a few rugs. Martha managed to find an old oil lamp that had been converted to electricity years ago and Jack then spent several hours converting it back to oil. They also managed to source an old china water jug and water pitcher and much to Lewis's amusement, even an old chamber pot for under the bed. Sheets and blankets turned out to be the biggest problem as Jack was pretty sure that anything they used would be strange but he just had to hope he wouldn't be that inquisitive so soon. By the time Melissa was tending a recovering patient they had done all they could.

They all repaired to the large kitchen and Jack got stuck into the internet. He found several HMS Andromedas straight away.

'Right, here we have a Cruizer class sloop, whatever that was. She was in the West Indies in 1785. Let's see, Nelson was in command in the Leewards from 1784 to 1787 so that narrows it down.' Looking up at his audience he announced with awe in his voice, 'it looks like that upstairs we have the Captain of a British warship that was out here serving under Horatio Nelson in about 1785 or so. Bugger me, it's all really true. What the hell do we do now?'

This was something they had discussed endlessly over the last few days. In the end, they had concluded that if they had managed to accept what appeared to be the impossible, then they should be able to convince their new guest as well.

'At least we are dealing with the Captain of a ship, so hopefully he will be well educated by the standards of the times. We now have a reasonably accurate idea of dates. Does anyone know what we could expect?'

Emma responded. 'I do know that the Royal Society had been established by then. My father's a member and I've been to the London club several times. Newton and other scientists had established the scientific method but the industrial revolution had yet to get really started. By our standards, they were still pretty primitive. I think Jack is right, it all depends very much on how well this chap is educated and if he has any sort of open mind.'

'I think we're going to have to give him some limited information and then just see how he reacts,' said Martha. 'Whatever happens in the longer term, he can't stay here. What are we going to do we do with him?'

'I've actually got a couple of ideas about that,' responded Jack. 'Martha, if you're happy to keep him here until he's fit, I think I can sort that out one way or another. We've got this charter starting next weekend but I am going to suggest that Melissa doesn't come with us, so she can stay here with him. That gives him about three weeks to physically recover and for us to try to literally bring him up to date. When we get back we will sort something out for the longer term. Is that alright?'

Martha nodded her agreement. 'Don't worry Jack. I agreed to take him in at the outset. I can hardly argue now.'

They talked into the evening and Melissa joined them when she was satisfied her patient was asleep. She immediately agreed to stay with him for the next charter and estimated that he would be fit enough to talk properly within another day. Jack saw his disability as an advantage. If was still bedridden, he wouldn't be able to see things before they were able to prepare the way for him. Luckily, his bedroom was in the rear of the house and faced only some trees and open countryside.

Charles surfaced from sleep and immediately felt a deep feeling of wellbeing. Although he was very weak, he was at last thinking clearly and quickly realised that he had survived his ordeal. Whatever had happened, he seemed to be in good care. He recalled falling off the ship and setting sail for the islands. He then vaguely remembered a beautiful girl giving him something to drink but little else. Turning to one side, he saw a glass full of water at his bedside. Grunting with effort, he managed to get a hold with shaking hands and take a drink. He immediately started coughing but got some of it down. His second attempt was much more successful and he finished the whole glass. Sighing, he lay back in his pillows which felt remarkably soft and looked around the room. It was fairly light and he suspected that it was either dawn or dusk although he had no way of knowing which. There was a wash stand by the window which was covered in some sort of colourful drape and a few rugs on the floor but little else to give any clue as to who his rescuers might be. The quality of the walls and ceilings seemed remarkable and he concluded he must be in a rich man's house. His last recollection, while in the boat, was of seeing an island in the distance that looked like St Lucia, so he supposed that that was the most likely location of this house. He dozed again.

The next time he awoke, the beautiful girl was back. She was sitting in a chair by his bed looking away.

'Good morning my Angel,' he croaked.

Her head turned quickly and he was able to take in her beautiful tresses and voluptuous figure. However, her manner of dress was most unusual. She was wearing trews of some sort and a colourful thin blouse that clung to her bosom. Seeing this, he recalled another vision of this same girl bending over him with no clothes on at all. He blushed at the recollection but smiled as well.

'So good to see you properly awake,' she said. 'Would you like some more water?'

Nodding his head, he accepted the glass from her and eagerly swallowed the contents. Clearing his throat, he found he could now talk more clearly. He settled back in his pillows and smiled at her. 'I seem to remember you in my dreams with less clothing. Pray tell me your name?'

It was Melissa's turn to blush as she realised he was referring to when she had tended to him in the dinghy. 'My name is Melissa and I see you have a good memory. What else do you recall?'

'Very little, until I woke up here. Bye the bye, where is here?'

'You are safe in St Lucia and we will talk more after you have rested some more. I think you should sleep again.'

Charles wanted to disagree, there was so much more he needed to know but again weariness overcame him and he drifted off to Melissa's glorious smile. When he came to again, she was still there sitting in the seat next to him.

'Have you tended to me the whole while?'

She jumped at his voice. 'Most of the time, although I have friends who have helped me. You will meet them soon. Now would you like something to eat?'

As soon as she said this, he realised he was ravenous and nodded.

She twisted the top off a curious metal tube and poured a hot liquid into a bowl which she gave him along with a spoon. He soon found out it was some form of broth, probably chicken and he ate it all despite it being remarkably warm. He then realised there was another bodily function that needed to be assuaged but had no idea how to broach such a subject to a girl.

As if reading his mind she said. 'There's a pot under the bed if you need it.'

He nodded.

'Fine, I will leave you for a moment and let you get on with it. I'll return in a few minutes.'

So saying, she rose and left the room. Charles found he was able to sit up and swing his legs over the side of the bed and aim into the pot with little difficulty.

Meanwhile, Melissa went down to talk to the others.

'He's fully awake now and quite compos mentis but still very weak. But I am worried that he is already getting suspicious. He is clearly surprised by my clothing and like an idiot I let him see me open the thermos flask. It was only when I saw his reaction to it that I realised even something as simple as that was outside his experience. We are going to have to be so careful.'

Jack looked at Melissa. 'I think you had better introduce me when you go back up and we will start off with a few half-truths to see how he reacts.'

'Alright but he is still very weak, so just enough to keep him content for the moment.'

They both went back up to the room but to their surprise, Charles wasn't back in bed he was by the window. The curtains were drawn and he was looking up into the sky. He turned to them with a look of astonishment and fear on his face.

'Pray, tell me, what in the name of God is that?' he asked pointing to the sky.

Jack got to him first and saw a helicopter flying slowly past, quite close. 'Oh shit, that's bollocksed it,' he muttered under his breath. 'Sir, please come back to bed and we'll talk.' He took Charles's arm and he and Melissa guided him back to the bed.

Charles was clearly quite agitated and Jack realised all his carefully laid plans had been blown out of the water.

'First Sir, let me introduce myself. My name is Jack Vincent and you are under my protection. Whatever you may see, you are perfectly safe here. May I have the honour of knowing whom I address?'

Charles looked at Jack and saw a man of about his own age, with strong features, a tanned face and dark hair. He looked into his eyes and saw only concern and honesty. Although he knew he had no choice, he also felt that this was a man he could trust despite the unusual way he dressed and spoke.

'My apologies Sir, I am Charles Lonfort, second son of the Earl of Hinchfield and Master and Commander of the Brig Sloop Andromeda. Please, please tell me where I am and what has occurred.'

'Please sit back and rest and I will do my best,' responded Jack thinking fast. 'Firstly, you are safe in a house in St Lucia. As to what occurred, we would like to know as well. We found you in a small ship's boat about forty miles out and rescued you. You were half dead through dehydration and badly burned by the sun. You also had yellow fever. We brought you here and you have survived the fever and are recovering. Now can you tell me how you came to be in that situation?'

Charles thought back to that terrible moment when he been swept off his ship. 'We were in pursuit of a blockade runner, an American, whom we had almost arrested in Dominica. It was a stern chase and we had the upper hand but we were hit by a terrible storm and the ship broached to the wind. I was already feeling unwell and lost my footing. The next thing I knew I was afloat. Someone had the presence of mind to cut a boat free for me and I managed to board and set sail for one of the islands,' and then in an agonised voice, 'now Sir why do you all dress and talk so strangely and what the devil did I see out of your window?'

Jack looked at Charles, thinking furiously and quickly came to a decision.

'That Sir, was a helicopter. I know you have no idea what that is. In this world it is used as a means of transport. I'm afraid there are many things you are going to find incredible. Can you please trust us to explain them in a manner you will understand?'

Melissa broke in. 'Yes Charles, please trust us. You have been through a great ordeal but there is so much more we need to explain and it is going to be difficult.'

Charles lay back and looked at them both. 'I have no reason to doubt that you have looked after me well and seem to have my best interests at heart but what is it you are so scared of telling me? I can see it in your eyes, both of you.'

Jack looked at Melissa, who smiled agreement at him. 'Alright Charles, may I call you that by the way?'

Charles nodded.

'What was the last date you can remember?'

Unsure of what they wanted, Charles thought back to the day he was swept overboard. 'The twenty eighth day of March, as I recall.'

'And the year?'

Charles frowned, now really unsure of where the conversation was going. 'Seventeen Eighty Five as I am sure you are aware.'

'Well Charles, the day and month tally but I'm afraid to tell you that the year is now two thousand and nine. You have travelled across the sea in your boat and forward two hundred and twenty four years in time.'

Charles looked nonplussed, switching his gaze between Jack and Melissa. He could only see concern and honesty. There was no hint of guile.

'You jest Sir, that is not possible,' but even as he said it he recalled some of the strange stories he had been hearing from locals. He even remembered his own words to his First Lieutenant about discoveries yet to be made. Could it be possible that he had travelled so far?

'That thing in the sky then, it is normal in your world?'

'Yes, that and many other things you will find incredible but we are still people like yourself. Your county, Great Britain still survives, as does your Royal Navy. I myself served for nine years in the rank of Lieutenant. There is so much to show you and plenty of time to do so. But we really feel we need to do this slowly. It will still be some time before you fully recover. Please, let me ask you again to trust us.'

Charles pondered Jack's words. The shock he felt at seeing that flying monstrosity was only compounded by what he had heard. But what choice did he have? However, if he believed for one moment that he had been told the truth, then there was an even worse problem, one that didn't bear thinking about.

'Jack, I'm not sure what to believe anymore but if what you say is true, how will I find my way home? Do you know how I got here and how I may return?'

'I can't make any promises Charles. We don't really understand what brought you to us. But I do have some ideas about how to get you home. Let's get you better first and then we will see.'

Melissa gave Jack a strange look.

'It's alright Melissa. I will tell you all when the time is right. Now, I think Charles that you need to rest and then we can think about showing you a few marvels.'

Despite all the incredible things he had heard, Charles felt a wave of fatigue overwhelm him and drifted off to oblivion once again.

Chapter 15

Charles showed remarkable powers of recovery. Within twenty four hours he was eating like a horse and chafing to get out and about.

Jack was in the kitchen talking to Martha and Melissa. Emma and Lewis had gone down to the boat, not the least, to deal with a five day old Mahi Mahi they had forgotten about in all the excitement.

'All our good ideas went out of the window literally, when he saw that damned helicopter. So, unless we lock him in, we are going to have to somehow introduce him to our world. I've looked at the view from the veranda and what I suggest is we get him down here and just let him see what there is. You can see the bay with ships with sails and without, cars going by on the main road and all sorts of things like telegraph wires and satellite dishes. Plus, I'm sure he'll catch the odd aircraft going into Castries but he's already seen one close up so that should be no surprise. Then, when he's made his own discoveries we can answer his questions. Guess we then just take it from there, any views?'

Martha pondered and replied, 'that seems a good approach. I wonder what he will make of a black woman owning the house he's living in?'

'Good point,' said Melissa. 'We mustn't underestimate the changes in social and moral values, just because he is going to be surprised by the technology.'

'Only one way to find out, Melissa. Let's go get him.'

So saying, the two of them went up to the bedroom to find Charles sat on the end of his bed dressed in a T shirt and towel contemplating the pair of trousers that Melissa had left him.

'Ah, my dear Angel, I understand the 'T shirt and underpants' you have provided but how on earth do I operate these things,' asked Charles glumly.

'Oh dear,' she exclaimed laughing. 'We really are going to have to start from scratch.' And she took the zipper and showed him how it worked.

Once he realised the function he smiled delightedly. 'So simple and clever, what else am I going to discover today?'

'How about this marvel of design?' said Jack opening the door to the bathroom. He let Charles put on the pair of slacks and then ushered him into the room. He explained the taps and how one had permanent hot water and one cold and then the shower, turning it on to demonstrate its purpose but strangely Charles didn't seem too impressed. When Jack explained the toilet and its workings, he was startled when Charles started to chortle quietly.

'I'm sorry, I don't wish to appear rude but my father has always been very keen on modern inventions and the washrooms in our house are not too different from these. I had hoped for something more amazing.'

'OK then, let's go down and sit on the veranda and we'll see a few more things.'

Charles looked puzzled again. 'Pardon my asking but what does O, K, mean?'

Jack sighed. This was going to be more difficult than anticipated. 'Actually, I have absolutely no idea. We just use it as a way of saying, alright or fine.'

Charles considered his reply. 'OK then, let us repair to the veranda.'

They all smiled.

They walked down with Charles and got him settled in a cane chair overlooking the bay. His eyes were everywhere taking in the sights. They opened even wider when Martha came into the room.

Jack looked at them both. 'Charles, may I introduce Martha. She is the owner of this house and has been kind enough to offer you shelter.'

Charles struggled to his feet and without the slightest hesitation bowed and then held out his hand. 'Madam, Charles Lonfort at your service.'

Martha beamed at him. 'A pleasure to meet you Sir, I expect we'll have much to talk about.'

Taking the bull by the horns, Jack interjected. 'Charles, thank you so much. We were all concerned about your reaction to the fact that in this age we hold all people, whatever their colour, in mutual respect. We know that it was quite different in your time.'

Charles looked at Jack and Martha. 'Indeed but that does not mean that all people of my time think the same way. As far as I am concerned, slavery is barbaric and should be abolished. There are many who feel this way, the problem is that the economic arguments are so strong. But,' he said with a smile, 'you can tell me all about how it was all brought to an end can't you.'

Martha smiled back. 'Yes we can. There's going to be so much to tell you. It's really hard to know where to start. Why don't we all sit down and we can start with the view from my veranda.'

The afternoon passed in a blur. The two things that Jack thought would completely surprise Charles were the cars shooting up and down the main road in the distance and the movement of boats and yachts in the bay without the use of sails. However, once the idea of an engine was grasped Charles seemed quite happy to accept the concept, pointing out once again that such machines were already making an appearance in his age, albeit powered by steam. What amazed him more were the lights that were turned on as dusk settled, both in the house and all around him. By the time it was dark, he was astounded at how much light was being generated, to the point that he couldn't even see the stars. Electricity was something he had great trouble understanding even when it was explained that it was the same energy as lightning or the static created when rubbing silk.

However, most of the time was spent talking about what had happened in society and the world. He was astounded when Melissa explained how many people there were now living on the planet. This led onto discussions firstly about how there could be enough food and then about medicine and how far the human race had come in understanding their own bodies. When they tried to explain modern concepts of social justice it became clear how big the divide in understanding really was.

Charles soon tired. He was still recuperating from a serious illness and that coupled with the marvels he had seen and heard, resulted in early fatigue and a request to retire. Melissa took him to his room.

He sat on the end of the bed and looked at her. 'You know I feel I am living in a dream. I cannot deny the evidence of my senses and all that has been imparted to me but if it wasn't for you, I think I might go mad. You rescued me and you nursed me to health. How can I thank you enough?'

'At the moment the best thing for you is to climb into bed and get some more sleep. We can talk all we want during the days to come. Now, is there anything I can do for you?'

He smiled back at Melissa. 'Thank you, no my lady, you have already explained that you are a nurse and what that means but I think I can look after myself now.'

He blushed at the recollection of what she would have done to him while he was in the grip of the fever.

Seeing him blush she smiled. 'Don't worry, it's my profession to look after sick people and you were no different. Just slightly more handsome than most.'

He looked her in the eye. 'And you are by far the most beautiful nurse a man could wish for.' And before he could stop himself, he kissed her on the lips.

For a second she responded and he felt the whole world start to turn. Then laughing, she pushed him away. 'Now tiger, you're still far from well and that would definitely be unprofessional!'

Charles looked glum for a second then grinned at her again. 'Then I must fully recover and then I won't require any professional services.'

Melissa smiled to herself as she left, vowing to explain to him sometime the different nuances of the word 'professional'.

Charles lay in bed, his mind in a whirl. He still could not fully believe all that he had been shown and told but the evidence was all around him. He knew that all he had to do was reach for the switch by the bed and the room would be instantly filled with light. He had seen things today that were impossible yet there they were. His hosts were strange yet still very human and this brought his thoughts back to Melissa. He had never come across any girl like her. In his time, no female would act and dress as she did. It was quite clear that moral standards were now extremely different. Women wore trousers for goodness sake! But she had a spark which would shine out in any age. He had no idea what the future was going to hold, how could he? But the one fixed thing in his mind, the one thing he held to as he drifted off to sleep was her smile, her golden hair and her smile.

Later that evening, they all sat around and talked about the day. Jack was surprised by how well it had gone. 'You know, I was amazed that he seemed to understand the technology so well.'

'I've been looking at the net,' said Emma. 'Steam engines were well understood by 1785. There had been several uses of them in ships and they were already becoming well established on land. It's not much of a leap to see how we have improved engines and machines in such a long time. His father appears to have been a forward thinker for his times and it seems to have rubbed off.'

Yes, he has far more trouble understanding social development,' said Martha. 'He was more than happy to accept the abolishment of slavery but when I talked about how things are funded through taxation he became quite upset.'

'You mustn't forget,' snorted Jack. 'That all his family's money must have come from being at the top of the aristocratic food chain. Things like, taxing income and then handing it to the poor, would seem mighty strange. Anyway, things have gone much better than I expected but we need to look forward now and decide on what we are going to do with him.'

Lewis spoke for them all. 'Jack you said earlier that you had some ideas on that. So come on, cough up and tell us what you were thinking.'

'Look, we seem to have two options, the first is to try to educate him enough and slowly bring him into this century. From what I've seen, I suspect we could do that. Although, how we would get him into the system would be interesting, you know citizenship, passport and all that. Let's face it he is the ultimate illegal alien. Maybe we could get the navy in HMS Suffolk to help there.'

'No Jack, he would end up in some government institution. I'll not let that happen,' responded an angry Melissa.

'Whoa, hold your horses I agree. I just mentioned it as one option. I take it none of us like that idea,' he said to a row of nodding heads.

'Well, we could try to do it ourselves or maybe there is something else, something that he would far prefer as well.'

They all looked mystified except Martha. 'You want to take him back don't you?'

'Back to where?' asked Emma and Lewis in union.

'To the Caribbean of seventeen eighty five,' replied Jack firmly.

Emma looked troubled. 'But how? We don't seem to have any control over this phenomena. You've said yourself that it seems to be random.'

'I've been thinking about that and I wonder what would happen if we went back and re-traced the route I took exactly when I encountered that slaving ship. I have a record of the track and timings on my navigation computer. I think Charles encountered the same ship himself when he arrived in the islands. I mentioned the story to him this afternoon and he described a very similar ship. If that's the case, I was briefly back at the same time as him. If we can repeat it but then turn away from an easterly heading, for example by heading up to Antigua, then we can then take him home.'

'Hang on just a second,' said Emma. 'Even if it does work, then we get stuck back in the past in a modern yacht. What would we do?'

'The same thing. Once we've dropped him off, we retrace our route again but keep sailing east and we should come back just like last time. Jacaranda is a traditional design, above the waterline at least, so it shouldn't be too hard to convince people she is a private fast trading ship. We can hide all the technology below decks.' He looked around seeing sceptical faces.

'Look, nothing may happen but I think we should give it a try before marooning the guy two hundred years from home and it's a risk I am willing to take. Who knows, I might get to meet Horatio Nelson for real. How cool would that be?' He added, beaming.

'I know your fascination with naval history, there are enough books in Jacaranda to testify to that,' said Emma. 'But if you think for one moment that you're going on your own you've got another thing coming. You go, I go.'

'Hey, I wasn't saying I would do this on my own and anyway it may not work but seriously there is always a risk we could get stuck back in the past and you must consider that.'

Melissa joined in. 'That's a risk I am prepared to take and don't you dare count me out either. At least if we go back we have a much better idea of what to expect. Poor old Charles had no warning or idea of what he was getting into. We do.'

'Well,' said Jack smiling. 'Looks like my crew are revolting as usual. Just remember that if we do get stuck, medical care is non-existent and life is pretty primitive, no internet, no phones, no toilet paper, even with what we know it will be culture shock all round.'

Jack could see that Lewis was looking uncomfortable. 'Lewis old mate this is not for you. If we do go back and get stuck, you are going to be in a very difficult situation. This is the age of slavery at its worst. Even if we could protect you as a free man, you would still be at the bottom of society. We really can't risk it.'

Lewis looked relieved. 'Thanks man, I wasn't sure if you wanted me to volunteer as well. It's not the sort of place I would like to end up.'

'But don't worry we'll need someone ashore and on the end of a radio. You can be our link for that and have a good laugh when we all sail back in after sod all has happened.'

They talked over the idea for the rest of the evening and agreed they would give it a try after the next charter had finished in just over two weeks. There was the usual week's gap between bookings after that and that should give them plenty of time to try out his idea.

They also confirmed that Melissa would miss the forthcoming charter to spend the time with Charles. She would help him with his modern education but also pick his brains as to what they might usefully take with them as insurance should they be marooned themselves.

Lying in bed later that night, Emma cuddled up to Jack. 'Is this really happening? Did we really spend most of the evening talking about sailing back to the time of Nelson? We must be mad. But it could be fantastic. Imagine going to Nelson's dockyard in Antigua and seeing it as it really was with no modern marina and fancy restaurants.'

Jack snorted. 'Yes, just a mosquito ridden mangrove swamp and a few buildings but my God you're right, I wonder if this will really work?'

Chapter 16

Paul gazed out of the window of the 747 as it banked around the corner of the beautiful green island to come in to land at Hewonarra International Airport. Sarah sat next to him, her head propped on his shoulder fast asleep, a legacy of several large gin and tonics. Sitting by the window in a club class seat, he had a grandstand view of St Lucia and it looked enchanting. As the aircraft turned, he could see two enormous cone shaped peaks jutting from the coast and several toy yachts moored in the bay between them. Just for once, he completely forgot about the business of making money and gazed longingly down, wishing he was on one of those boats right now. Paul had always loved the sea, learning to sail as a little boy on the south coast of England and progressing through his teens to ocean going yachts. During his short time in the army he had made maximum use of the facilities available to military personnel at the Joint Services Sailing centre in Gosport. It suddenly came to him how little he had actually sailed in recent years. In fact, the last time he had been out was on Jacaranda in the days before everything changed. He suddenly realised how much he was looking forward to his two weeks away and was really grateful to Sarah for bringing him here. He still didn't know where they were staying. She just kept giving him a sly grin every time he asked.

The aircraft touched down with its usual thump and in no time the doors were opened. A rush of warm, island scented air, assailed them as he reached up and grabbed their hand baggage before thanking the very cute young hostess who had kept their glasses topped up all the way across the Atlantic.

No airport tunnels or even busses here. They, along with all the other passengers, were required to walk across the tarmac to a slightly scruffy looking terminal building where a bored looking official checked passports and directed them to the baggage retrieval.

'At least we didn't have to take our own bloody bags off the plane,' he said to Sarah, looking around at the well worn building.

'God yes, it is a bit third world. Still where we're going should be a little better', she responded with another secretive smile.

'I am not going to rise to the bait anymore, sorry,' he responded, smiling back.

Eventually, their bags arrived and they joined the queue for customs, where a clone of the immigration officer took his own sweet time checking the passengers through.

Slightly hungover and starting to sweat profusely, they finally managed to get through the doors to the main terminal. Sarah was clearly looking for someone in the crowd.

Suddenly, Paul caught sight of two people standing by the main doors. They hadn't seen him yet but he instantly recognised Jack and Emma despite their clothing. He turned to Sarah, grabbing her arm and turning away from the door. 'Please don't tell me you've chartered a yacht called Jacaranda?'

Sarah looked slightly alarmed. 'Yes, I know you love sailing and I found them on the internet. She looked beautiful. What's the problem? And stop squeezing my arm you're hurting me.'

Hastily he let go of her. 'Sorry my love, it's rather a shock, you see I know the owner and his crew rather well. We go back a long way. He used to work for the company but left under rather a cloud shortly before you joined us.'

'Oh God, is that going to be a problem?' She suddenly looked sick.

Paul was thinking furiously and he suddenly realised that it wasn't actually a problem at all. When Jack left, Paul hadn't been involved and he had even helped Emma out a great deal. His motives might be suspect but no one knew that.

'No, no why should it be? I'm sorry. It was such a surprise that's all. Actually, it's time I got back together with them and you'll like them, they're great people. In fact, bloody well done I can't think of anything I'd rather do than sail that boat with them out here'. And he gave Sarah a great big hug before turning back towards the concourse. Sarah was relieved, for a second she thought she might have made an awful mistake.

Paul walked towards Jack and Emma and was amused to see the looks of recognition and surprise on their faces. They looked disgustingly tanned and fit, wearing faded shorts and T shirts.

Jack got in first. 'Paul you old bastard, you must be our charter but hang on, I have it in the name of Wilson.'

Sarah held out her hand. 'You must be Jack Vincent. Hi, I'm Sarah Wilson, Paul's girlfriend. Sorry, this is all my fault. I made the booking as a surprise holiday for Paul. It seems it's an even bigger surprise than I intended.'

Jack smiled back at them both. 'No worries, this could be really fun. Hey, welcome to St Lucia. Let's jump in the luxury transport and we can talk on the way to the boat. Paul, we've got so much to catch up on. How was the flight by the way?'

'Fine, fine, the usual but Emma what on earth are you doing here? Last I heard you were still working in London for that travel magazine.'

'Not anymore,' smiled Emma. 'You're now looking at the second under flunky responsible for cooking and crew morale on the good ship Jacaranda, where I work for a pittance, for Captain Bligh,' she said casting a loving glance at Jack.

Paul smiled back but couldn't miss seeing the looks they gave each other and the pang of jealousy it generated in him. In other circumstances she could have been looking at him like that.

'Come on,' said Jack, taking Paul and Sarah's bags. 'We've got the old jalopy outside. We need to get you both to the boat and into some suitable clothing. Didn't you know long trousers and Lacoste polo shirts are illegal in St Lucia?'

It took over an hour to drive right across the island to get to Rodney Bay. The roads were good in some places but dreadfully pot holed elsewhere. When they hit the capital Castries, Paul discovered that the Caribbean could do traffic jams as well as anywhere else in the world. But it didn't matter, as they chatted happily all the way, the time flew. Jack pointed out interesting parts of the island as they travelled and they discussed itineraries.

They agreed that they would rely on Jack's local knowledge and put themselves in his hands. Emma asked if they had any special requests on the alcoholic or culinary front and again they were content to take what was offered. The one subject that was not broached was that of Jack leaving the company or what had been happening since. Paul knew it would have to come up at some time but wanted to pick his own moment.

They finally arrived at the marina and Jack got hold of a trolley and they walked down the jetty to the boat. Sarah gasped when she saw the boat in the flesh and Paul was genuinely overwhelmed when he saw her again, the beautiful classic lines, the soaring varnished mast and gleaming decks. Just for a second, he wondered whether he had got it wrong, that this should have been his life and then he remembered he had enough money to buy ten Jacaranda's and that was a far more satisfying thought.

That evening, they sat in the cockpit enjoying the local rum. Paul and Sarah had changed into more casual clothing but had to put up with the ribbing from Jack when he saw Paul's shorts had creases ironed into them.

'It's alright Paul,' he said. 'They'll look the real thing once they've got some decent food stains and faded properly after two weeks in the sun. At least you've not got socks on with those sandals.'

'You know, I bloody well hope you treat your regular customers with a bit more respect,' retaliated Paul. 'How on earth do you make any money if you're so effing rude?'

Emma joined in and laughed. 'Yes well, you're not real customers, you're friends and that means we can be as rude as we like. I know we'll get it back in spades anyway.'

'Yes and that reminds me before I get too pissed on this firewater you serve but just to make it clear, that is how I want it to be. I know we are paying to be here but can we forget that now and make this fortnight like old times please?'

'You've got it mate but even so we will not ask you to do the washing up or clean the heads.'

'When did I ever do either of those things?'

'Good point, pass the rum.'

The next day they headed south. Jack had decided to go down to Grenada then head slowly back north over the fortnight. He initially planned to sail the one long leg overnight and allow his guests to catch up on some sleep. Sarah had done some sailing but was very tired from the flight. However, Paul was insistent that he do his share so they ended up splitting the night watches for which Jack was very grateful. Before he turned in, they spent an hour or so chatting. They were cruising along, powered by a warm trade wind under a starry sky with a half moon casting a silver trail over the water. Jacaranda's wake was picked out by a trail of silver phosphorescence.

'By God, this is wonderful,' exclaimed Paul. 'I'm beginning to understand why you walked away from London.'

'Maybe but being kicked out of my job might have had something to do with it you know.'

'Er, yes we need to talk about that sometime but can it be later? This just doesn't seem to the moment and you need to get your head down. I seem to remember that naval aircrew need eight hours sleep a day.'

'Yes and what they get at night is a bonus!' they both said in chorus.

'God, it's good to hear all that old crap being regurgitated again,' said Jack sleepily. 'Right mate, she's all yours, head south, don't hit anything and give us a call if you need me. See you at dawn.'

After a few days in Grenada, they travelled lazily north, spending a day here and there, up through Cariacou and then Union island. They spent several days in the Tobago cays the stunningly beautiful anchorage behind the great arc of the World's End reef. For some reason, the water was always clearer there than anywhere else in the Caribbean.

Jack and Emma managed to have an evening on the beach while Paul and Sarah watched a video on board. They pulled the dinghy up on one of the deserted islands and lay in the sand looking up at the stars. With no light pollution, the stars of the evening sky were stunning.

Emma leant on one elbow looking down at Jack. 'Our guests seem to be enjoying themselves but I'm so glad you got out of that world when you did.'

Jack looked up at Emma, her loose hair half covering her face. The silver moon shining through her tresses and making her beautiful eyes look like pools of darkness. He really didn't want to talk about Paul at such a perfect moment. 'I couldn't agree more.'

Meanwhile on Jacaranda Sarah had found a DVD of Pride and Prejudice and despite Paul's good intentions of keeping her company, he soon found his attention wandering. Jane Austen was definitely not his thing. Slipping away to the rear of the saloon he rummaged around in the large cocktail cabinet looking for refreshment. Suddenly, his fingers encountered a rolled up object that was clearly not alcoholic in nature. Carefully pulling it out, he discovered a chart of the area with all sorts of odd notations on it. It was hard to make out in the dim light and he didn't want to switch one on and interrupt Sarah's viewing. However, it was quite clear that Jack had been plotting something on the chart that was way out of the usual. Thoughtfully, he rolled it up and put it back in its hiding place. He would have to have quiet chat with Jack later.

They gave Mustique a miss. Jack said the anchorage was too rolly and sleeping would be uncomfortable. He didn't like the place anyway, it was too much like a theme park for the mega rich. The next stop was the little island of Bequia and that exercised its charm on them all. Then they were heading back to St Lucia with the end of the holiday suddenly in sight.

Their last but one stop was on a mooring between the Pitons, the amazing cone shaped hills Paul had seen as his aircraft arrived in St Lucia. They were in fact old volcanic plugs that had never erupted. It was almost like being in a Norwegian fjord. They grew straight out the water, almost a thousand feet high with shear sides making a stunning backdrop to the bay. That evening, the plates had been cleared away and they were enjoying yet another rum in the twilight. Some music was playing on the cockpit speakers in the background.

'Will you two please stop doing that!' Paul exclaimed.

Startled, Jack and Emma, both turned to look at him.

'You two spend half your time just looking at each other and grinning like idiots, it's most off putting.'

'Sorry,' said Jack. 'It's just that when I was three she hit me over the head with a doll and I've never trusted her since.'

'Only because you hit me with a toy brick,' riposted Emma smiling fondly. 'But you're probably right, I always travel with a doll so just behave or you know what's coming.'

'Anyway, now I've broken up the love in Jack. I think it's time we broached the subject of what happened a few years ago. We really should clear the air.'

Emma got up and looked at Sarah. 'I think we should let these two have a moment to themselves. How about helping with the washing up?'

The two girls went below to grateful smiles from the two men.

Paul settled back on his cushion and took a settling swig of his drink. 'The first thing you need to know is that you are actually looking at the Managing Director of Dwyer Investments. Sir Nigel is standing down and I am taking over.'

'Bugger me, you old fox, does Nigel know what a prat you really are? He'll regret it. No sorry mate, bloody well done. Hang on, now I get it, you only tell us at the end of the charter when it's too late for me to put up my prices, smart move.'

Paul grinned. 'You've got me there but tough luck you charge far too much for this old scow anyway. Now look, about when you were fired.'

'I bloody well wasn't fired. I left before the old bugger had the chance.'

'Yes but don't you want to know why?'

Jack looked serious. 'You know, that's a good question. Part of me wants to find out, as whatever it was, it must have been a stitch up of some sort. But there again look at me now.'

'So, you're quite happy to let things lie?'

'Not only am I happy to do so. I wouldn't have it any other way.'

Paul decided that he wouldn't pry any deeper. It was quite clear to him that Jack was totally settled in his new life and more importantly, no threat to him.

'Good, I'm glad that's settled. To be frank, I was worried that you still might want to dig into things and knowing I am taking over the business, I was worried you might want me to do the digging.'

Jack looked at his friend. 'Paul, you can see how happy I am with Emma. I just hope you have the same luck with Sarah, she seems really nice.'

'Thanks for that. Oh by the way, there was one other thing' he said looking speculatively at his friend. 'I wasn't meaning to pry but I discovered a strange sort of chart at the back of the booze cabinet. It seemed to have some very odd detail on it. What are you up to? Some sort of treasure hunt?'

Jack's face showed a start of guilty surprise. 'Oh shit, you weren't meant to find that. I knew I should have hidden it somewhere better. Paul, can I ask you as a friend to keep quiet about it just for the moment. You are sort of right, it is a chart I keep to log certain things but now is not the time or place to discuss it.'

Before Paul could reply, the girls came back up into the cockpit and so he just nodded at Jack. 'OK, let's talk later.'

The next day was a short coastal hop up to Marigot Bay. Jack had planned it so they would have their last evening apart from when they returned to the marina, in one of his favourite spots. They left the Pitons late in the morning and had a leisurely sail up the coast past the town of Soufriere and the island's west coast.

Jack had left the navigation to Paul as he often did with guests for this particular leg of a charter.

'So, now we are approaching Marigot, I'll buy the beer all evening if you can point to the entrance and get it right,' said Jack cheerily as they looked up from the electronic map on the chartplotter to the green coastline.

Paul studied the land carefully. There were a couple of sandy beaches and headlands so he bloody well should be able to see it but he couldn't. The chart showed an inlet between two headlands but where it was, was a complete mystery. 'No, you've got me it should be about there but I can't make it out.'

'An honest answer,' said Jack triumphantly. 'And that means you buy the beer.'

'Oi, who said anything about me buying? All you said was that you would buy if I got it right, not the other way round.'

'Drat, foiled again,' said a cheery Jack. 'Now look, if we head south a bit more. Now you can see the red buoy just off the entrance. Look, another boat is coming out.'

Sure enough, a mast followed by the hull of a yacht appeared out of the greenery and suddenly it all came into focus. The entrance was now visible but Paul reckoned that without seeing the outgoing yacht he would still be searching.

'Bloody hell, how did people ever find the place without GPS?'

'Not only that, once we get closer, you will see that the lagoon inside is hidden by a sand bar and it's almost impossible to see what's at anchor. This was why it was so good for pirates and smugglers. The place has an amazing history. There is even a story of an English fleet hiding in the lagoon while the French just sailed past and you can see why. Luckily for us, it's now the home of several good restaurants and the best happy hour bar in St Lucia.'

They turned Jacaranda into wind and dropped the sails and then motored into the narrow steep sided entrance. Jack had already booked his usual mooring inside the lagoon. Getting Jacky in was always a bit of a squeeze but he had done it many times before and the local boat boys came out to help as usual.

Once settled Jack turned to Paul. 'Well, we'll need the tender to go ashore, so LAUNCH THUNDERBIRD ONE.'

Paul grinned back, he always enjoyed this bit. In his opinion it was the best boy's toy on the boat. Going behind the wheel he found the large red button that some wag had labelled 'large red button' and pushed it. A square section of deck at the rear of the boat slowly opened on hydraulic jacks and stopped when vertical. Paul clambered down the little ladder and climbed into the rigid inflatable boat stored there on a ramp. This was Jacaranda's garage and apart from the tender it also held a couple of windsurfers and all the normal junk you find accumulating in a yacht. Once settled in, he pushed another button on the wall and the boat tilted back as another panel opened up below Jacaranda's overhanging stern. Soon the little boat was stern down just above the waterline and he pushed the final button and a winch smoothly let the tender slide backwards into the water. He hit the starter for the fifty horse power outboard, clambered forward to unhitch the winch line and then slowly motored out. He tied up alongside the starboard side where Jack had secured a set of boarding steps.

'You know that has just got to be the most over engineered outrageous way of getting a dinghy into the water,' he called up to Jack as he clambered on board.

'Yeah but what fun eh?' and they grinned at each other like two overgrown schoolboys.

That evening, the four of them sat in the bar where happy hour never ends. A band made up of local expatriates was giving it large in the background. A flock of stuffed toy parrots adorned the roof and swayed to the gentle breeze. Their chairs were placed to look out of the harbour entrance towards open sea where the sun had just set. The sky was still just light and the clouds were showing the last burned orange of yet another spectacular sunset.

'Isn't this the best place in the universe right now?' said Emma feeling mellow, looking at the others and sipping a rum punch.

'Yup, said Paul. 'What a shame we have to leave. Maybe I'll get my own boat and come out here like you two. It'll have to be bigger and better than Jacaranda though.'

'Bollocks,' snorted Jack. 'Within two days you'll be back at your corporate desk, planning the downfall of yet another financial institution and loving every minute of it.'

'I suppose so but now I am the boss, it does make you look at things differently. You know its one thing to climb the mountain but quite another to reach the top. You can't really climb any higher. Oh shit what's in this rum? I'm getting all maudlin. Right Emma, you need a dance.' And so saying, he grabbed her and dragged her willingly to the little dance floor in the corner.

Jack sat back with a sigh. He was going to miss Paul. In some ways he could be a right twit but he was a damned clever twit and had helped Jack so much in the past.

Later that evening, Paul and Jack shared one last drink in the cockpit. The girls had already gone below. Paul looked speculatively at his friend. 'Right me old mate, are you going to come clean about what that strange chart is all about?'

Jack sat back and considered what to say. He knew Paul would not rest until he got some sort of answer and he also knew that Paul was very good at spotting untruths. With the booze undermining his guard, he decided what the hell, he probably wouldn't believe him anyway.

'All right old chum, you asked for it,' and he launched into the whole story.

Paul sat quietly, initially a look of astonishment and disbelief building on his face but slowly as Jack provided more and more detail he seemed less sceptical.

'Let me get this straight, there is some form of time warp thingy out to the west of here and you have experienced it for yourself? My God but this rum is stronger than I thought.'

'Scoff if you like but the navy are taking it seriously and are looking for evidence. Not that they've got anything out of me.' And Jack recounted his conversation with the Captain of Suffolk.

He also told Paul about their house guest and the fact that Melissa was there looking after him. Funnily, Paul wasn't that surprised to find that she was out here as well but was worried what he would say to her if they met.

'Bloody hell and you're saying you've got a chap from 1785 staying at your place and you're going to try and get him back in this yacht?'

'Got it in one, I don't expect you to believe me. I'm not sure I would believe me if I was in your place but there it is.'

Paul looked at his friend. His story was outrageous but he had never known Jack to lie and clearly he believed all that he had said. And dammit if this was true there must be some advantage he could get from it.

'Jack thank you for that, there is only one more question I have.'

'Go on then.'

'You are going to let me come along aren't you?'

Chapter 17

Melissa and Charles talked for over two weeks. As Charles's health rapidly improved, so did his inquisitiveness. For the first few days after Jack and Emma had left on charter, they had stayed inside the house. Melissa, with Martha's help, had tried to slowly introduce Charles to the modern world.

He was fascinated by all he saw and heard. What surprised him most was that he seemed to be able to understand most of what he was told quite easily. It didn't take him long to realise that although his tutors knew a great deal, they often only understood things at a superficial level. Early on Melissa had shown him a thing they called a 'television'. When she turned it on, he was completely startled to see moving and talking pictures appear from nowhere but he soon became familiar with it although much of what he saw and heard he really couldn't put into any context in his mind. However, when he asked them how it worked it was clear that they really didn't know and this was true of many of the machines in the house. After a while, he realised why. With so many miracles available to these people, there was no way anyone could fully understand them all.

His first foray into the kitchen proved to be a bit of a disaster. Martha had shown him how her coffee machine worked and as good coffee was one of the passions of his life, he made a special effort to follow the instructions. Unfortunately, they all then assumed that he had grasped more of the general concept of the operation of electrically powered machines than he really had. The next morning having risen early and finding himself alone in the kitchen, he had successfully managed to get the coffee bubbling away nicely. Flushed with success, he then attempted to make some orange juice in the blender as he had seen Melissa do. Unfortunately, he had not realised that you needed to put the top on it and therefore was completely amazed at how far it could project the contents across the room and over himself. At the same time, the toast in the toaster was starting to burn and as luck would have it that was exactly when Melissa walked in.

She took one look at Charles liberally splattered with orange as was the rest of the kitchen and the smoke pouring out of the toaster and was caught between the desire to burst out laughing and stop the place burning down. In the end, she managed to do both and then had to apologise to Charles who had such a woeful look on his face.

'I am so sorry my love,' he offered as she gave him a cloth and directed him how to help clean up the mess. 'I was so successful with the coffee maker, I thought I'd be able to use some of these other devices. I clearly need more education.'

'No, don't worry,' and she gave him a conciliatory hug. 'We can't expect you to manage all this after only a few days but I suggest in the future that you limit yourself to the coffee maker. You're obviously quite good at that.'

He beamed at the compliment and they sat down to a cup of his really rather good coffee. In the end, he was able to consign all the machines into the mental category of things that were just improvements which he could expect after so much time had passed. However, when the girls started to explain how society now worked he was very surprised. He found the story of the abolition of slavery very satisfying but as he learned more about social development he was at turns delighted and horrified.

'Let me be sure I understand this,' he said to the girls one evening. 'Everyone who earns money has to give a large amount of it to the government so they can hand it to out to poor people. Why does anyone work at all?'

Melissa found that quite hard to answer and in the end, they realised that this was the biggest gulf to bridge. In the modern world even a prisoner had a better standard of living and life expectancy than an aristocrat would have had in Charles's time and this really took time to sink in. He had originally assumed that Jack and his friends must be aristocrats or at least rich people. It slowly began to dawn on him that they considered themselves to be pretty ordinary.

After a week, Melissa took him out for his first ride in Martha's 'horseless carriage.' Although he had got quite used to seeing cars driving along the road in the distance, he was still unprepared to actually travel in one. Melissa got him seated safely with his seatbelt on and climbed in behind the wheel.

'Now, I'm going to start the engine and you will hear it rumbling from the front.' So saying, she turned the key and fired it up. Glancing over at Charles, she saw he was sitting staring straight ahead gazing fixedly at something in the distance.

'It's really quite safe you know.'

'Madam, that's easy for you to say, you've been brought up with these infernal things,' said Charles through tight lips. 'Pray tell me again, how fast did you say this machine will go?'

'The maximum speed limit in the island is actually forty miles an hour but most people ignore that, so we could probably get her up to sixty or seventy on a clear road.'

Charles turned even paler.

'I'll have you know that experts in my time state that any person travelling faster than twenty miles an hour will be crushed by the resultant forces. I understand that this is incorrect but please take care,' responded Charles in an even tighter voice.

Grinning to herself, Melissa slowly moved the car forward, watching him from the corner of her eye. They reached the bottom of the lane and luckily the road was reasonably quiet. Turning left to go along past the marina she very slowly accelerated up to forty.

Charles was astounded. The ride was unlike anything he had experienced. The road was incredibly smooth with no ruts or potholes and he felt no forces on his body at all. The only change as they sped up was a slight increase in noise from the front of the vehicle where presumably the engine was working harder.

Melissa didn't take him too far on the first day but after that, it became a daily routine and by the time Jack was due back she had driven Charles all around the island. As an extension of Jack's idea to let him make discoveries himself it worked extremely well. While they drove, they talked about what they saw. One day she took him to Marigot Bay. He had told her the story of the arrest he had made there. Looking down into the lagoon from the overlooking road, he was amazed by how much he recognised but also how much had changed.

Melissa saw that Jacaranda was secured to a buoy in the lagoon and pointed her out to Charles.

'You know, that's the most familiar sight I've seen. It seems most odd to see a vessel that would be almost no stranger to my time moored where I moored my ship.' His voice sounded quite wistful.

On the way back, on a quiet section of road, she had let him have try at driving and was astounded at how quickly he picked it up. She had greater trouble explaining licences, insurance and why she couldn't really let him drive all the way home but he accepted it as yet another part of the baffling world he found himself in. As they descended the road back into Castries that afternoon, she saw that HMS Suffolk was back alongside the harbour wall and stopped the car opposite so Charles could study her. A young sailor was walking past and she lowered the window to ask why the ship was back in harbour so soon.

'Yes ma'am, we're undergoing a maintenance period,' he cheerily responded. 'Going to be here for another few days. I can think of worse places to be alongside.'

Charles turned to Melissa. 'I know that that massive ship is a direct descendant of my own but the only thing I recognise is the flag flying at her stern' and he pointed to the white ensign on the flagstaff at the rear of the ship. Then with a sigh, 'but at least some things seem to have been retained. From what Jack told me before he left, some of our traditions and spirit remain.' He was unusually silent all the way back to the house.

Apart from Charles's ongoing education, Melissa was having real concerns over her developing personal relationship. He had made no further attempts to kiss her, for which she supposed she was grateful. She kept telling herself that this was a man out of his time and with any luck due to return soon and then she would never see him again. That was easy to say but when you spent most of your day with a gallant, good looking and intelligent man, from no matter when, good resolutions were hard to keep. And to prove that he was very human too, that evening as she wished him good night, he took her in his arms and before she could stop him, kissed her long and hard. She could have pushed him away, she could have resisted him but, dammit she didn't want to. When they came up for air she looked him in the eye.

'This is definitely not a good idea and we both know it. We're going to try to get you home in a few days and then we'll be separated by an impossible distance.'

'I don't care,' he whispered in her earlobe.

'This won't work.'

'I don't care.'

'Dammit, nor do I.' They fell through the door and onto the bed. Very shortly Melissa found out the one thing that humans were very good at that transcended all time.

The next morning Melissa crept back to her room before Martha or Lewis were up. They had both agreed that they would keep their liaison discreet. What they got up to in private was no one else's business. Things would just get more complicated if they were honest with everyone about their feelings towards one another.

She showered and dressed, by which time she could hear the sound of others stirring. She cheerfully made breakfast for everyone and bade Charles what she hoped was a normal good morning when he strode into the kitchen with a bounce in his step and a smile for everyone.

That morning, she took him around the top of the island and they stopped for lunch at the little restaurant on Pigeon Island which overlooked Rodney Bay from the north. To Charles's amazement, as they sat at their table, he looked in the distance and saw the telltale white squares of a square rigged ship appear around the southern headland. As they watched, a two masted brig under full sail approached the island. When it was a few hundred yards away he was startled by the report of a long cannon firing. It was answered by a similar gun from the old lookout emplacement at the top of the hill behind them.

'What on earth is going on Melissa?'

She couldn't hide her amusement. She had picked this spot in the hope that this would happen. 'Sorry Charles but I thought you would like to see some of the things we do for amusement these days. That is the brig Unicorn and she sails every day with tourists on board. The cannon is used to illustrate the story of when this island was used by the pirate Jambe de Bois or Peg Leg. His real name was le Clerc. It's all just a bit of fun.'

She was surprised to see he looked upset and sad. 'I'm sorry Charles, have I done something wrong?' she asked and reached out and touched his hand.

He cradled her hand in both of his and looked into her eyes. 'No my love but it has reminded me so much of home and that we're to be separated just after I found you.'

Melissa didn't know what to say, she felt the same and she berated herself for allowing things to go so far. Except that she knew in her heart she would never regret it.

They returned early to the house, neither in much of a mood for further talk. When they got there, they saw Jack's motorbike leaning against the wall and a strange hire car in the drive.

'Oh good, Jack and Emma must be back, I hope the charter went well.'

When they went inside, the two sailors were talking to Martha on the veranda but to Melissa's surprise someone else was with them. As he turned around she realised with a shock that it was Paul Smythe, someone she had thought was gone from her life and the last person she wanted to see.

'Hello Melissa, I hope this isn't too much of a surprise.'

'Paul, what on earth are you doing here?'

Before Paul could speak, Jack answered for him. 'Melissa, Paul was the charter we've been on for the last fortnight. His girlfriend booked it as a surprise for him. She's had to go back home but Paul discovered our little secret. I didn't intend he should know, he sort of found out by accident and look he's volunteered to stay on and help us with our return project.'

Melissa looked tight lipped at Paul. 'I can't say I am glad to see you. You were an absolute shit to me when we last spoke.'

Paul smiled at her. 'Yes, you're right and I'm not here to open old wounds. Can we just put it behind us? What Jack and Emma have told me is just so fantastic, I couldn't go home without offering to help.'

Emma spoke to her friend. 'Come on Melissa, Paul maybe have been an asshole but he has been a good friend to Jack and me,' she glanced apologetically at him as she said it. 'And he could help us sail the boat and who knows what could happen? A spare pair of hands could be invaluable.'

Melissa realised she was outnumbered and rather than make a scene she reluctantly agreed. She would talk to Jack later.

Charles was looking rather bemused by the whole exchange. It was clear that Melissa was not too happy but that the others were, so he would reserve his judgement. He introduced himself to Paul and they all sat down to talk.

The conversation centred on how and when to make the return attempt. They looked at all the data they had about the original event. As Jack didn't really have hard evidence about what factors might be critical, they looked at everything they could think of. Clearly, being in the same place and heading in the right direction were key factors but these were easily reproduced. Other considerations were the time of day and even the phase of the moon. Jacked checked his almanac and found that the moon was full in two days time as it had been on that day last summer. They all agreed that they would take Jacaranda out the next afternoon. They had to sail out to the south west a fair way and then they could turn back and follow the original track aiming to be in the right place at the right time just after dawn the day after tomorrow.

Melissa and Charles had also been considering what might be worth taking with them in case they were caught in the past.

'The first thing I thought about were medicines,' said Melissa. 'So we've been to several pharmacies and bought loads of antiseptic, antibiotics and other useful modern drugs. We also reckoned anything electrical would be a waste of time, even battery powered, they would have too short a life.'

Jack agreed. 'Yes, they would be impossible to explain and have to be thrown away sooner rather than later. There was no internet or GPS back then.'

'But then Melissa asked me what I would value from what I have seen here,' interposed Charles. 'We talked about money as you all seem so rich but you don't seem to be able to get hold of quantities of gold or silver readily and frankly I still don't understand how your money works. However, I have plenty of funds in my time. My father is one of the richest men in the country. What I would value and what I believe would be the most useful commodity is information. There's so much knowledge here that we could use, so Melissa and I have been buying books.'

'Hang on,' said Jack and Emma almost together. Emma carried on with what they were both thinking. 'Can we really do that? Won't we end up rewriting history? This is the old time paradox thing isn't it?'

Melissa smiled. 'We haven't included any detailed histories or contentious books like Darwin for instance. But we have got lots of stuff on medicine and basic science, engineering and the like. I suppose the fact that we go back at all will effectively change the past anyway. Surely it's only a matter of degree?'

Jack agreed. 'We're in completely unknown territory here and I want all the help I can get. Remember, we're not planning to remain and in theory will only stay long enough to drop Charles off before we come back. Let's take the books.'

'This may be a silly question but what about weapons?' asked Paul. 'It's a pretty rough and ready place back then.'

Jack looked slightly sheepish at the question. 'Well no one is meant to know but I do carry a couple on board. They are well hidden but we should be alright. I'll show you if we need them alright?'

Paul nodded.

The basics decided, Jack headed off to the supermarket to get provisions. Melissa went with him to give Emma a break. Charles also asked to come, saying they would need as many hands as possible to buy all the coffee he was planning to take with him.

On the way in the car, Melissa voiced her concerns to Jack.

'Jack, I know you think he is your friend but I have seen another side of Paul and I just think you need to be careful with him about.'

'I do understand and you might be pleased to know I haven't told him absolutely everything of our little secret. But I can't see where the harm is and we could honestly use another pair of hands.'

Charles, understanding some of Melissa's concerns, turned to her. 'Fear not my lady any problems with your old friend and he will have me to deal with.'

She smiled back and hugged his arm.

Meanwhile, Paul had returned to Jacaranda. Using his laptop and the marina Wifi system he accessed his e-mails. Sarah hadn't been too keen to leave without him but he had told her that he and Jack had identified a rather good business opportunity and he wanted to stay on for another few days to look into it. She wasn't happy but there wasn't a lot she could do. Anyway, what was the point in being Managing Director if he couldn't take time off when he wanted to?

He skimmed his inbox, not intending to read any of the business e-mails, they could wait, when his eye was caught by one from the boss. Nigel tried not to use e-mail unless he really had to, so he opened it with interest which soon turned to dismay and then panic. The e-mail read:

Paul,

With the Auditors here soon, I thought I would do a few checks of my own especially over that time when we made that big loss and Jack Vincent was fired. All looked well until I looked into

Jack's private account. There is no record there of any of the transactions that should be reflected from his trading account. It was something he was clearly quite meticulous about, the rest of the time. Yet strangely there is no record of him or anyone else deleting anything from that account. It doesn't make sense to me, it almost seems that some sort of malfeasance took place and with the audit imminent we need to sort this out, please come and discuss as soon as you return.

Nigel

Shit, shit, how the hell was he going to explain this? There was no indication in the e-mail that the boss suspected him but a convincing explanation was going to be virtually impossible to come up with and once the boss realised that, he would look at everyone's accounts and the game would be up. He sat staring numbly at the computer. At least by staying out here, he had given himself some thinking time and by God he was going to need it. He sent a quick holding reply, explaining that he would be back a few days late, his mind working furiously.

Soon, despite his worries, his mind turned again to Jack's fantastic story. He would still be inclined to disbelieve the whole thing except for the mountain of evidence that Jack had presented once he had seen the map. The fact that the Royal Navy was aware of strange things happening and was apparently taking them seriously as well was another strong supporting factor. Then he had met Charles and he was even more convinced. The man had a manner and tone of speech that was not of this century that was for sure. No, unbelievably this was real and his mind was whirling to see what advantage he could obtain. He suddenly remembered something Melissa had said about when she and Charles were driving back through the capital Castries. A germ of an idea began to form. Yes, that might solve his problem. It certainly wouldn't do any harm.

Chapter 18

Dawn was just breaking. It was half past five in the morning and Jacaranda and her crew had about two hours to go before their rendezvous.

Jack and Emma were snuggled together on watch, drinking coffee and watching the sunrise.

'We should do this more often darling,' said Emma. 'The sunrise is more spectacular than the sunset.'

'Our guests don't usually seem that motivated this time in the morning for some reason.'

'Must be all that booze you force them to drink.'

Just then Charles poked his head out of the hatch. 'Good morning to you both.' He called cheerfully.

'Sleep well?' asked Emma.

'Madam, in all my time at sea I have never slept so well. Your accommodation is better than my stateroom at home in England and the way this vessel sails, is quite astounding. Pray how fast are we going?'

Jack looked down at the instruments. 'Oh, cruising at about ten knots or so.'

Charles smiled. 'In these conditions, my Andromeda would be hard pressed to make even half that and she is over twice the size of Jacaranda.'

'If you saw what this yacht looked like underwater I'm sure you would understand.'

Melissa then appeared. 'Morning campers, looks like a nice day.'

They had all noticed that Charles and Melissa had ended up in the same cabin last night. Melissa had given them all a hard look as she followed him to bed and they had all tacitly agreed to pretend not to notice.

A call floated up from below. 'Seems we're all up, how about I do some breakfast?'

A chorus of agreement met Paul's suggestion and within ten minutes more mugs of coffee and bacon sandwiches started appearing in the cockpit.

'So, where exactly are we?' asked Paul as he plonked himself down with his sandwich and coffee.

Jack looked at a hand held GPS as the main chartplotter had been stowed below along with other evidence of modern technology. 'We're south west of St Lucia and west of St Vincent. I've put in a waypoint for our rendezvous position. We need to get there at just after half past seven. At this speed, we'll arrive slightly early but we can slow down a bit when we are closer and should be able to make it quite exact.'

'Fuck me, what was that?' exclaimed Paul, as a roaring noise shot past the boat.

'That me old son is a Lynx helicopter. HMS Suffolk must be around somewhere. In fact right about there,' said Jack pointing towards the horizon ahead where the shape of the Frigate could just be seen. She was bows on and clearly at high speed as witnessed by the white wave being flung up at her bow.

The Lynx, having gone past Jacaranda now turned hard and came back and hovered alongside the stern. They could see the pilot staring at them and in the cabin door there seemed to be someone lying down with a rifle.

'What the hell is he doing?' asked Emma.

'Shit,' exclaimed Jack. 'That's a half inch recoilless sniper rifle. We used to use them for shooting out the outboard engines of high speed drug smuggler boats. What the fuck is he doing pointing it at us? Emma, pass me the hand held radio.'

Jack held the radio up so the pilot could see it and then went half way down the saloon ladder so he could hear it over the noise of the aircraft's engines.

'Lynx helicopter 472, this is sailing vessel Jacaranda do you read over.'

'Jacaranda this is 472, read you loud and clear. How do you know my call sign over?'

'It's written on your door in bloody great white numbers you twit. I used to fly those things. What the hell do you think you are doing pointing that sniper rifle at me?'

There was a few moments hesitation before the reply. 'Er, OK Jacaranda we are under orders to detain you. Please standby to be boarded.'

'What the fuck are you talking about? We are in international waters and you have no powers of arrest. I have done your job and I know the rules. Now point that fucking gun elsewhere or I will put out so many Mayday calls out your ears will be bloody burning.'

'Negative Jacaranda, my orders are clear and we are jamming your communications.'

'Look you fucking twit, that gun is designed to shoot at outboards of fast moving craft. It may have escaped your notice that we are sailing at about ten knots and currently heading straight towards your ship not away from it, so it serves no purpose but to scare the hell out of me and my crew.'

A new but familiar voice came over the radio. '472 this is mother, do as he asks, pull back and put the rifle away. Jacaranda, my apologies, they seem to have got slightly carried away.'

Jack immediately recognised Robbie's voice but that did not ameliorate his anger.

'Robbie, what the fuck are you doing? We are in international waters, you have no mandate to board me and you certainly are not allowed, by any law I know of, to jam my radios.'

'Simple law mate, I am bigger than you and have bigger guns, sorry but its orders. I will personally come over and explain. Suffolk out.'

'Emma quick,' called Jack. 'Go below and see if we can get on line with Inmarsat. He may be jamming VHF and HF but I'll bet he's not jamming the satellite frequencies. He has the same system and will want to keep it open for his own communications. I'll bet he doesn't know we've got it, our antenna is not obvious.'

Emma shot down to the saloon to turn on Jacaranda's computer. Meanwhile, they all looked over to Suffolk who was approaching rapidly.

Emma called up from below. 'Yes Jack, we can get on line. I presume you want me to put the webcam on this and put it live on to our website?'

'Absolutely,' called Jack. 'And then ring Martha and get her to copy it onto her computer as well. That way, if they shut down my site, we'll still have the evidence.'

A few moments later, a hand appeared at the top of the hatch holding a small high definition web camera. Jack took it and gave it to Melissa.

'Melissa, you're our cameraman OK? Try and keep it concealed when they board but also get as much as you can.' She nodded grimly and took the little device cradling it in her hand and immediately pointed it at the helicopter that was now about five hundred yards away.

'One last thing, Paul you asked about weapons. Go down to the chart table, underneath it and inboard there is a little brass catch. It looks like a screw head. Give it a tug and you will find a rifle and a pump action shot gun. Bring them up please, oh and there are some boxes of ammunition as well.'

Paul nodded and went below.

'Surely, you are not going to use guns?' asked a clearly very confused Charles.

'Not if I can help it but if they board me with weapons, I have every right to defend myself. They know that and so do I and whatever this is about, I am going to do my damnedest to make them look in the wrong.'

'I understand' said Charles. 'I only hope it's not my fault that you're being put into this danger.'

'God, you may be right. This may well be about you. Though how the bloody hell they found out I don't know. Look Charles, it might be best if I ask you to go below and stay out of sight. This is going to be the biggest game of bluff I have ever played and if they see you it will weaken my hand.'

Charles didn't look happy but nodded and went below.

Paul then came up with the weapons. 'What do you want me to do with them?' he asked.

Jack looked at the two guns. 'Give me the shotgun and put the rifle on the deck in clear view OK?

'Load them?'

'Yes, we'll have some rounds in the magazines but definitely none up the spout. This is for bluff. We can't win this but we can maybe make it so difficult they will have to back down.'

Emma called from the saloon. 'We're streaming onto the website Jack and I've just spoken to Martha. She is recording it all. She is also getting some of her friends to record and has gone on Facebook telling people to look at our webcam. Knowing how these things work, we will be watched by half the world soon. If they shut down our site, she will let us know and we can switch our output to her. She also said that there was a big fuss in Castries early this morning. Suffolk left in a real hurry and on the way out her wash did some damage to one of the cruise liners and several local boats. There are some really pissed off people back there.'

'Well done Emma. Her Majesty's Royal Navy are going to get one big fucking surprise if they're not careful.'

By this time Suffolk had gone past Jacaranda and then made a spectacular heeling turn through one hundred and eighty degrees to match her course and speed. As soon as she was in position, a large RIB was lowered and cast off heading straight towards them. Jack didn't need binoculars to see the person in the bows was his old friend and he was accompanied by five other sailors all of them armed with SA 80 rifles.

As the RIB drew alongside, the helicopter moved back in with its rifle once again aimed at them.

Jack leaned over and yelled at Robbie. 'If your fucking helicopter does not piss off with that stupid rifle now, you'll never get on board without shooting me is that what you want?'

Robbie said something to the radio attached to his lifejacket harness and the aircraft withdrew back to its previous position.

Jack could have put his boarding ladder in place to help Robbie on board but didn't see why he should make anything easy for him. So it was with some difficulty that Robbie eventually made a leap for the side of the boat and hauled himself on board. Jack had to smile, it would have been much easier if the guard rails were still there but they had been removed for authenticity as Charles had advised that health and safety was not an eighteenth century issue.

'That's enough,' yelled Jack over the noise of the helicopter. 'No one else on board until we've spoken.'

Robbie signalled the RIB to hold off and then radioed the helicopter to move even further away so they could speak.

'Hello Jack,' he said looking around from the deck. 'Going to invite me down?'

Jack gestured him forward and he jumped down into the comparative peace of the cockpit. His eyes narrowed when he saw the shotgun in Jack's hands and the rifle leaning against the saloon bulkhead.

Looking at Melissa and Paul who stared stonily back, he asked. 'Are you going to introduce me then?'

'No,' Jack was not going to give an inch.

Robbie, looking uncomfortable, broke the silence. 'I am instructed to put this sailing vessel under my orders, search her and escort her back to St Lucia. Do you understand?'

'And I refuse your illegal order. We are in international waters.' He looked at his GPS. 'Our position is thirty eight point five miles from Castries on a bearing of zero six nine. Which even you must know is outside any internationally agreed border. You have no authority on my vessel and absolutely no right to be on board bearing arms.'

'Doesn't seem to have stopped you,' said Robbie pointing towards the shot gun.

'As you well know, I have every right to defend myself from fucking pirates.'

Robbie winced. 'Look Jack, I am acting under orders. In fact, you wouldn't believe how high up those orders have come from and I'm afraid you have no choice.'

'So, let me get this straight. Someone in your command or even the British Government has ordered you to illegally seize this vessel and arrest all those on board. One simple question, why?'

'Oh come on Jack, we both know you have an illegal alien on board. You should have talked to me when you had the chance.'

'I have absolutely no idea what you're talking about,' responded Jack. 'I think you need to be clearer.'

'Hang on a second,' said Robbie. 'Are you recording this?' and then he saw the glint of the lens of the camera in the blonde girl's hand. 'Won't help you, you know, we're jamming your radios and you won't physically get anything off.'

Jack gave Robbie a conspiratorial grin. 'One word Robbie, Inmarsat. Smile you're probably being watched by half the world now and it's too late to shut us down.'

'You slippery, sodding, bastard.' But there was a hint of admiration in his tone.

'Careful now, we wouldn't want the whole world to know what bad language the Captain of a Royal Navy warship uses, now would we?'

Robbie looked nonplussed for a second. He hadn't wanted to do this in the first place but the signal he had received from Fleet headquarters had given him absolutely no option. However, this changed everything and he was going to have to try to carry out his orders while doing as much damage limitation as he could.

'Look you silly ass, talk to me without that bloody camera, please? As you value any friendship we may have left.'

Jack realised he had pushed his old friend about as far as he could and signalled Melissa to turn the camera away.

'You've got two minutes, no more. What can possibly justify what you have just done?'

Robbie drew a mental breath. 'We both know that you encountered exactly what I asked you about when we last met and you have direct first hand evidence to that effect. The government will do just about anything to get hold of that and if it's not us the bloody Yanks will soon get to hear about it and you know how they overreact.'

'You had better tell me how you know this first before I answer anything.'

Robbie now looked distinctly uncomfortable. 'Can't tell you old mate but remember Sun-Tzu.'

Jack looked confused but ploughed on. 'Well, I'll offer you a compromise. We were heading back to St Lucia anyway. I'll not let anyone on board but once we are alongside, I will allow a thorough search of the vessel, as long as the St Lucian authorities conduct it as well. Otherwise, we just go back on candid camera.'

'Alright but we follow you all the way and nothing or no one leaves the yacht. We will be watching closely, agreed?'

'Agreed.'

Motioning to Melissa to point the camera back at them, Jack said into its lens. 'We've come to a compromise. Jacaranda was going to St Lucia anyway and we have agreed to be searched on arrival but once this is finished, then I'm afraid the lawsuits may well start.'

Robbie could think of nothing more to say. He nodded at the camera and then took his leave. As soon as the RIB had gone, Jack looked at his GPS and checked their position. The autopilot had continued to do its job and they were still on track. He was surprised to see how little time they had left. Their encounter had lasted a lot longer than it seemed.

Paul looked at Jack. 'What the hell do we do when we get into Castries?'

'Who said anything about going back to St Lucia,' replied Jack. 'We have a different destination remember?'

Paul nodded. 'You really do think this will work don't you.'

'Well, we're completely buggered if it doesn't aren't we. Can you watch the helm. We only have a few minutes to go and I really need a pee.' So saying he shot down into the saloon leaving Paul and Melissa together in the cockpit.

Paul smiled weakly at her. 'Well that was fun, I wonder what happens now?' Inside he was thinking furiously. *'This was not going as planned and he would have to do something soon or it was all going to go horribly wrong.'*

Jack was also thinking hard. Robbie had clearly tried to tell him something when he mentioned Sun-Tzu the famous ancient Chinese strategist. And then it came to him, the quote 'keep your friends close and your enemies closer,' he suddenly understood what Robbie had meant. Shit, no time for that now he had one other thing to do and now was the time.

He went into the galley and looked at his sharks. Just like last time they were all lined up, grinning their inane grins at him. In the middle was the bone shark with the green eyes and as he looked into them he felt the same shudder and Jacaranda began to heel as the autopilot lost control.

'Sir, Sir!' called the Officer of the Watch to Robbie, as he climbed the stairs back onto the bridge of Suffolk. 'Sir, look ahead, I can't believe it but I saw it happen with my own eyes.'

Half a mile ahead of the ship, where moments before, a beautiful sailing vessel was heeling to the wind, there was nothing but empty sea.

'Oh shit, how the hell am I going to explain that?'

Chapter 19

As Jacaranda began to heel, Jack heard a cry and horrible soft thud from the main saloon. Rushing through the door he saw Emma lying on the floor, a small pool of blood forming around her head. He mentally cursed himself for not warning everyone what was liable to happen. She had clearly slipped and hit her head on the side of the saloon table. He could see a trace of blood there as well.

He yelled up the hatch. 'Melissa, come down as quick as you can, Emma's knocked herself out.' He knelt down and checked her breathing, which mercifully sounded normal.

Melissa pushed past him and started checking her over thoroughly.

'That's a bad knock she's taken. Help me get her on the saloon berth there.' Charles had come down by now and the three of them carefully carried Emma to the settee and made her comfortable.

'What's happening up top?' asked Jack as soon as he saw that there was little he could do for Emma in the immediate future.

'Paul has taken the wheel and is steering and that warship has vanished,' replied Charles in a strange voice. 'Can it be that I'm home?'

Jack looked over at the sat phone and sure enough, the screen reported no network. Yes, it looked like it had happened again. The only problem was that the suspicion in his mind was getting stronger by the minute and he knew he was going to have to act soon. He was now torn between his concern over Emma and what he needed to do urgently in the cockpit.

'Melissa, what can we do for her?'

'Sorry Jack but all we can do is keep her comfortable and wait for her to wake up. At the least, she will have one hell of a head ache. At worst, she will be concussed. Oh Christ, please don't tell me we are somewhere with no hospitals?'

'Sorry but it does look that way. Look, I must go up top. It seems your warnings about Paul the other day were right.'

She gave Jack a surprised look. 'OK, I'll stay down here with her. You go up. I'll call if she wakes up.'

Jack nodded and turned to Charles. 'I think you need to come up and hear this.'

He turned and climbed the ladder considering how to handle what he needed to say. Jack was normally a pretty mild character and it took quite a lot to wind him up but now he was seeing red and he had to force himself to keep calm, knowing that blowing his top would not be productive.

'YOU UTTER, FUCKING, TREACHEROUS, LYING, DISLOYAL, BASTARD.' He yelled at Paul. 'Now I know where you were yesterday afternoon you shit. You were betraying us to the navy, WHY?'

Paul was standing by the wheel and clearly not expecting Jack's attack.

'What? I don't know what you are talking about,' he blustered.

'The Captain of that ship is one of my closest friends. I asked him how he knew about us. He wouldn't answer directly but he mentioned something. A clue to an old phrase we knew from Staff College. He was telling me in a coded way that one of my friends was now my enemy and that could only have been you, you fucking shit!'

Paul was now looking thoroughly flustered. He looked at Jack who was clearly livid and even Charles was starting to frown at him. This was not going to plan at all. It even seemed that Jack's mad theory was correct. That bloody warship had simply vanished and at the same time the autopilot dropped out because all satellite lock had been lost. He needed to think and he wasn't going to be given the time. Suddenly, it came to him that it didn't matter. Why the hell should he justify himself? Years of suppressed envy overcame him. All the worry over his future. If he was actually where they all thought they were, he could wipe the slate clean. He looked down and saw the shotgun and the rifle. Kicking the rifle behind him he grabbed the shotgun, pumped a round into the chamber and pointed it at the two men.

Seeing the shock on their faces only spurred him on. 'Can you remember when we first met Jack?'

Jack was completely thrown by the odd question. His anger urged him to ignore the gun and just go and smash in Paul's smug face but common sense held him back. He knew Paul was good with weapons.

'What the hell that has that to do with anything?'

'I'll answer it for you then. It was at HMS Sultan, where we both attended the Admiralty Interview Board.'

'So what?'

'What was the result?'

'I passed and joined up but in the end, you decided to join the army and went to Sandhurst instead.'

'Not quite, I failed and went to the army as second best. What happened when we both went flying training? I'll spare you the answer. You passed and I got chopped. Every time I tried to do something you did it better and then there's Emma.'

'What on earth has she got to do with anything?'

'Just like everything else, you got her. When you introduced us you weren't together but as soon as I showed any interest in her, you bloody well took her back. You know, when you left the navy I got you the job with Sir Nigel because I wanted to get the better of you just once. And then, despite your complete lack of knowledge of the financial world, you started out performing me.'

The penny dropped with Jack. 'So that's it. It was you, you son of a bitch. You got me fired. Let me guess, you didn't cover your tracks well enough and you got found out so you decided to tell the navy as some form of insurance policy.'

'Got it in one and guess why no e-mails got through to Emma after you were fired?' I could access her e-mail account on line, so I deleted them before she could read them and even then she's bloody well stuck by you. I had to put up with second best again with that stupid blonde.'

'I heard that, you arrogant pig,' said Melissa who had just come up to the cockpit after hearing all the noise. Her eyes opened when she saw the gun in his hands. 'Christ, what the hell are you doing now?'

'Something I should have done ages ago but now I have the ultimate way of getting my own back. In about twenty minutes if you are right Jack, this boat will return to our time. Except you lot aren't going to be on it. I'll tell the navy some cock and bull story which no doubt they'll believe and Sir Nigel bloody Dwyer will not be able to touch me,' he almost shouted with a mad glint in his eye.

Still unsure of what was really going on, Melissa looked him in the eye. 'I've no idea what planet you're on but Emma is out cold and we need to get her some medical attention.'

'You won't get it in seventeen eighty five if that is where we really are. She can stay with me on the boat and go home but you lot are staying here.' So saying, Paul reached behind him and pushed the red button.

Jack immediately saw what Paul was intending to do and any self-restraint he might have felt evaporated in that instant. Without thinking, he rushed at Paul. He should have gone for the shotgun but instead, in a blind rage, he simply reached for Paul's throat. Paul saw him coming and reversed the shotgun, slamming the stock into Jack's gut and then bringing it up hard into his chin. 'See, they teach you some useful things in the army,' he gloated as Jack fell to the cockpit floor like a sack of potatoes, blood pouring out of a cut on his chin.

'And you, caveman, you keep back, this gun is capable of cutting you in half,' he said, as he saw Charles beginning to tense.

Melissa caught Charles's arm. 'No, it's true, that shotgun is lethal and this contemptible prick has clearly lost his mind.'

Paul grinned at her. 'Thank God this is the last time I will have to listen to your whining, you stupid cow. Now, you and Charles, drag Jack into the tender or he can stay on board full of buckshot.'

Charles and Melissa got hold of the semi-conscious Jack and half dragged him to the stern while Paul moved the other side of the cockpit table keeping it between them and keeping the gun trained on them both. He risked a quick glance down into the saloon and saw with satisfaction that Emma was still out cold on the settee. He suddenly realised that this really was the answer to everything. He would bring the boat back with just him and Emma. He was sure he could make up some story to satisfy her and the navy. And even if it all went wrong back at work, he still had the vital information of what was going on here which would no doubt be worth good money. 'Yes, this would work,' he laughed to himself.

He forced the three of them into the tender and then reached over and pressed the release button. Soon the tender was trailing behind Jacaranda on the winch line. Sighting carefully he fired the gun and the line parted. The tender dropped back quickly into Jacaranda's wake.

'Just one last thing,' he put down the shotgun and picked up the rifle.

On the tender, Charles had found a bucket and managed to slosh some seawater onto Jack, who spluttered and started coming round. When he started to focus he looked about and seeing Jacaranda several hundred yards away, quickly worked out what had happened.

Without warning, there was a snicking noise and part of the top of the outboard engine shuddered. It was followed by the report of a gun from the yacht.

'Oh shit, he's shooting at us. The mad bastard is trying to kill us now,' screamed Melissa.

'Everyone down,' yelled Jack and they did their best to hide, even though they all knew the side of the boat didn't offer any real protection. Five more shots followed the first one, all hitting the engine.

'At least he's pulled back from being a murderer but there again I suppose he feels he doesn't need to kill us,' said Jack after the shots had stopped. Looking up, he saw that his yacht was now too far away for even such a good shot as Paul.

'But he has shot up the engine. Presumably, he doesn't want us to follow him. Now there's a surprise.' Then he noticed flames starting to leap around the top of the engine. 'Oh shit, Charles, quick, give me a hand.'

The last round must have caused a spark and the top of the engine was starting to burn. The last thing they needed was the fuel in the main tank to catch light. He showed Charles what to do and they quickly undid the clamps of the wrecked engine and dumped it over the stern. It dragged behind the boat on its steering wires but the fire was quickly extinguished.

And then he started to laugh. It started out as a small giggle but soon was a full throated belly laugh.

Melissa and Charles looked at him as though he was mad.

Seeing their expressions, he wiped his eyes. 'Sorry, but Paul was so pissed off at feeling second best and now he thinks he has got one over on us. There's only problem.'

'And that is?' asked a puzzled Melissa.

'Oh quite simple, he has completely forgotten that Paul Smythe is a complete and utter wanker!'

On Jacaranda, Paul watched with satisfaction as the disabled and smoking tender disappeared astern. He was pretty sure he had only hit the engine. But then he found that he didn't actually feel concerned whether he had hit one of his ex-friends or their boat had caught fire. After all, they meant nothing to him anymore but he was proud of his marksmanship. Let them stew or fry out here, it was not his problem.

After an hour, he was beginning to panic. He had faithfully kept on course. As a precaution, Jack had put a waypoint in the GPS for the position where he had emerged back into the twenty first century. Even without the satellites, he was pretty sure he had sailed through it and absolutely nothing had happened. As far as he could tell, he was still back in the past. Maybe it was time dependant? No, that couldn't be right, his timing was spot on. Was there something more? Yes, that must be it. There must be something that Jack had done that he hadn't told his friend about.

He would have to backtrack and ask him. The barrel of a gun should convince him to come clean. He dropped the sails and started both engines. It should be quite simple to double back. They could hardly have gone far without an engine, even if they had oars on board.

An hour later, Paul was in a state of panic. He was absolutely sure he was back at the exact position where he had jettisoned the tender. So why was the sea completely empty in all directions?

Chapter 20

'Pardon me Jack but once again we seem to be talking different languages. What exactly is a wanker?' asked a puzzled Charles.

Melissa stifled her own chuckle and answered for Jack. 'Don't worry Charles, it's just modern slang. It means fool or idiot but,' and she turned to Jack who was just recovering from his fit of giggles. 'But what are you doing? It's hardly a laughing matter. We are now stuck out here in a disabled boat.'

'Well, if my old friend Paul had actually bothered to listen to the safety briefing I gave him at the start of his charter, he would have remembered that the tender is also our auxiliary liferaft. We have enough food and provisions to last us some time and more importantly there is this, Ta da!' And he opened a compartment at the rear to expose a small Tohatsu outboard engine. 'We often use this tender for fishing and as we can go a long way out, we always carry a spare engine. This is only ten horsepower as opposed to fifty but we can still get about eight knots or even more out of it, especially without the weight of the main engine.' He rummaged around in a locker and came up with a set of wire cutters and reached over and cut the steering wires that were holding the big engine onto the back of the boat and it sank into the depths.

He lifted out the smaller engine and clamped it in place.

'Sorry but the steering wheel is now useless. We'll have to steer using the tiller but what the hell. Now, where are we going to go? Charles, where would you recommend?'

'That rather depends on how far you think this boat will go,' replied Charles.

Jack knew the main fuel tank was full but the spare engine was a two stroke and could not run off the main tank. Checking the locker he could only find an almost empty bottle of two stroke oil. That was not so good. He thought carefully. 'We have enough fuel in the engine itself and enough extra oil to probably get three hours out of it. So at a conservative eight knots that gives us a range of about twenty four miles, bugger.'

Charles looked thoughtful. 'With the current against us, we'll never make St Lucia. It's going to have to be St Vincent then, which is not so good.'

'Oh, why is that? Surely, it's another British island?' asked Jack.

'Unfortunately, it has rather an unusual history. For many years the local Indians were very hostile to Europeans but they let escaped slaves take sanctuary there. There's now quite a large population of mixed race and they don't like us. Yes, it is nominally British, it was handed back two years ago by the French but much of the island is quite wild. We will have to be very careful. The capital is Kingstown but it is right down at the bottom of the island and I don't think we can make it that far. Anyway, what effect would it have if we sailed in, in this boat?'

'Hm, see your point,' said Jack as he rummaged around in another locker. 'We will have some security. We have these.' And he produced a flare pistol and a small automatic hand gun.

'What are they?' asked Charles looking blankly at yet more strange devices.

'Oh right, well this is our equivalent of your flintlock pistol except it fires up to eleven bullets without reloading and this is a pistol that fires a red flare for emergency situations but it is also a very good close quarters weapon. God, I really hope we don't have to use them. What do you reckon Charles?'

Charles regarded Jack and the weapons. 'Jack, this is my century now and you must understand that you will find things are very different. People are expected to look after themselves. There's none of your social welfare or health and safety that Melissa told me about. The islands in your time were completely tame but here and now they are dangerous places. I know you served in you navy but did you ever confront anyone? Did you ever have to defend yourself at a personal level?'

Jack looked worried. 'No, I had my share of warfare but it was all very impersonal. What are you suggesting?'

'You all looked after me well in your time and I was the novice but here and now I strongly suggest that you defer to me. I am a naval Commander and probably know enough to keep us alive and get us back to civilisation. Please don't take this the wrong way but I don't think you and Melissa would last long here on your own.'

Jack actually looked relieved. 'Charles, I couldn't agree more.' And he looked over at Melissa who just nodded her head at him. 'As far as we are concerned you're now the boss.' And he gave Charles a jaunty salute. 'So, what should we do now?'

'Firstly, show me how that pistol works. I would suggest that I am the best person to put it to use, if it should be needed.'

Jack spent the next few minutes showing Charles how to use the gun and once again was surprised how quickly he was able to grasp the concepts of modern technology. They also decided that Jack should keep the flare pistol as backup, especially when he explained that if the flare hit someone, it would keep burning even underwater.

With the new chain of command and their destination settled, Jack started the outboard and they set off for the large grey island in the distance.

As they motored on, Jack raised the issue of what they were going to do once ashore.

'That moron Paul is not going anywhere in time. He doesn't know how to get back but if we can retake Jacaranda, I'm pretty sure we can sort things out fairly fast. And I really need to get back to Emma.' All the activity up until now had blunted his concerns but they all came rushing back at once. 'Christ, I need to get her back. Melissa, tell me she is going to be alright, please?'

'Jack, it was a nasty thump to the head but there is no reason why she shouldn't fully recover. I couldn't find any sign of a fracture and just before all the fuss happened she seemed to be settling down. She'll be alright as I said, with a nasty headache for a while.'

'I wonder what that bastard will tell her when she comes round? Some pack of lies about how we were attacked by pirates and he bravely fought them off I wouldn't wonder. Oh God, I don't care about anything else. We have just got to get her back.'

Charles interrupted Jack's increasingly hysterical tirade. 'Jack, calm down, we've got to think this through carefully. We'll never retake Jacaranda while she's at sea. Paul has that rifle and anyway Jacaranda is much faster than us. I'm afraid the only way to resolve this is to get some help. If I can get us back to my people, with Andromeda we could easily make him change his mind.'

'Sorry but the worry is not going to go away. First, we are going to have to guess what Paul will do. You know, once he realises he is not going home, he will probably try to find us again, so I can tell him what he has missed. Once he has that information anyone care to guess what he will do to us? I can't see his shooting being so careful next time around.'

Charles pondered for a few minutes. 'We could try to get round to Kingstown but overland it would be too dangerous and probably not possible in this vessel, if as you say we have insufficient fuel. However, if we can get ashore we might be able to buy passage on a fishing boat or even barter for one of our own. But my squadron is to the north and I have no idea where the Windward Island forces are at the moment. They are usually based in Grenada, so there is not much hope that there will be any in St Vincent at any particular time.'

'What are you suggesting then?'

'We head north and look into St Lucia and if there is nothing there, we keep going. We're bound to encounter Andromeda or one of the other Leeward squadron ships. We should go straight past Martinique and Guadeloupe. French islands will not be the best place to go for help even if we are at peace. Even if we encounter nothing on the way, Antigua is not that far and we are bound to find help there.'

They all agreed, although Jack had reservations on how they were going to acquire the necessary transport. First things first, as he had been taught in the navy, when in a survival situation concentrate on the achievable and getting to land was the first priority.

The first thing they did, once underway was to do an inventory of their possessions. There was a good amount of survival kit, although some of it was useless in this age. Emergency radios and hand held GPS systems were clearly of no use. There were two large jerry cans of water and a solar still that meant water should not be a problem. They also had enough emergency food to last them all about a week. Rummaging around elsewhere in the boat, Melissa also came upon a pair of small binoculars and the locker full of fishing gear. Both latter items Charles felt would be excellent for barter with any local once they got ashore.

However, once they settled and he could start thinking, it suddenly hit Jack that this wasn't the peaceful Caribbean he knew. This was an area of islands held by countries with barely restrained hostility to each other and where slavery, disease and an incredibly short life expectancy were the norm. Suddenly, the reality of the situation was filtering through. He had already lost Jacaranda and Emma. This was definitely not what he had planned for so naively only a few days ago. He looked across to Melissa who also seemed to be in mild shock and took her hand.

'We are going to get through this. We will get home.'

She looked back at him. 'Thank you Jack. I know if anyone can do it, you can,' and then looking up at Charles, 'and we have one of the best people of this age with us.'

'I thank you for your trust my lady. You all showed great kindness to me when I was lost and fear not, I will do the same for you.'

The little boat droned steadily up and down the large swells making reasonable progress. It wasn't long before the lee of the island started to take effect and the seas started to settle down. With smaller waves to contend with, they managed to speed up and it wasn't long before they could start picking out landmarks on the shore. Just then the engine stopped. Jack looked in the little tank and sure enough it was empty. He soon filled it with neat petrol from the main tank and dosed it with two stroke oil but even though he used as little as he dared, there was not going to be enough to fill another tank after this.

'Where would you recommend we head for?' asked Jack as he studied the approaching shore.

'Strange as it may seem, you may know better than I,' replied Charles. 'It's an island I have never visited. It's outside my patrol area. My knowledge is only based on general information.'

Jack thought for a moment. 'In my day, there are three bays on this coast that offer shelter. They all have settlements but I have no idea which ones are currently inhabited. I suggest therefore we go for the northern most one called Chateaubelair. That reduces the distance we have to go when we leave and with a name like that, maybe there is a plantation and some form of civilisation that can offer help.'

So saying, they headed towards the top of the island until Jack could make out the large bay with a peninsula and little island jutting out into the middle.

'I suggest we land on that island first. This boat is very conspicuous. We can haul her out and then take stock, hopefully without arousing any suspicion,' suggested Jack.

'Good idea,' responded Charles. 'Although I wouldn't be too sure we won't be seen. Look over there.' And he pointed to a small boat that could just be seen against the trees of the shoreline. 'There are always plenty of locals out fishing. It's one of the main ways they survive.'

'We'll keep out of their way as much as we can and just hope to sneak in. I certainly don't recommend waiting for dark. A landfall with no light would be just too dangerous. Right, everyone keep a sharp lookout.'

They covered the last few miles towards the island carefully trying to avoid several small boats on the way in. When they got close enough they could see a rocky beach with vegetation growing almost right to the waterline. Jack knew that most of the island was very steep to and so they headed for the beach as the best option for getting ashore and hiding the tender. With their landing area facing west it also had the added advantage that the island blocked most of the view from shore.

They scraped the bottom a few yards out and jumped over the side to pull the tender up onto the beach. Although not a large boat, it took considerable effort to get her fully out of the water and Jack's idea of hauling her into the bushes for concealment didn't look too promising. Instead, they broke off some large branches and collected palm fronds, laying them over the boat. Hopefully, from seaward it would break up the outline.

They retrieved some food and water from the boat and all sat down to consider what to do next.

Charles opened the debate. 'If we get back to civilisation, we need to account for ourselves. I can say that my boat reached St Vincent and I recovered in the care of some locals and I suggest we say that you two were also there having been shipwrecked during the last hurricane season. You were not able to travel and the locals convinced you to stay until rescued. When I was washed up, you helped me recover and we set off together once I was well. How does that sound?'

'You're the boss, if you think that that's believable,' replied Jack. 'I suggest that Melissa and I are brother and sister. I hope you can come up with a plausible background, family names and all that?'

'Oh I think so, after all we're not in your age and even a blatant lie will take months to be confirmed. You will have gone long before that. Let me think on it. I have several friends at home that you can become and that will make my explanations more convincing.'

Before they could talk further, they were interrupted by a splashing noise and around the corner appeared two large fishing boats crewed by several tough looking blacks pulling at the oars. In the bow of the leading boat was an extraordinary sight. The man was large and quite fat, with a crown of what looked like feathers. He wore a simple loincloth but also what appeared to be an elaborate coat with gold piping and epaulettes.

'That's a French Naval officer's coat,' said Charles. 'This doesn't look good. Quick Melissa, hide behind the boat and Jack get the weapons.'

'The problem we're going to have,' said Jack nervously. 'Is that they won't recognise the pistol as a weapon. I hope you don't have to shoot one of them to prove it.'

'So do I but let me take the lead. They probably speak French. I am fairly fluent. How about you?

'My French is reasonable, as to whether this lot will understand my version of it is another matter.'

The two boats grounded and the fat man followed by his tough looking crew advance towards Jack and Charles, striding up the beach and gesturing angrily.

When they arrived, they stopped in front of Charles who had moved forward to greet them. Before he could say anything the fat man started shouting angrily in some strange language and pointing towards the partly hidden boat.

Charles shouted back in French and the fat man switched, although Jack could barely understand him, so strong was the accent.

'What's he saying?' he asked Charles during a pause in the conversation.

'Something about devil boats and trespassing on his island but I think that what he really wants is to see our boat He obviously has had reports of us travelling here without sails or oars. Actually, this is all bluster, I think he is also quite wary because, of course to him, we could actually be real devils.'

Suddenly, there was a triumphant shout and a scream from behind the tender and one of the locals who must have crept around behind them appeared tugging a struggling Melissa behind him by one arm.

Jack started shouting at the leader, while Charles pointed the pistol at the man and shouted at him to release the girl.

Suddenly, Melissa managed to twist free but stumbled onto her knees. The man raised what looked like a large machete and started to strike downwards towards her.

Without thinking, Charles fired the gun. The man spun violently and fell forward next to Melissa, a pool of blood appearing between his shoulder blades.

There was a moment of silence. Then the fat man took a threatening step forward and started shouting even louder.

'Jack, he has just said that now I have fired our weapon we must be prepared to die.' So saying aimed the pistol at the fat man's feet and fired four rounds in quick succession.

The look of astonishment on their faces would have been comical if the situation wasn't so serious. Charles then pulled the barrel of the gun up and pointed it directly at the fat man's face.

'Leave us now monsieur or this devil will kill you all!'

The fat man looked unhappy and frightened at the same time. He was even less happy when Charles explained that they must all go in the smaller of the two boats.

They backed off slowly to the boat with Charles keeping pace The pistol unwaveringly pointing at the fat man's face. They were almost there when one of the men suddenly shouted and rushed at Jack who was off to one side ensuring the bigger boat was kept clear.

Jack yelled at him to stop but he kept coming, so he pulled the trigger of the flare gun. There was a loud crack and a red streak shot out and hit the man in the arm. He screamed as the phosphorus flare started to burn into him and he ran towards the shore, hurling himself into the sea to no avail. Even with his arm below the water, the flare kept burning. The other men took flight and ran to their boat pushing off as fast as they could. On the way they hauled the man in the water into the boat half conscious, the flare having at last burned itself out.

They turned to Melissa who was kneeling by the body of the fallen man. She looked up with tears in her eyes.

'Oh Charles, he's dead. We should never have come here.'

Charles knelt down and put his arms around her 'I had no choice my love. He was going to strike you with that.' And he pointed to the large machete in the man's outstretched hand. He gently pulled her up and away from the corpse and she buried her face into his shoulder.

Charles looked over at Jack. 'Well, we've acquired some local transport. That boat has a mast and sail and is quite large enough for us to use to go north. We must unload all our belongings from the tender and prepare to sail.'

Jack shook himself. He had never seen a man shot and it was terrible. Despite all his years in the navy, he had never actually killed anyone and now after only a few hours in this place he had seen someone shot at close range. His mind told him there was no choice but his heart felt leaden.

'Sorry, what did you say Charles?'

'I said, we must load up that boat and take our leave as soon as we can. We can't rule out them coming back soon and in greater force. It will mean an overnight sail up to St Lucia but we have time to clear the north of this island before it gets dark.'

Charles went over to the dead body and removed the clothes. They were rough and ready homespun but enough to give each man at least something to wear that wasn't two hundred years out of time. Unusually, Melissa had been wearing jeans and a faded T shirt. With some quick work to fray things even more, Charles felt sure they would pass a quick muster as survivors clothing and they could then be disposed of quickly before anyone discovered the zips.

They stripped the tender, taking all the food and water and a few of the modern gadgets. Jack wanted the small binoculars and the box of fifty rounds for the pistol but everything else they left. Their final act on the beach was to puncture the main fuel tank and let the petrol pour out all around. They then clambered into the wooden boat and once they were afloat, Jack fired the flare pistol into the tender. For a second nothing happened and then a great gout of flame shot up and the boat started to burn, producing a tall oily black cloud of smoke.

'That should give the locals something else to think about,' he said despairingly, realising that yet another token of their real life was disappearing in the same day.

The principles of sailing have never changed but Charles had to show the two of them how to handle the primitive rig on the boat which was crudely built and lacking in anything like creature comforts. By the time they had cleared the north of the island, which as usual proved to be windy and rough, the sun was starting to set. A spectacular sunset finished the day and despite Melissa's protests that she was quite capable of standing a watch, the two men split the night as they sailed slowly north.

St Lucia was a disappointment. There were no British ships in any of the anchorages. However, if Melissa and Charles needed any confirmation that they were in a different world it was the lack of large resort hotels and any meaningful signs of civilisation that confirmed it. As they slowly sailed past Rodney Bay, even Pigeon Island was just that, an island separated from land by a considerable gap. In Jack's time, it was connected by a causeway and road formed from the spoil of when they had dredged out the mangrove swamp that had become his marina and his home.

Reluctantly, they agreed on another night at sea. They passed Martinique, mainly in the dark. As they cleared the top of the island they could see smoke and flames shooting out of the large volcano on Mount Pelee that towered over the capital at St Pierre. Jack knew that there was going to be a tragedy there in the near future but decided to keep his council. There was enough to worry about without telling Charles the result of that particular chapter of history.

Midday the next day, they entered Portsmouth in Dominica and to Charles's delight, there swinging around her anchor, was his Andromeda. She looked slightly odd, her foremast was clearly repaired and she showed other signs of storm damage. The black paint used to disguise her function had mainly washed off but enough was left to make her look quite shabby. To Charles's eye she was the most beautiful sight in the world. Now he knew he was home. He explained the state of her to his guests as they approached. When they were within a few hundred yards a voice called to them. 'Boat ahoy, your business please.'

Charles stood up and cupped his hands to shout back one word. 'ANDROMEDA.'

A flurry of activity started on the quarterdeck. That reply was only given when the Captain of the ship was approaching by boat. They immediately saw several telescopes trained upon them and Charles waved and grinned back at them.

As they bumped alongside, Charles could see the smiling face of his First Lieutenant beaming down at him, along with many of his crew, even the irrepressible Mr Bevan. Bosun's calls played as he once again trod the sanctuary of his own quarterdeck. His two passengers were helped up after him. The crew were particularly entranced by the long legged blonde girl who by their standards was practically naked. He briefly introduced them as fellow survivors and ordered an awed Mr Bevan to take them down to the great cabin and get them refreshment. Their meagre belongings were also hoisted on board and taken down below.

Tom turned to Charles. 'Sir, thank God you're back and well again. We've been here ever since the storm, repairing damage but are ordered to sail forthwith back to St Kitts. Sir, Captain Nelson has been arrested!'

Chapter 21

'Where the hell was that tender?' Paul stopped the engines and let Jacaranda drift while he thought. *'Jack had mentioned that they could use it as a liferaft so there was no reason for them not to still be here, unless the smoke he had seen had turned into a real fire. In which case it could have sunk but they were all good swimmers so where were they? There could only be one conclusion, either they had burned with the boat or drowned in the meantime.'* Paul knew there were plenty of sharks in these waters. Whatever had happened, they were probably gone now. He was surprised to feel no remorse.

His reverie was interrupted by a weak voice coming up the hatch.

'Hello, Jack, anyone, what's going on?'

'Shit, another problem,' he thought desperately. *'He would have to come up with something convincing to tell Emma. Oh God, once he had convinced her, he would not be able to continue hunting Jack, not if he wanted her for himself. One thing at a time.'*

He looked down into the saloon and saw Emma sitting up with a hand to her head. 'Hi, you're back with us,' he said in a solicitous tone as he went to her side. 'Look, lie back you must have slipped when the boat heeled. You banged your head really hard. You've been out of it for several hours now. How do you feel?'

'Well, apart from this terrible headache, not too bad.'

'Hang on a second.' Paul went to the medicine cabinet and rummaged around until he found some painkillers. He got a glass of water from the galley. 'Here, take these.'

As Emma gulped the water, he was thinking furiously about how was going to explain the absence of the rest of the crew and the tender. Suddenly, inspiration came to him.

Emma finished the water and pills and lay back with a sigh. 'Where is everyone else?' she asked.

'Look, Emma, there is no way I can say this easily. They're no longer with us.'

'What, what do you mean? Have they gone somewhere? Where are we? What has happened?'

Paul took a deep breath and launched the lie. 'Emma, you remember the navy ship and their Captain coming over?'

'Yes, yes and then he came to an agreement with Jack and left. I remember all that.'

'And you remember that helicopter that kept following us?'

'Yes, of course.'

'Well, just after their Captain left, we must have gone through Jack's waypoint because the warship vanished and the autopilot lost its navigation signal which is why the boat heeled over and you slipped.'

'Yes, that's the last thing I remember.'

'Well, that damned helicopter managed to follow us through whatever it was that we came through. Unfortunately, something must have damaged it in the process and it started to spin and flew into the sea.'

'Oh my God, were they alright?'

'I'm so sorry Emma, we'll never know. As you can imagine, Jack was not one to leave fellow aviators in trouble. The helicopter was floating, so he launched the tender and he, Charles and Melissa went over to see if they could help them. I'm sorry, there is no easy way to say this but as they got to it, there was some sort of explosion. I don't know, maybe they had depth charges or something on board but the whole bloody thing just went up.'

Emma was starting to look alarmed. 'What are you saying?'

'I've been searching the sea ever since and I'm so sorry but there is no trace of them or the helicopter. I'm afraid they're gone.'

Emma looked blankly at Paul. 'No, that can't be right, let me see.' And before he could stop her she clambered up to the cockpit. There was no one else in sight. She hit the big red button and saw that the tender had indeed gone.

'Oh my God,' she cried and sat down shaking with tears pouring down her face as the reality of what Paul had said started to sink in.

Paul sat down next to her and put his arms around her. She turned to him and sobs wracked her body as he held her close.

'Well that went well,' he thought smugly.

'Oh God, what are we going to do now?' she asked with a tear stained face.

'I've been searching for several hours now and we have to face the fact that they must have been taken out with that explosion. There is nothing else I can think of to do. All I can suggest is that we head for the other waypoint and try to return home.'

'What will they say when we get back?'

'Let's cross that bridge when we come to it,' and then belatedly, Paul realised his lie would be exposed the minute they got back. He would hardly be able to avoid the navy when they returned and the presence of one shining helicopter on the back of Suffolk would destroy his stupid bloody story in seconds. Damn it, what now? Hang on, what was so wrong with the here and now? He had Emma, who else could she turn to? In time they would become a couple he was sure. They had prepared Jacaranda to be authentic to the time period, removing all modern gadgets from the upper deck and bending on her oldest set of stained sails. Charles had been pretty sure that she would pass muster as an unusual but contemporary vessel and she was stuffed with things that could make him very rich in this age. All those books for a start.

'We can try to go to the place he said would get us back. Is that what you want?' Paul asked.

'Oh I don't know, it's so hard to think, there has just been too much happening in the last few days.'

'Look, there is nothing more we can do here I think we should give it a try don't you?'

She nodded miserably and so Paul started the engines and re-engaged the autopilot in heading mode. Now he found himself once again going back to the same position but this time hoping desperately that nothing would happen. If Emma knew anything more about what Jack did to facilitate the event she didn't offer any information which was hardly surprising the state she was in and he didn't ask.

Sure enough, when they got there, nothing happened.

When she realised the transfer wasn't going to happen, Emma was surprised but she felt so numb she also found she really didn't care. With Jack gone, her life was over anyway. They had had a tempestuous love life over the years but the loss of him after the problems in London and recent reunion had made her realise once and for all that there would never be anyone else in her life, ever and now he was gone. Just like that. She was stuck back some time in the past with Paul and she just didn't care.

Paul realised that Emma seemed to be sinking into apathy and did his best to keep her engaged. Once they had both agreed that they seemed to be stuck, he tried to generate a debate over what to do next but it was an uphill struggle. They stopped Jacaranda and he went down and made some sandwiches. He also brought up a couple of beers. Whether alcohol was a good idea on top of painkillers he wasn't sure but he hoped it would keep Emma from thinking too much about their situation.

'We should go and anchor for the night. Somewhere quiet where we can take stock. There must be places that are safe. I know, Jack mentioned that Marigot Bay was used as a refuge. How about that?'

Emma just nodded.

'Right those painkillers and the beer are sending you to sleep. Let's get you below for a kip. Don't worry, I can get us into Marigot on my own. That is as long as I can find it without GPS.'

She gave him a wan smile and allowed him to take her down and make her comfortable in the saloon where she was asleep in minutes.

As soon as she was settled Paul got Jacaranda under way again. Although he no longer had GPS, he had a full set of paper charts and the autopilot would still follow a compass course. As he approached St Lucia, he found that the old skills he had been taught when he was young had not deserted him. Taking fixes with a hand bearing compass, laying out tracks and dead reckoning all came back quite easily and to his surprise, they made the entrance to Marigot Bay quite easily. Emma was still out cold as they made the entrance, so Paul took her in on his own. He dropped the foresail on the deck but kept the mainsail up so that if anyone was watching they would not see that he was actually surreptitiously using the engines as well. Looking at the place, he decided not to go right into the lagoon but rather he anchored in the entrance, as there was more room to swing and they would not be so visible to anyone looking from ashore.

Emma joined him in the cockpit. It was clear she had been crying. Her eyes were red and she looked awful. Paul decided to let her work it out of her system in her own time. He knew she was a very intelligent and tough person and sooner or later she would start the process of acceptance and he would definitely be there for her then.

Meanwhile, he had a real problem he needed help with. 'Emma, no matter how you feel, we are definitely in the past. Look this is Marigot Bay. We were here only a few days ago but look, no houses, no hotels, no buoys marking the channel, absolutely nothing, it's spooky. If we needed more evidence that Jack was right this is it.'

Emma looked around and for the first time, Paul saw a spark of interest in her eyes. 'Yes,' she said in a small voice. 'Jack was right,' and immediately burst into tears again.

Despite his earlier decision, Paul put his arms around her again and gave her a hug. 'Look girl, it's just you and me now and we still have to face things. This reality is not going to go away.'

She sniffed and looked up to him with trust in her eyes. 'Thank you Paul. Just give me some time to sort this out in my own mind.'

'Of course, of course but we need to discuss one thing now. We can't stay here. You were the one who did all the research at home when Charles was with us. Have you any good ideas about where we should go now?'

She thought for a moment. 'Well, if we stay locally here, it's a choice between the British or French islands. Many of the British ones have only just been handed back after the American War of Independence. The French islands are probably better managed and populated. I guess we could go north to the Antigua area and meet up with the Royal Navy.'

'I'm not sure that's necessarily a good idea. They might show a little too much interest in this yacht. I think we should try to avoid the military.' An idea was beginning to form. 'You speak French don't you?'

'Yes and I know you do too. Are you suggesting we try one of the French islands then?'

'Yes, I am. Where is the capital of Martinique at this time, do you know?'

'In our time it was Fort de France in the bay in the middle of the island but back then, I mean now, God this is confusing, it's at St Pierre at the top of the island.'

'Look, we can't hide forever. We're going to have to go somewhere, so let's give that a try. How about it?'

She nodded and Paul decided not to press her further. Not much later, he got her to take some more painkillers and she went below to lie down, this time in the large comfortable bed in the rear cabin. As he bade her goodnight, he looked at her trim figure and cute breasts and realised with a surge of lust that with any luck soon, all that would be his.

Paul spent an uncomfortable night mainly sat in the cockpit. It was so eerily dark and quiet he felt distinctly uncomfortable. It felt like unseen eyes in the mangroves were watching. It was so different to his last visit. For comfort, he retrieved the shotgun and cradled it in his arms as he dozed and catnapped until daybreak.

The next morning, Emma seemed more settled, although she was very quiet. Her headache had cleared up but clearly her heartache had not. They worked together in harmony to get Jacaranda ready. It wouldn't take long to sail up to the north of Martinique. Paul estimated about seven hours.

Just before they left, as they shared a quick breakfast, he made a couple of last suggestions.

'Emma, we really ought to get into character if we are going to make contact. I have Charles's old clothes down below which would be suitable and you should put on one of those old dresses that we brought along for insurance. Oh and one final thing, will you marry me?'

She gave him a surprised look.

'We need a story to tell local officials and it will be much better if we tell them we are husband and wife. It could save a lot of awkward questions. We can concoct some more detail on the way north.'

She smiled for the first time and looked him in the eye. 'Paul I would be honoured to be your wife,' but then added. 'But it will only ever be for practical purposes I'm afraid.'

Paul smiled back. He could bide his time.

The Mayor of St Pierre, Jean le Clerc, looked out of his office window at the wide bay before him. Behind him, the volcano rumbled gently, a sound he was so used to now, he completely ignored it. Unlike his ancestral namesake, he looked nothing like a piratical ruffian, more a contented middle aged banker. However, many a competitor had fallen into that trap. His bland fatherly visage hid a calculating and rapacious mind. He had climbed to the top of the social and commercial tree of the Caribbean's most prosperous port with flair and intelligence and not a little ruthlessness. In the bay, he could see the bustle of activity around the warehouses and commercial vessels anchored out. He thanked the lord for the stupid British who tried to control trade with their islands by banning foreign vessels which only resulted in more trade for him.

However, none of this was in the forefront of his mind. It was focused on the strange looking vessel sailing in from the south. She was unusually slim and had an incredibly tall mast. The speed she was cutting through the water was amazing, particularly in such light winds. What was even more unusual, as he focused his telescope on the decks, was that there appeared to be only two crew, a man and a woman. This was unheard of, how did they manage so large a vessel? The thought crossed his mind that the other crew could have been taken by the fever but she was flying no cautionary flags, merely the French ensign at her stern.

He called out to his secretary. 'Michel, run down to the guard boat and tell them that I will be accompanying them to visit our new arrival. They are not to leave until I get there.'

His call was acknowledged by scampering feet from his outer office.

He turned to get his coat and fit his wig securely. He then took one last look through the telescope to see the woman in the bow of the boat let go a most peculiar anchor. It seemed to be attached to some form of metal chain. She then helped the man lower the mainsail, seemingly effortlessly into a large bag tied along the boom. Most unusual, he had never seen anything like it.

The guard boat cut through the water towards Jacaranda. The crew of six oarsmen were joined by two armed soldiers with the two bewigged and official looking personages of the Mayor and Harbour Master in the stern. As they approached closer, the Mayor could start to pick out other unusual features. What was that metal pipe sticking out below the stern of the hull? There was a black discolouration all around it. And how was that ridiculously tall mast held up? There was virtually no sign of any ropes, only some very thin lines going to the masthead. Surely they couldn't be made of metal? The more he saw, the more disquiet he felt. The conversation with the crew was going to be most interesting.

They came alongside the incredibly smoothly painted hull and climbed on board using a small ladder the man had hooked onto the side. The Mayor was first on board followed by the Harbour Master and the two soldiers.

The two parties confronted one another. The man looked ill at ease and kept looking at the muskets held ready by the soldiers. The woman, who was a real beauty, just looked forlorn and almost seemed disinterested in the whole situation.

The man introduced himself in French but with a very strange accent. He seemed to have difficulty answering the simplest of questions and the more he spoke the more suspicious the Mayor became. The final straw was when he was unable to produce a set of ship's papers. The simple question seemed to completely surprise him and despite his bluster, he wasn't able to offer any sensible explanation as to why he didn't have any.

The Mayor had had enough, everything about this boat was irregular and the crew were clearly breaking the law. More importantly, he wanted a good look around, especially below decks. Turning to the Harbour Master, he had a quiet word. He immediately nodded and issued instructions to the two soldiers.

'I am sorry monsieur but you have no papers and your story is quite unbelievable. I'm afraid you leave me no choice. I am placing you and your wife under arrest. A night in my cells may incline you to talk more honestly.'

The man looked shocked and for a moment the Mayor wondered if he was going to offer some violence. However, he took one look at the two tough soldiers who were now both pointing their muskets directly at him and he seemed to sag inside. They were led away into the guard boat and Mayor le Clerc was free to examine his new prize.

Chapter 22

Andromeda sailed north that afternoon heading for St Kitts where Captain Nelson was being restrained. Tom explained to Charles and the other two shipwrecked mariners that two of the American vessels had sued Nelson for illegal seizure, in the courts at St Kitts. The local Governor had supported the action and to all intents and purposes, Nelson was imprisoned in his own ship until the matter was settled. It didn't help that Admiral Hughes was offering no help and had even hinted that he was on the side of the merchants. The information and new orders for Andromeda had arrived two days ago in one of the small cutters that plied the islands.

Tom also explained what had happened during the squall. The American must have escaped or foundered as they never saw him again. During the height of the storm, their topmast had carried away and one of the two forward nine pounder bow chasers had broken free causing a great deal of damage. The repairs had taken some time but Tom admitted to deliberately lingering, in the hope that his Commanding Officer had survived and would turn up. He was extremely glad to have been vindicated. Finally, he also told them about the visit he had subsequently made to the Major in charge of the fort to discuss the consequences of the musket shot that had warned the American ship. When the Major had tried to pull rank on a mere Lieutenant, Tom had pointed out that as the de facto Commanding Officer of a Naval Warship, he in fact outranked the Major and made it clear in no uncertain terms what would happen the moment Captain Nelson heard of the incident. He of course neglected to mention that the good Captain would probably not be visiting any time soon and left the Major with the fear of God inside him.

Charles laughed at the last part. He would have been delighted to have given the admonishment himself but it was clear that Tom had done a good job and had obviously enjoyed every minute of it.

He introduced Jack and Melissa using their real Christian names but with the surname of De Winter, as he had friends at home with that name. They had already put more detail into their story. As soon as Charles could, he checked the previous summer's shipping reports and found a suitable vessel that had been wrecked in a hurricane. It seemed that Jack and Melissa must have been the only survivors. Surprisingly, little was asked of them. The story was clearly not that unusual and they seemed to be accepted with alacrity. This was especially the case with Mr Bevan, who was clearly smitten with Melissa. He took every opportunity he could to follow her around, much to everyone's amusement.

Domestically, having a woman on board proved a bit more of a problem, especially when it came to accommodation. Jack and Melissa were given Charles quarters despite their protestations. It was deemed quite acceptable for brother and sister to share a cabin. Charles moved into Tom's cabin and so on down the line. No one seemed to mind however, as it was only for a few days and Melissa was proving to be a hit with the whole crew. Charles was able to find some clothes for Jack but unsurprisingly there were no suitable female clothes on board. However, within a few hours, Charles had tasked his sail maker to produce a simple wrap around dress from some spare linen and the proprieties were then all met.

Shortly after sailing, Jack and Melissa were standing on the small quarterdeck watching all the bustle around them and trying to keep out everyone's way.

'All I can say is thank goodness for C S Forester, Patrick O'Brien, Julian Stockwin and the rest,' mused Jack. 'You know in some ways this is almost familiar.'

'I assume you're referring to all those books you read about this period,' replied Melissa. 'I'm glad you know what's going on. I thought I was a pretty good sailor but I haven't understood half of what they've been a saying.'

'We can pull up our mainsail with one winch. On this ship, they need about a dozen men and twenty ropes but isn't it bloody marvellous!'

Melissa looked at Jack and smiled. She was glad for him that, at least temporarily, he was enjoying himself. She knew he had read extensively about the navy of this era and the opportunity to witness it first hand must be fulfilling a dream.

'There is only one thing all those books fail to mention,' he remarked.

'Oh, what's that?'

He lowered his voice. 'Its quite clear, that despite all this warm sea and fresh air, they really don't believe in washing. The pong is quite overpowering.'

Melissa laughed. 'Of course it could be argued that humans aren't designed to be washed every day and you are experiencing the real smell of humanity as it should be.'

'Huh, you wait until you start missing all those potions and lotions you modern women smother yourselves with day and night, then we'll see.'

Just then Charles came over and tipped his hat to them.

'Well, my good friends, how do you like my world?' he asked with a grin.

Melissa just laughed and grabbed his arm as the ship lurched over a wave.

Jack looked at Charles. 'It will be even better if we can find out where Jacaranda is and do something about it.'

Charles nodded seriously. 'Yes, I'm sorry we have to go north for the moment but before we left I put the word out with the locals and offered a small reward for any sightings. It's the best we can do for the moment and it really doesn't matter where we are. We can get to any of the islands in a matter of days. I expect Captain Nelson will have us back on patrol fairly soon and then we can see what we can do.'

At the mention of Nelson, Jack's eyes lit up. 'I take it you will introduce us?'

'If you wish, although he is just another naval Post Captain you know.'

Jack decided to keep his council on the matter. He might let Charles in on the secret some time but for the moment he was just overawed at the prospect.

Charles really wanted to head straight to Antigua where hopefully most of the remainder of his crew were recovering but his orders were quite specific and so they skirted the volcanic island of Montserrat just as dawn was breaking and headed directly north to anchor in the bay at Basse Terre once again.

Charles was immediately ordered over to HMS Boreas where he met a surprisingly subdued Nelson.

'Damned merchants have got it in for me Lonfort,' he grumbled the moment they were alone in the great cabin. 'I'm closeted here at their whim and even my Admiral seems unable or unwilling to offer me any support. The only solace I have is that my Fanny is such a good companion. She at least lights up my day.'

'Indeed Sir. From what you say, I gather you may travel ashore. On parole I assume?'

'Yes, at least the lawyers allow me that solace. Now, tell me of your recent travails. I hear they have been varied.'

Charles briefed Nelson on most of what had happened over recent weeks with one obvious exception. He explained that the fever had taken him several weeks to recover from and also that he had been able to rescue two English castaways. Nelson listened but his heart didn't seem to be in it anymore. It was almost as if someone had doused his fiery spirit. Being restrained from doing his duty seemed to have removed his spark.

'I would be delighted if you could all join me for dinner this evening. I don't expect your two new acquaintances to dress for the occasion but some civilised company will no doubt be a joy for them. Fanny will be joining us.' And then with smile. 'Would you like me to invite the Governor's daughter? I could send a note up if you wish?'

To Nelson's surprise, Charles declined. 'If you wouldn't mind Sir, I am not so sure that would be a good idea. We are all just returned from sea and I would rather be able to present myself at my best.'

Nelson politely acquiesced but from Charles's demeanour, he wondered whether there was something else in his subordinate's response. Maybe one of the castaways had also cast a spell?

Charles left his written report and took his leave promising to return at sundown. On climbing on board Andromeda, he informed his two friends of their invitation.

Melissa immediately started to panic. 'Oh my God, what will I wear? I can't dine with Horatio Nelson dressed like this. What would he think?'

Jack started to laugh. 'After all we have been through and you worry about what to wear! Thank the Lord for the female of the species.'

Charles interceded on her behalf. 'My dear, he does understand that you were recently shipwrecked but if it is any consolation I will accompany you both ashore this afternoon and no doubt we can find something suitable in a millinery in town, even at such short notice. However, you two are really going to have to confide in me why you are so in awe of this man.'

Jack looked thoughtfully at Charles. 'Charles, you may remember that we agreed not to go into too much detail about your immediate future, indeed it was at your request. Can I just say that your Captain will become a very well known and admired man and leave it at that please?'

'I had gathered it was of that ilk, yes but thank you for that at least. Now some lunch and then ashore.'

Later that afternoon, Jack and Melissa were dressing. Charles had managed to find a simple but elegant frock coat, trews and leggings for Jack which were taxing his dexterity as he tried to work out the fastenings and even which went on top of which. Melissa emerged from the little side cabin and Jack stopped his fiddling and just gaped. She was wearing a simple pale blue dress with low bodice gathered in a high waist. Her hair was tied up with some form of comb and even with hardly any makeup, she looked completely stunning.

'By God, you'll give Horatio Nelson apoplexy when he sees that cleavage. Do you really want to change the course of history? Who the hell will win Trafalgar?'

She smiled back. 'Get used to it. This is apparently how they all dress. It seems Jane Austen left that little bit out. It must be something about not having invented the bra yet.'

'Well, for God's sake don't sneeze or it could all really be bustin' out all over.'

They emerged onto the quarterdeck into a beautiful Caribbean evening. A warm wind was blowing from ashore bringing the scent of the land. Melissa smiled at the beauty of the evening, much to the admiration of every male on deck. Jack felt a sense of detached unreality. Here he was, in an anchorage he used every other week of his life but he was on the deck of an eighteenth century warship. He was dressed in leggings and a frock coat and about to dine with Horatio Nelson. Then a dagger pierced his heart. Emma wasn't with him and for a moment he almost turned and went below but he gathered himself up. He would tell her all about it as soon as they were together again. And that would happen he vowed to himself.

The dinner went surprisingly well. It was a small gathering, only Nelson, Fanny Nisbet, Charles and the castaways. With Charles's help, Jack and Melissa had concocted sufficient detail for their story to avoid any suspicions.

When they were introduced, Jack was completely overawed. But such was Nelson's charm that within a few minutes, he had put the whole room at ease. As the evening progressed, he studied his host and his lady. Nelson was much smaller than he imagined and of course still had both his arms and eyes but it was his manner and charm that held Jack captive. He was also very obviously human, as witnessed by his gallant reaction to Melissa when they were introduced. Frances Nisbet was definitely not what Jack expected. Of course history had side-lined her pretty much once Emma Hamilton entered the equation but even so Jack was quite puzzled as to the attraction. No great beauty, Fanny was taller than Nelson, with a pale complexion and slim figure. It was only when she spoke that Jack realised that here was a quite determined and forthright lady. He suspected Nelson liked her not so much for her looks but her obvious intelligence and wit.

The meal consisted of a fiery mulligatawny soup, followed by roast beef and then cheese. They drank Madeira. Jack knew that this was one of the few European wines that managed the trans-Atlantic passage without spoiling and the quality was excellent.

'So Jack, apart from your rather unfortunate voyage to the West Indies, do you have much experience of the sea?' asked Nelson as they started on the cheese.

'Oh yes, the sea and sailing have been part of my life for many years,' responded Jack. 'But only in small craft,' he added hastily, realising that any detailed discussion of maritime issues could be dangerous ground.

'I joined the navy at thirteen you know. Far too young but that is the way we do it, so I suppose you could say that sailing has also been my life as well. Take some advice. If you have any sons, don't send them to sea too early. I sometimes feel I have spent all my life inside wooden walls.'

Jack suddenly felt a wave of sympathy for Nelson. His life was so different from anything Jack had experienced and here he was now unable to even do his duty while a court case was pending. He wondered what would happen if he told this proud little man what was in store for him but immediately dismissed the idea. He wouldn't be believed and even if he was, he got the impression that it wouldn't allow it change him one bit.

Fanny looked over at him, 'What are your intentions now Mr De Winter? I understand you were on your way to Antigua to take ship home. Is that the case still?'

'Why yes Maam,' said a thankful Jack, glad to be back on firmer ground. 'Melissa and I had just been visiting our uncle's estate in Grenada and were heading home as you correctly point out. I am hoping to press Captain Lonfort to take us with him to Antigua if that is where he is heading next.'

Nelson broke in. 'It is no secret. Charles needs to return there to embark the rest of his crew, so I'm sure he will be able to offer that service.' And he raised an eyebrow in Charles's direction.

'Of course Sir, it would be my pleasure. I assume you will you have other orders for me?'

'Indeed, indeed, if you would repair on board tomorrow we will talk in detail. Ladies my apologies for talking of naval matters. Now who would like some more Madeira?'

All too soon they were taking their leave. As Jack took Nelson's hand to make his farewell, he couldn't resist one little remark. 'Sir, thank you very much for your hospitality. I know your present circumstances are unfortunate but I have the feeling that much more will be expected of you in times to come and that you are the person to achieve great things.'

'Why, thank you Jack. I get the feeling there is a lot more to you than meets the eye as well. May your next voyage be more productive.'

As Jack and Melissa prepared for bed she looked over at him. 'So what was it you said to the great man as we left? I hope you weren't telling him to keep an eye out for the future or something else unfortunate.'

Jack burst out laughing. 'Dammit, why didn't I think of that? No, just wishing him luck in the future, a sentiment he echoed to both of us. You know he's the most perceptive man I have ever met. I wonder what he really thought of us.'

'Hopefully, we'll never know. Right, I'm off to bed, see you in the morning.'

The next morning, everything changed.

Just after Charles returned from his morning meeting on Boreas and before the ship could be got ready for the short hop to Antigua, another brig sloop entered the anchorage. She was flying the signal that she had urgent despatches and as soon as her anchor was in the water, her Captain was in his boat heading for HMS Boreas. Shortly after, the signal for the Captain of Andromeda to repair on board was seen and Charles found himself heading back to Nelson's ship.

He was ushered straight into the great cabin where Nelson was in conversation with the newcomer. Introductions over, Nelson looked directly at Charles. 'I'm terribly afraid to tell you this Lonfort but one of the urgent despatches I have just received is in regard to you.'

'Sir?' asked a puzzled Charles.

'There is no way to soften this blow I'm afraid. I have news of your family. Your father and brother have both perished. My information is that they were travelling together in a carriage which was swept away by a sudden flood.'

The blood drained from Charles's face. 'But James was a fine swimmer. How could that happen?'

'You need to read this,' and Nelson passed Charles the despatch and also a personal letter. 'But to answer your question it seems your brother was trying to rescue your father and in the process they were both lost. You realise that you are the Earl now?'

Charles just nodded and scanned the despatch which in bald terms told him no more than Nelson had done already. The letter was from his mother and he would read that later in private.

'Sir what....?'

Nelson interrupted before he could go any further. 'I have another despatch here. It seems that the Admiralty are being quite understanding for a change. I suppose they can afford to be in these quiet times. They are ordering you and Andromeda home. Whether you wish to continue with your naval commission in light of these events, I leave up to you. You can make your decision when you return. Oh and if you want to give passage to your two guests, I would not be adverse.'

Charles just nodded and shortly after took his leave. When he returned to Andromeda, he went to his cabin and read the letter from his mother. She gave some more detail on the accident and hoped that he would be returning. She pointed out all the duties that would now fall to him as the Earl. Charles was not too worried about this. He knew his mother was quite capable of running the estate in his absence. She had been doing it for many years, as his father sank further and further into the bottle. But he now had some difficult decisions to make. Did he turn his back on the navy to take up the life of an aristocrat? And more importantly, how was he going to help his friends now that he had to return to England?

Chapter 23

Paul and Emma were put in a cell in the town's court building. If Paul needed confirmation of where and when they now were, he only had to take one look at the conditions to know. He presumed that as they were a 'married couple', they were given the privilege of a cell and separate small room with a bucket but he wouldn't bet his life on it. There were two beds made of planks and covered with sacks stuffed with what smelt like old straw. There was a small barred window that overlooked the town square and that was about it. When they were delivered there by the two soldiers, the jailor took over and simply pushed them in and locked the door. All Paul's shouts for food and water were ignored but just before it got dark, the door was opened and a plate with some bread and cheese and a pitcher of water were handed to him.

'Come on Emma, we need to eat,' he cajoled his partner as he sat down on his bed with the food. But just like the whole afternoon, she just sat on the bed with her knees pulled up to her chin and ignored him. He knew how she felt. The shock of the last few days were nothing compared to what had happened in the last few hours. They had now lost the boat and everything else to link them with their world and for Emma, losing Jack as well must have compounded the situation tenfold. At one point, pity almost got the better of him and he came very close to telling her the truth. In the end, he held himself back. If they were really on their own in this world he needed her on his side.

Eventually, he managed to get her to drink some water and they fell into an uneasy sleep. Sometime in the night, there was a small scream and Emma jumped across into Paul's bed and hugged him.

'Rat,' was all she said. Paul panicked for a second until he realised she meant she must have heard a rat running around the cell. He had to smile to himself. Rodents had never bothered him. But as he gave her a comforting hug back he wondered what she would have said if she had known the truth. Rat would have been the nicest epithet.

Shortly after it got light another plate of bread and cheese was pushed through the door. Once again, all Paul's questions were ignored.

Jean le Clerc was a very worried man. Once he had the strange craft to himself, he went down below. His own boat would return after delivering the couple to a holding cell but meanwhile he had a few minutes on his own. The first thing that struck him was the quality of the fittings. The main saloon would not be out of place in a palace, yet here it was in a small cutter for goodness sake. He looked in the two main cabins and found the same level of luxury there as well. But what really worried him was that there were so many things he didn't understand. Everywhere he looked, he saw strange devices. In what he assumed was the galley, he found some sort of cooking range but how it worked was beyond him. In the main saloon, he found a quantity of books. They were all written in English but that didn't bother him as he spoke it as his second language. When he looked inside them, most was totally incomprehensible but some things he could understand and the contents were really worrying. Propped up by the door, he found what he assumed were guns of some sort. They were like nothing he had ever seen. One had two very large barrels, one above the other but there was no sign of the firing mechanism. The other had only one slim barrel and once again no visible sign of how it worked apart from a trigger in the normal place. He tried pulling it experimentally but nothing happened.

He decided two things. Firstly, no one else was going to see the inside of this boat and secondly, he was going to have a very serious conversation with her previous owners. He would wait until tomorrow morning. If those two were used to this level of luxury, a night in the town cells would no doubt concentrate their minds. He took the two weapons and as many of the books that he could find up onto deck and when his boat returned, he had them taken ashore to his residence. He also left strict instructions that the boat was now in quarantine and no one was allowed on board. On the way home, he arranged with the Harbour Master to have a twenty four hour guard mounted to enforce the restrictions.

That evening, he started to catalogue the books. The more he read, the more puzzled he became and in some ways the more scared. If what he understood was right, the contents of these tomes were both impossible but also the greatest opportunity of his life. Something here was very strange and he needed to get to the bottom of it.

Sometime after 'breakfast' the door was flung open and two guards motioned for Paul and Emma to follow them. They were taken through the town which was bustling, crowded and very smelly. The vast majority of people were black but quite clearly subservient to the smaller number of white people. All the time, there was the constant background grumble from the volcano that towered above the town. They walked slowly uphill and the streets gradually opened out as they left the commercial area behind them and started to see some quite elegant houses set back from the road with ornate formal gardens. They were taken to one of the largest, which occupied a small hill and had a commanding view of the harbour and town. On reaching the front door, they were handed over to a well dressed but clearly quite capable manservant who took them upstairs to a light and airy room. Seated behind a large oak table was the man who had introduced himself as the Mayor the previous day. He didn't get up when they arrived and didn't offer them a seat. Instead, he gestured to the objects strewn across the table top and simply said, 'you two need to offer me an explanation. Who are you?'

Paul thought for a moment. The desk was strewn with their books and also the two guns. This man had clearly suspected something when he came out to Jacaranda and now he had had time to follow up his suspicions. The chances that he understood much of what was before him were pretty slim but he must have some idea.

'Given the way you have treated us, why should I answer that?' He looked squarely at the man.

'Quite simple, this is my town and anything I command will happen. You are in my power.'

'Very well,' said Paul and he reached forward quickly and grabbed the shotgun before the man could react. He pointed it at the man. 'Now, let me rephrase the question, who are you? You arrogant shit.'

The man smiled. 'That won't help you. It doesn't work.'

Paul smiled back, pumped a round into the breech and fired it through the large window behind him. The report was deafening and almost drowned out the sound of the window disintegrating.

There was a second of silence. The look of terror on the man's face was actually quite amusing. However, very quickly the door was flung open and the manservant who had brought them to the room flew in. He halted when he saw the tableau of Paul pointing the weapon at his master.

The Frenchman started to smile but Paul outguessed him. 'There are another five rounds in this weapon and it reloads itself. Would you like me to demonstrate again? Tell your man to leave us alone.'

The Frenchman nodded again and beckoned to his servant to leave. He reluctantly closed the door behind him.

As soon as the door was closed, Paul smiled again. He looked at Emma who had remained motionless throughout the exchange and gestured her to one the large leather chairs. He decided to take a gamble. He would need friends in this place and this chap seemed to be top dog. So, before seating himself, went up to Frenchman handed him the shotgun and put out his hand. 'Monsieur Paul Smythe and my wife Emma, a pleasure to make your acquaintance Sir. Now, who do I have the pleasure of addressing?'

The Frenchman looked nonplussed for a second as he took the gun and then a look of understanding crossed his face. He put the gun down on the table and put out his hand, 'Monsieur Jean le

Clerc, Mayor of this town at your service Sir. My apologies, we seem to have started off on the wrong foot.'

Paul sat down in the other chair and looked steadily at the Mayor. 'I have no doubt that you have seen the inside of our boat and have looked at those books and guns, so you realise something extremely strange has occurred. Believe me when I say we feel the same. However, we have not eaten properly for some time and in exchange for a good breakfast, I will show you how that gun works. Then we really need to talk.' He mentally held his breath. It was clear to him that this was an intelligent man who would probably respond to honesty and avarice.

The Mayor called out to his manservant who had obviously been listening on the other side of the door. 'Raoul, tell the cook to place some food out in the dining room and we will be down shortly and then arrange for this window to be repaired.'

It was to be the start of a very close friendship.

They ate a good breakfast but Emma kept very quiet. Jean tried to get conversation out of her but her answers were monosyllabic.

'Madam, you seem to be rather upset and I can only apologise. Maybe I was a bit rash with my treatment of you. Will you accept my apology?'

Emma gave him a wan smile. 'Of course Monsieur.'

Paul played the concerned husband 'I wonder Monsieur le Clerc whether you could find a place for my wife to retire. She hardly slept at all last night as you can imagine.'

'Of course, of course, my wife Marie will look after her.' And so saying, he called his manservant again and asked him to find his wife. Shortly thereafter, a rather portly middle aged woman was introduced. Le Clerc explained that Emma was tired and in need of rest and they left together. As soon as the women had gone, he turned to Paul.

'Monsieur, who are you?'

Paul had been thinking hard on what approach to take and decided, as usual, that sticking as close to the truth as possible was the best course of action. But before he started explanations, he decided he needed some information himself.

'I would like to ask you something before I give an explanation if you wouldn't mind?'

'Very well, ask away.'

'Are you aware of any odd incidents happening at sea out to the west of these islands? Stories of strange vessels or people?'

Le Clerc looked surprised at the question but then a degree of understanding crossed his face. 'Over the last few years there have been some odd events as you describe. Are you suggesting that you are linked to them in some way?'

'Yes, where I come from we have had the same things happening. Our two worlds seem to cross over out there for some reason.'

'You say two worlds. Is yours different to mine then?' asked le Clerc who was starting to wonder where this was going.

Paul knew this was the key question. He just hoped that this man had enough of an open mind. 'My wife and I come from your future.'

Le Clerc looked at him for a second and then burst into laughter. 'Very good Monsieur and I am the King of France.'

Paul knew this wasn't going to be easy. 'How do you explain those two guns in your study and the books you have? I can assure you that those books have information in them about medicine and science that could make you the richest man in the world.'

At the words 'richest man in the world' le Clerc's eyes opened wide and Paul realised that this was the key. His earlier assessment of the man was right. He might almost be dealing with an eighteenth century version of Sir Nigel. In which case, this was a game he knew how to play.

'Let me give you a simple example. You asked about the weapons we had on board. Let me show you how they work.' So saying, the two men went back up to the study. Paul ejected the cartridges from the shotgun and showed them to the Frenchman.

'In this heavy paper case we have black powder and shot all assembled as one, so there is no need to load them separately down the barrel like your muskets. We then load the cartridge through the breech.' And he showed him how the cartridge was inserted. He then demonstrated the rifle and explained that it used a metal cartridge but essentially worked the same way. He showed him the small telescope on top and explained that unlike the shotgun it had a range of many hundreds of metres.

Le Clerc looked with fascination. 'But how do you fire the cartridge? You have no flint or method of making a spark.'

Paul smiled back. 'Simple, if you look at the base of the cartridge you can see a small round piece of metal. It's filled with an explosive that is set off by being struck. When I pull the trigger a small metal pin hits it and the whole cartridge is set off.'

He took the rifle and looked out of the window. In the distance was a small church with a weathercock in the shape of a cockerel on top of a small spire. 'How far away would you say that church spire is monsieur?'

Le Clerc looked at where Paul was pointing. 'At least five hundred metres, don't tell me you think you can hit it with that weapon?' he asked in a disbelieving voice.

Paul knelt down and took aim through the telescopic sight. 'Watch the cockerel monsieur.' He squeezed the trigger. There was a massive report from the gun and almost instantly the weathervane started to spin.

Le Clerc looked astonished. 'If we had these weapons the French nation could conquer the world,' he looked hard at Paul. 'Would you know how to make more?'

Paul decided to try and dodge that one. 'I take it you are starting to believe what I told you about where we come from?'

'I can't see anyone from this world being able to produce such things but if I could make them I would not only be a great patriot, I would be able to name my price.'

'Don't you mean our price?' responded Paul.

Le Clerc thought for a moment. He was suddenly realising the possibilities that were opening up. What he was seeing now was probably only the tip of the iceberg. He was going to have to keep this man close and ensure that he was able to get everything he could out of him. In the future, of course, he could always be disposed of.

Paul watched the expressions on le Clerc's face and was pretty sure what was going through his mind. One step at a time. Once he had his confidence he could worry about making himself indispensable.

'Yes,' le Clerc said with a smile. 'Yes, I did mean 'our price'. If you will work with me, I am sure we can come to a mutually beneficial arrangement.'

'Thank you Sir but I would have to insist on you returning my vessel and furnishing me with suitable ships papers.'

Jean le Clerc considered the request and then held out his hand.

'Agreed.'

Chapter 24

Charles was in a quandary. He needed to sail for England but he also needed to stay in the islands to find Jacaranda and Emma. What was he to do? His first action was to discuss the situation with Jack and Melissa. They were immediately sympathetic over his loss for which he was grateful but it didn't take Jack long to realise the problem that was looming.

'What has Nelson actually ordered you to do?' he asked with worry in his tone.

'He has been reasonably vague. He asked me to transfer some of my crew to the new ship, so we will sail home with slightly reduced numbers but I still have to go to Antigua to collect most of those we put ashore. After that I am ordered home. I suppose the actual route I take is my decision but of course the conventional way would be to head north and look for the westerly winds up near Bermuda.'

Jack thought for a moment. 'We've told everyone that we were on passage home from Grenada when we were shipwrecked. Do you think Nelson would allow you to sail south first, to take us there to assure our relatives that we survived the storm that in theory caused our shipwreck? It would only add a few days onto our passage but would allow us to cruise down the whole island chain.'

Charles considered the idea and could think of nothing better. 'I don't see why he would object. I will discuss it with him tomorrow just before we leave. But Jack, even if he refuses, I will do it anyway. I owe you my life in more ways than one. The worst that their lordships could do is reprimand me and I will probably have to resign my commission anyway when I return.'

However, that worry turned out to be unnecessary. When Charles broached the subject, all Nelson had to say was that he could choose any route he wished. There was no deadline on his return to England apart from any that Charles wished to impose on himself.

With that settled, Andromeda sailed for Antigua. If anchoring off St Kitts felt strange to Jack, then sailing into English Harbour was even more unsettling. The fort on the end of the spit overlooking the bay was the same. Except that this time the battlements were fully intact. There were real guns pointing through the embrasures and the Union flag was flying proudly from a mast at the point. The bay was virtually empty and Jack had to admire the way Charles and his crew handled such a big ship under sail alone. He would have never attempted to do so in Jacaranda. Once anchored, they all went ashore to the dockyard. Charles wanted to see his men and check up on any intelligence and Jack and Melissa just wanted to look around while they had the opportunity. Once again, the place was uncannily familiar. In Jack's time it was the most restored piece of architecture from the past in any of the islands. So, much of what he saw he recognised. The large capstans on the point were there. The buildings looked very much the same but instead of large yachts moored stern-to all around the jetty, there were just a few work boats and two large cutters moored alongside. However, the place was full of bustle. Sailors and artisans were working everywhere he looked. It would not take long he realised for the dockyard of the future to become the dream and for him to accept this place as the reality. He shook himself, that would not do and they set off to find Charles and see if he had heard any reports of strange looking vessels in the islands. They found him in the Head Quarters office right at the end of the main building on the first floor. Once again Jack had déjà vu. The last time he had been here was on a Thursday night when the landlord of the French restaurant and bar it had become, laid out musical instruments for anyone to play. He had spent some riotous nights here in the past. Not now though.

They found Charles seated at a desk reading some reports. He jumped to his feet as soon as he saw them, 'some good news my friends. I was just reading a report from the Captain of that cutter down there,' he pointed to one of the vessels alongside. 'They were sailing past St Pierre in Martinique last week and noted an odd looking vessel at anchor. She was and I quote 'very slim with a single tall mast and painted pale blue'. I think we know were Jacaranda is,' he exclaimed with a triumphant note in his voice.

Jack and Melissa exchanged delighted looks but Jack immediately saw a problem. 'Martinique is a French island, won't that cause us problems?'

Charles considered the question. 'We're at peace with France and there is no reason why we shouldn't pay a visit. It shouldn't be too difficult to find out what is going on once we are ashore. After that we will just have to see. Taking Jacaranda back should be quite simple unless there is a French warship around which would be unusual but of course we have to find Emma first.'

Jack looked grim. 'Jacaranda is secondary Charles. Getting Emma back is my only priority.'

His friend nodded sympathetically. 'Just don't expect me to sail Andromeda back into your century to get you home.'

'One of your ship's boats will probably do but it would be much better in Jacky. Let's just get down there and see how the land lies. Oh and there may be one further problem.'

Charles lifted an eyebrow.

'That volcano, I can't remember when but I am pretty sure it is due to erupt soon and we definitely do not want to be anywhere near it when it does. We can check when we get on board Jacky. I'm sure the date is in one of my pilot books.'

Charles pondered. 'Interesting, everyone here feels it's still safe. After all, it's been like that for years now but I agree. We shouldn't waste any time.'

Andromeda sailed the next morning. It was early spring and the wind was starting to become more south easterly which meant they were hard on the wind all the way. Jack spent most of his time on deck fretting. The closer they got to Martinique, the more worried he became. The cutter Captain's report had not mentioned any sightings of crew on the strange ship but that of course meant nothing. It didn't stop him imagining all sorts of things that could have gone wrong. The only solace he took was the thought of getting his hands around a certain ex-friends neck but even that was secondary to his concerns over Emma.

Early the next morning, they ghosted around the top of Martinique in the fading breeze and dropped anchor in the crowded harbour. The town was spread before them along the wide open bay and up the sides of the green clad mountain that brooded over the scene. Smoke was pouring out of the top from several fissures and every now and then a rumble could be heard like muted thunder. All the way in, Jack had been searching for a sight of his yacht but apart from half a dozen merchantmen there was no sign of her.

As soon as they were secure, Charles joined his friend by the taffrail. 'Don't worry my friend. We know she was here only a few days ago. We'll go ashore and I am sure we'll be able to discover where she went.'

Jack just nodded and asked when that would be.

Charles pointed over to the Harbour Master's boat which was already heading their way. 'As soon as we have cleared in with that man,' he said.

Paul had been busy. The first thing they had decided to do was to move Jacaranda out of the bay where she was attracting far too much attention. Unfortunately, the coast of Martinique had no little bays or inlets they could use unless they took her right to the bottom of the island, so they had to compromise by taking her south of the bay and anchoring her out of sight of the main town. The day after their initial meeting, Paul and Emma took Jean down to the boat. They raised the mainsail to sail forward and although he used the electric anchor winch, he got Emma to pretend to pull it up by hand in case anyone ashore wondered how it was doing it all by itself. As soon as they had turned away, he started the engine whose exhaust was away from shore and slowly headed out to sea. Jean le Clerc was astounded even though Paul had already explained what he would see and hear. Once they were clear to the south, they headed back to shore and anchored around the point. It wasn't ideal as the yacht was still in plain view of anyone sailing past to seaward but she was away from prying eyes ashore and firmly under the guns of the small fort that covered the southern end of the bay. The Fort Commander had been given strict instructions to keep her guarded and safe.

Once Jacky was as secure as possible, Jean wanted to know what would be the best way to proceed with his new found knowledge. It was very clear to Paul that he was fascinated by the two guns and saw being able to replicate them as his first priority. Unfortunately, Paul knew that the technology to make steel of sufficient quality would take many more years to develop. The techniques of modern steel making were in one of the books they had brought along but even armed with the knowledge it would take years to make it reality.

They visited the local gunsmith but Paul could immediately see that breech loading, cartridge firing weapons would not be possible in the near future and that was what Jean wanted to hear. Paul needed to keep his new benefactor happy and racked his brains for a solution.

That afternoon they sat in Jean's study looking out of the newly repaired window.

'So Paul, you have seen what we have in the town. What do you think?'

Once again Paul decided that honesty was the best policy and besides he thought he had come up with an acceptable idea. 'Jean, look again at the barrels of either of those guns. Do you think that anyone could make metal of that quality today?'

Jean looked at the beautiful blued steel of the rifle barrel. 'Would it be that difficult my friend?'

'Yes, I'm afraid so. I can show you in one of those books how it is done but it would take years to build the factory to make it.'

Jean frowned. This was not what he wanted to hear. 'So you are saying we cannot do it?'

'Yes, in the short term but I have another idea, if you will allow me to explain. Apart from loading your muskets through the muzzle, what is the other big problem with them?'

Jean thought for a moment. 'I suppose it's keeping the powder dry in the firing pan.'

'Exactly, you put powder in the pan and then need the spark of a flint to set it off. Any dampness and your weapon is useless. I reckon that in a matter of weeks I could produce a musket for you that would solve all these problems.'

Jean started to look interested again.

Paul ploughed on. 'Remember the little metal cap in the base of the bullets I showed you?' We could make a small copper cap that we place over the touchhole of a musket, the hammer then strikes it. Inside the copper cap we put the same explosive that we use in our bullets and you have a musket that will fire in all weathers.'

Jean immediately saw the advantages but also saw a major problem. 'And how do we get this explosive?'

Paul smiled back. His interest in the evolution of firearms was now proving to be more than just a hobby for a rich London financier. It could literally save his life. 'I know the formula. You mix nitric acid and mercury and then add some ethanol, that's the pure spirit found in any alcoholic drink. When we were at the gunsmith's this morning I checked what chemicals he has and the acid and mercury are available in reasonable quantities. All I need is a way of producing neat alcohol.' He looked up at Jean who was starting to laugh.

'My friend,' chortled Jean. 'Look up at the mountain behind us. Can you see a red roof sticking through the trees right in the distance?'

Paul looked where Jean was pointing. 'Yes, up near the top, why?'

'Because Paul, that is my sugar plantation and it also has the biggest distillery on the island. I assure you getting quantities of alcohol will not be a problem.'

Emma was trying to keep herself busy. Apart from when she helped to move Jacaranda, she found herself solely in the company of Jean le Clerc's wife. '*Marie le Clerc must be the most boring woman on the planet*,' Emma thought to herself for the umpteenth time. She showed absolutely no inquisitiveness into who Emma was and how she had got there. She seemed completely devoted to her husband and prepared to believe anything he told her. There seemed to be only one topic that motivated her and that was the volcano. When she wasn't boring Emma to death with talk of embroidery or the cost of bread in the shops, she was grumbling about the mountain behind them. It wasn't that she seemed to be scared of it rather it was the incessant noise. It couldn't be dangerous as Jean had said it was safe but he wouldn't say when it would quieten down.

Finally drawn on the subject, Emma asked her why she was so concerned. 'Surely if it is safe, then why do you worry?'

'Oh, Jean says all the experts have been consulted. It has been like this for many years now and is quite safe. You know we sent the children to Fort de France a while ago because it seemed to be getting more active. But we don't want people leaving or the town would die, so to show how safe he feels it is he brought them back only the other day.'

Emma remembered Jack telling her something about the volcano here but while she had been on board Jacaranda they had never stopped in Saint Pierre and she was racking her brains to remember. If she could get back on board she knew there was something about it in one of the pilot books. She also had another reason for wanting to get back. Before they moved Jacaranda, Paul had given Jean le Clerc a tour down below and demonstrated some of the technology. He had briefly turned on the chartplotter which operated through the screen of the television as well as the repeater screen in the cockpit. Jean had had the same reaction to it as Charles initially had and Paul realised that it was probably a demonstration too far and had quickly turned it off. But she had got a quick glimpse of the screen and not surprisingly it showed their track up to the time they had come here and then an estimate of it based on ships speed and heading once the satellites had been lost. There was something about it that looked odd but she didn't have the time to analyse what and the problem was gnawing away at her subconscious. She was going to have to ask Paul or Jean to be allowed back on board. She already had what she felt was a good excuse. All she had to do was get away from this bloody woman and find Paul.

Her chance came a few hours later. Usually, Jean and Paul lunched on their own. Talking about whatever it was they were hatching together but today the women were invited. She found the two men in an expansive mood waiting for them in the dining room. It seemed that whatever they were trying to achieve had met with some success. During lunch, she discovered that Paul had given Jean the idea of using percussion caps for muskets. She really was going to have to talk to him once they were in private. Even such a small technological development could totally change history and it scared her. Towards the end of the meal, she seized her chance. They were talking of going up to Jean's plantation and distillery for the weekend, something to do with more experiments. Marie was delighted, although it was closer to the volcano it was behind a large ridge and much more sheltered.

'Paul, if we're going away, would it be possible to make a quick trip to Jacaranda? All my cosmetics are still on board and I really need some shampoo.'

Paul looked at her. At last, she seemed to be coming out of her shell and anything that encouraged her was to be supported. He looked over at Jean. 'Is that alright with you Jean? We could send your manservant down to help her. It would only take a couple of hours and then we can all leave for your estate this evening. I am sure your wife would be interested in our lotions and makeup as well.'

Jean nodded. 'As long as we are all ready to go by four o'clock. I don't like to arrive in the dark.'

After lunch, Emma and Raoul the taciturn manservant took a small horse and cart through the town and along a track to the fort. The soldiers lent them a boat and they rowed out to the yacht. Raoul seemed disinclined to board the yacht. He had clearly heard some of the things that had gone on and seemed to have a dread of Jacaranda. He offered to stay in the dinghy while Emma got her things.

Emma went below and immediately turned on the television and chartplotter. While they were warming up she went to the forward shower and retrieved all her makeup and shampoo. She then returned to the chart table and studied the picture. She soon realised what had bothered her. Just to be sure, she grabbed the hand held GPS they had used for the navigation on the day as they had hidden the cockpit display below decks. She also hurriedly searched for the pilot book she remembered. It was in the rack along with all the other navigation publications and stuffing them both in her bag she went back on deck. Her mind was whirling in mounting excitement. If she was right, then maybe Jack was still alive but that would mean Paul had been lying all along. Why? Either way, he had some serious answers to provide and maybe, just maybe, Charles, Jack and Melissa were not actually dead.

Chapter 25

The Harbour Master was courteous when he came on board. Merely asking their business and apologising for the fact that the Mayor would not be able to meet them as he was away at his plantation.

Charles explained that they were purely visiting before heading back across the Atlantic and wanted to take the opportunity to purchase some of the produce of the island and any good wines that might be available. The English islands, he explained, were not good at supplying wine of any quality. The Harbour Master beamed at this and told Charles where the best vintages could be obtained, carefully omitting to mention that he owned the particular establishment in question. Jack and Charles had decided not to enquire about Jacaranda. They didn't want to run the risk of arousing suspicions before they had even got ashore. Formalities over, they were free to use the port facilities.

Charles sent several parties ashore to purchase fresh food and animals for the journey. He briefed the officers in charge to keep their ears out about the strange boat that had been in the harbour but to not appear too interested. Charles, Jack and Melissa then proceeded to the recommended wine emporium. The quality was indeed good and Charles indulged himself. He at least would be sailing back across the ocean soon. On departing, they enquired as to the whereabouts of a good place to dine and were given directions to an establishment down near the waterfront but away from the bustle and smell of the working dock area.

They were seated at a delightful table on the first floor overlooking the bay. The beauty of the view leant itself to comments to the owner who came over personally to serve them. It was not often that a warship's Captain and more importantly, a beautiful young lady dined in his establishment and he looked forward to a pleasant exchange and a good tip. After ordering wine and food, Charles started chatting amiably to the Frenchman. 'This is a beautiful place monsieur. It seems to be the busiest port in the Caribbean.'

'But yes,' he beamed in reply. 'Unlike you English, we trade with everyone and you can see the town is very rich because of it. Our Mayor, Monsieur le Clerc, has made a policy of open trade.'

'Ah, I have heard of this man he must be very farsighted. There must be a lot of innovation going on. Lots of new ideas being tried out.'

'Indeed, we see some strange sights here. The other day this fantastic boat came in. She must be something to do with the Mayor as her crew are at his residence this weekend. A boat that size and only two people on board, a man and a woman. The whole town has been talking about it for days.'

Jack who had been keeping out of the conversation felt a great weight come off his shoulders. Emma must have recovered and was definitely on the island and hopefully not too far away. He looked at the restaurateur. 'We didn't see this boat as we came in Has she sailed away?'

He laughed. 'No monsieur, they have anchored her just behind the southern point over there by the fort.' And he pointed towards the bottom of the bay. 'We think the Mayor moved her because everyone was so interested and he wanted to get her out of sight but many people still sail past to look, what a fantastic vessel.'

'You said they were at his residence this weekend. How do you know this?'

'My apologise monsieur, this may be a large town but it is quite small for gossip and the young girl off the boat is very beautiful. So everyone is interested. When I said residence, I meant his plantation up in the hills. If you look up there in the distance you can see the roof. It is very grand and he even has his own rum distillery.'

Just then the food arrived and the man bade his leave. Although the meal was very good, they ate quickly and left as soon as was decent, heading back to the ship to plan what to do next.

That afternoon they met up with the other shore party officers and learned much the same story. The whole town was fascinated about what their Mayor was up to now and who were the crew of the strange beautiful boat. Charles suggested they launch one of the ship's boats and go and scout out Jacaranda's anchorage. He gave the task to Mr Bevan but made it clear that he was not to go close. Merely confirm she was there and see how an approach might be made from shore if possible.

Meanwhile, they discussed what to do next.

Jack was keen to take action as soon as possible. 'Let's just march up to the plantation and confront them. I know that place. In our time it still exists as a working rum distillery.'

Melissa was the voice of caution. 'And what do we do when we confront them Jack? Presumably, Paul has convinced them that he is the owner of Jacaranda and must have some sort of deal going with this Mayor. It will be his word against ours.'

'Yes but Emma will be able to tell the truth.'

'I suspect the Mayor will not want to know that. Especially if they are up to something lucrative. Which knowing Paul, will be the case.'

Charles was concerned about the bigger situation. 'Look, you two may be private citizens but this is an English warship and I can't afford to set off a diplomatic incident. My crew will be wondering what the hell is going on as well. I've sent half of them off to surreptitiously ask about a strange vessel. Mr Bevan will be back soon with tales of an odd looking blue hulled yacht. In all fairness, I cannot ask them to get involved in this even if they were prepared to believe what I told them it was about.'

'Sorry, you're absolutely right Charles,' replied Jack worriedly. 'You have done all I could ask. I am going to have to work this out. Why don't you just drop us off and head home, dammit you have enough worries of your own now.'

'Excuse me,' butted in an angry sounding Melissa. 'None of this 'I' crap. We will work this out together. Emma is my friend as well and I want to see Paul sorted out as much as you do.'

'Oops, sorry Melissa, yes you're right but I can't see how Charles can help us more without causing all sorts of problems.'

Just then there was a knock and the door. Tom and the young Midshipman entered.

Mr Bevan spoke first. 'Sir, I took the ship's boat out for some training as you suggested and we went down to the south. There is a small fort on the point with about six guns and anchored under the guns is this strange boat. She is very slim and has an amazing mast. Her hull is light blue. I assume that is the one you are looking for?'

'Yes,' replied Charles. 'That's the one. What about approaches to the fort?'

'All I could see Sir, apart from the fort is a track that comes along from the town and a small jetty but to approach the jetty you have to go past the entrance to the fort. You couldn't do it unseen, even at night if that is what you wanted to do.'

Tom broke in, he could not contain his pent up feelings any longer. 'Sir, what is this all about? We have clearly come here to find this strange yacht. All the crew are wondering what the hell is going on and you can include me in that. Surely, this isn't in our orders?'

Charles sighed and looked at his friend. 'I am sorry Tom, I should have explained earlier. No, this is not in my orders although coming to Martinique is within their scope. For reasons that I cannot explain right now, the story about Jack and Melissa being shipwrecked in a hurricane is not quite true. That strange boat is called Jacaranda and it belongs to Jack. It was stolen from him and they were marooned on St Vincent where I found them. Not only was the boat stolen but Jack's wife was on board and we have reason to believe they are here as guests of the town's Mayor. Please trust me when I say that there is good reason for all this.'

Tom thought for a second. 'It sounds like a simple act of piracy to me Sir. Why can't we simply report it to the Mayor and recover Jack's wife and the boat?'

'For several reasons Tom but mainly because they would dispute ownership. Even if Jack's wife was able to corroborate the story and we are not sure what she knows, as she was wounded when the boat was taken, we believe the Mayor has a vested interest in keeping hold of her. And don't forget we are at peace with France, so any accusations of piracy that included French nationals would take months if not years to sort out and we don't have the time. Our orders do require us to sail home sometime this year.'

Mr Bevan could contain himself no longer. 'Sir, they are our friends why don't we just take her back? Once we have sailed away they would have to prove they weren't pirates and anyway we would be in England by then.'

'I wish it were that simple but we would still have to rescue Jack's wife and she is not on board. She is up there in a house inland.'

'Then we should go and get her Sir.'

Charles looked at the determined young face. He wished he could see everything in such simple terms of black and white. Before he could speak further Tom broke in.

'Sir, I think I speak for the whole crew. We know you have some sort of special relationship with Jack and Miss Melissa and they clearly helped save your life when you had the fever on St Vincent. If there is anything we can do to help them then we should do it. Maybe Mr Bevan is correct, we should rescue Jack's wife and then retake his yacht and just sail away.'

Jack looked at them all. 'Tom, Charles thank you for your support but this is not your fight. Just leave us here, we will sort it out.'

'With respect Jack, that is just rubbish,' retorted Tom. 'You saved our Captains life. If we can repay the debt then we will.'

Charles made his decision. 'I cannot and will not involve the whole ship and I cannot act in any official capacity but I will not leave this island until we have done exactly what Tom has just outlined. We will rescue Emma and recover the yacht.'

Chapter 26

Paul and Emma arrived at Jean's plantation separately. They set off at the same time but the ladies and their entourage travelled in a horse drawn coach and the men were given horses. Once again, Paul found himself doing something he hated. By the time they arrived, his sore behind reminded him why he never took up riding in the first place. Of course, as he was staying in this time, he supposed he would just have to get used to it.

The plantation house was magnificent, a white colonial style building with a veranda all the way around the first floor, which allowed the rooms to catch the best of the breeze. It was set in manicured grounds and through the trees one could glimpse the blue sea in the hazy distance far below. In the background, there was the continuous clanking sound from a water wheel that turned night and day. It was used to crush the sugar cane for the distillery whose aroma perfumed the air in competition with the local flora.

The men gathered in the library. In addition to Paul, Jean had invited several of his friends. There was the local doctor and a lawyer as well as Monsieur Bouchier the gunsmith, who Paul had met the other day. Jean had arranged for him to deliver some of his supply of acid and mercury so they could try a few experiments over the weekend. On arriving, Jean gave them all a quick tour of the distillery. French rum, unlike everywhere else was made directly from the sugar juice of crushed sugar cane. This was a uniquely French method. All the other islands used fermented molasses for the base drink. '*Typical bloody Frogs,*' thought Paul sourly. '*They always have to do everything differently.*' But he had to admit the product slipped down very acceptably when it came to the tasting part of the tour.

By the time the ladies arrived, they were all well into it and Jean had to prize them away from the tasting area to their rooms to change for dinner. Paul had a sudden flash back to a Scottish castle and returning to his room to meet with a certain amiable lady. Who knows, maybe Emma would start to accept her lot and become more amiable as well. It was about bloody time.

A black manservant showed him up to his room and when he entered he saw that Emma was already unpacking the bag she had filled up from Jacaranda.

'So good to see you my dear,' he mumbled in a rather inebriated voice. 'Apologies for not greeting you on arrival but we were being given the rum distillery tour and very good it was too. How was the boat, all in order I hope?'

Emma looked at him with a jaundiced smile. 'All in order indeed, including the track on the chart plotter.'

Paul looked at her, suddenly confused. 'I have absolutely no idea what you mean.'

'Very simple, the main chartplotter will continue to give an estimate of the ship's track based on the log and compass readings even when the satellite signal is lost. I checked it when I was on board. You told me you spent two hours looking for the others after the helicopter had crashed. The chartplotter says you sailed towards Jack's exit point and then turned around, presumably when you didn't return home. Seems to me there is a large discrepancy between your account and what the boat actually did. Now tell the truth you bastard!'

Paul slumped into a chair and looked at Emma. He could see she was pretty pissed off but he couldn't tell her the truth that was one certainty. He was going to have to lie once again.

'Oh Emma, I am sorry. I thought it would sound better to you if I said I searched for hours rather than just heading off to the return waypoint.'

'You got that right,' she said through clenched teeth.

'Yes but look, the explosion was massive and there was nothing left on the surface. There was no way anyone could have survived. What was the point in hanging around for hours? I honestly thought the best thing was to head home.'

Emma didn't look convinced. 'When nothing happened why did you turn back?'

'Yes, well, er, as there was clearly something I should be doing that Jack hadn't told me about I had no recourse but to head back and search the area and wait for you to come round. Melissa had said the thump on your head wasn't serious and you would come round quite quickly and she was right.'

'It might have scrambled my brains for a while but if I've got this clear and I'm pretty sure I have. You didn't search thoroughly at all. You set off for the return point and it was only when it didn't work that you came back to search properly. They could have been alive, YOU BASTARD.'

'Look Emma, I may have panicked. No, I did panic but come on, we had just been chased by the Royal Navy and then gone through some sort of bloody time warp for God's sake. Then my friends get blown up by a sodding helicopter. But honestly, I am sure they weren't there after the explosion. Look, I'm sorry but I'm only human.'

'So am I and I will never forgive you, never. Got it? And as soon as we have some freedom again, we will go down to St Vincent and St Lucia and see if we can get any reports of anyone shipwrecked. You may say you are sure they died but clearly you weren't or you wouldn't have gone back. Do you understand?'

Paul realised that Emma was not going to be moved but at least she still swallowed the story about the helicopter.

'Yes Emma, I'm sorry, I really am. We will go as soon as we can alright?'

Suddenly, something else occurred to Emma. A chill ran down her spine. 'Paul, why haven't you asked me about what Jack did to get Jacaranda through the time warp? You say you went back to search in case they had survived BUT YOU NEVER ASKED ME! Now why is that?' and then it hit her. 'For some reason, you decided not to go back, didn't you? You could have asked me when I came round but you never did. At some point, you bloody well decided to stay in this benighted age. Now, why would that be I wonder?'

Paul didn't like how close to the truth Emma was getting. 'Look Emma, with what we know we could do so well here.

You're right about me deciding to stay. It's such a wonderful opportunity.'

'And you didn't think to ask me what I wanted?'

'Well to be frank, it was hard to get a word out of you. When I proposed we come here you seemed content enough, so I assumed you were happy to go along with me.'

Emma considered this and to be fair to Paul he had consulted her at every stage but he knew she was probably concussed and had the tragedy of her three friend's deaths on her mind. 'Well, I'm starting to think clearly again and I don't want to stay in an age with no medicines, no concept of female equality or social justice. Where life expectancy is about forty and more to the point, no BLOODY SHAMPOO! I have a pretty good idea what Jack used to get us through, even if I don't know exactly how he did it. And whatever we find when we go and look for Jack and the others, I then want to go home. You can stay here for all I care. Have you got that?'

'Yes, yes,' he said placatingly. 'But we have to get le Clerc to trust us fully first and I need to demonstrate that we are of value to him. That is what this weekend is all about. We are going to try to make fulminate of mercury tomorrow. If that is successful, then we can get the gunsmith to make some percussion caps and le Clerc will be in our debt. Now, will you please go along with me that far?'

Emma realised that she didn't have much choice. To get back to Jacaranda and sail south she needed Paul. 'Fine but as soon as we can, we go and look for the others and then I go home. Frankly, I don't care what you do. Oh and you sleep on that sofa tonight.'

Paul breathed a sigh of relief. He would talk to Jean and make sure that there were plenty of obstacles placed in their way to stop them taking Jacaranda back to sea and in the meantime he was sure he could slowly talk Emma round.

Jean and his wife had lent them both suitable clothing and so shortly afterwards, they went in search of the other guests. In the end, they had a surprisingly amiable dinner. Emma had clearly regained all her faculties and despite her private misgivings, charmed the pants off all the men.

'*What an asset she will be in this age,*' thought Paul as he downed yet another glass of wine and looked at her over the dining table. With her raven hair set up high and gorgeous deep brown eyes, she looked every inch the aristocratic lady. And who knows in this age, it shouldn't take that long to be able to buy into the aristocracy. The future had so many wonderful opportunities.

When they retired though, Emma made it quite plain that her threat for Paul to use the sofa was real. Up until now, even though they had shared the same bed, it had been totally platonic. But with Emma out of her shell, she clearly felt differently and he was not going to push his luck. He would ensure that they never made it back somehow and he knew she would eventually be his. He could wait.

As she lay alone in her bed, silent tears streamed down Emma's face. Her heart cried out for her Jack and if he was still alive she vowed to herself she would find him. And then she would return to her world. Paul had better get that through his stubborn bloody head.

The next day was great fun. After breakfast, the men went to a large barn in the distillery where Monsieur Bouchier had arranged for the delivery of a glass cask of nitric acid and a small bottle of mercury. Jean had instructed his distillery staff to prepare the purest alcohol they could from the still. Paul tested it and although it was not totally pure, felt it would probably do for his purposes.

'Now, gentlemen the only explosive substance currently known to man is black powder. I am going to show you a new one. It will not replace black powder because it is too unstable as you will shortly see but as we have discussed, it can be used to initiate an explosion.'

So saying, he took a large glass beaker and carefully poured a measured quantity of nitric acid out of the glass jar. He then took a small amount of mercury and poured it into the acid. He stirred the solution with a glass rod and the mercury slowly dissolved. Next, he took another, even larger glass jar and filled it with a slightly smaller amount of the alcohol.

'Now watch gentlemen and do not be afraid of the reaction.' He took the acid mixture and slowly poured it into the alcohol. Immediately the solution started to froth and bubble. Despite his warning, the men all took a step back in alarm.

'No, it is quite safe at this stage.' As the reaction slowed down, white crystals started to appear in the liquid. After a short time, Paul was able to pour the liquid through a paper filter and then wash the residue with water. There, gleaming in the sun, were pure white crystals. The men all crowded around curious to see the product.

Paul picked up a few in his fingers and squeezed them. 'As you can see, this is quite safe but wait until it dries out'.

Paul laid the filter paper out in the open and they all returned to the house for coffee. On returning, the crystals had dried in the hot Caribbean sun.

'Now for the fun bit,' grinned Paul. He carefully shook a few tiny crystals out onto blacksmiths anvil that he had asked Jean to provide. Taking a small metal hammer, he tapped them. There was a loud crack and puff of smoke as the crystal exploded. Murmurs of astonishment greeted the demonstration.

'As you can see, the crystals are now very unstable and any impact or indeed friction will set them off. Now who would like a try?'

One by one they all had a go with the hammer. Initial trepidation turned into delight as they all realised that the small quantities were relatively harmless. Paul looked on as the bewigged and frock coated men turned into little schoolboys playing with a new toy.

Jean turned to them all. 'Paul thank you, you have delivered as you promised. I look forward to your next demonstration when you and Monsieur Bouchier have made the new firing caps for our muskets.'

He turned to a slave servant and indicated that all were to be given a glass of his finest rum. Looking at them all he raised his glass. 'We will confound our enemies and rule the world. Gentlemen to the Glory of France!'

Chapter 27

In the end, Jack and Charles had to settle on a relatively direct approach. The plantation house was a good five miles outside the town and up a steep and heavily wooded incline. They would have to use the one and only track, as the Caribbean undergrowth was just too thick elsewhere. There were also several little villages en route, so to approach totally unseen would be nigh impossible. Despite literally, a ship load of volunteers to help, they decided to keep numbers small. The town supported quite a large militia and the last thing Charles wanted was some form of pitched battle.

Despite protestations, Charles ordered Tom to stay on board and get the ship immediately ready for sea. He could not afford to have his second in command ashore with him and he was determined that he was going himself. Melissa was a different case and no amount of arguing was sufficient. In the end, both Charles and Jack gave in. They knew a hopeless case when they saw one. Charles also decided to take his previously successful shore party of Mr Bevan and his Coxswain John Cummins but their job would be to act as back up, whereas the other three would try the more direct approach.

When it came to how they would retrieve Jacaranda, Jack seemed unconcerned.

'As long as it's dark, we don't need a boat to get out to her,' he explained.

Charles looked puzzled.

'It's your mind set,' he explained. 'No one from this time thinks of swimming. For some reason, you're all afraid of the bloody sea. I know you can swim Charles but even you don't think of doing it deliberately. I'm damned sure no one in the fort will expect it either. As soon as we get down to the beach, I will swim out to seaward and approach with Jacaranda between me and the shore. Once I'm aboard, I can slip the anchor and motor out. A boat moving fast, with no sails up, should confuse them enough for me to get clear.'

Charles had to acknowledge the truth in Jack's remark. Not one of his sailors could swim and the soldiers in the fort would be even less inclined to believe that anyone would do such a stupid thing.

They also thought hard about weapons and clothing. Carrying swords wasn't common practice in normal times and muskets would be most suspicious. In the end, Charles settled on a pair of his favourite flintlock pistols hidden inside his cloak. Jack took back the automatic pistol which he hid in the back of his waistband. He just hoped he didn't have to demonstrate, once again, what it was and how many rounds it could fire. Once was enough. But there again, if it meant getting Emma back, anything would be acceptable. Mr Bevan and his Coxswain also carried a concealed pistol apiece plus an assortment of knives. When it came to Melissa they had a real problem. Ladies of this age simply did not carry weapons and when it came to riding a horse, their intended mode of transportation, there would be even greater difficulties. She solved it in her normal direct fashion and demanded Charles hand over some suitable male clothing. She then disappeared into the sleeping cabin to reappear some time later looking sufficiently male to allay suspicion.

'Good God,' exclaimed Jack. 'What did you do with your boobs?'

She smiled a superior smile back at him. 'I simply wound some material round them and squished them up. How do I look?'

Charles got in first. 'You are still the most attractive sailor on this ship, even with your lovely hair in that scarf, my dear.'

Melissa's cheeks dimpled. 'Thank you Charles, at least someone appreciates my skills at disguise. Now gimme a gun. I'm one of the boys now.'

So, with that settled, the five of them rowed ashore just as they had on previous days.

On Andromeda, Tom took charge of getting the ship ready. By the time the shore party returned she would be able to slip her anchor and depart at a moment's notice if necessary.

They were able to hire horses from a local stable, five for them and spares for those they hoped to be bringing back. By late afternoon they were heading up the track towards the plantation. They would have gone faster but Jack was no horseman. He was given the oldest, most staid nag the stable owned but still had trouble at anything faster than a walk.

'Bloody uncomfortable thing,' he grumbled. 'And dangerous at both ends. I can drive a car, a yacht, even a sodding helicopter, so why can't I make this bloody thing do as he's told,' he said pulling on the reins and kicking his heels as his horse stopped once again and started to eat grass at the side of the road.

Melissa laughed at his discomfiture and took the reins from Jack and pulled the horse back into line. 'You have to show them who's boss right from the start, otherwise they will do what they want. You obviously haven't impressed this guy one bit.'

'You know, I'll just bet that when you were six your bedroom was full My Little Ponies and when you were twelve daddy took you riding every weekend.'

She just smiled sweetly and rather smugly back at him.

'Bollocks to that, you just pull him along and I'll sit here and admire the countryside.'

Even though he was prepared for the differences, the last time Jack had come up here it was in a hire car and the track was a tarmacked main road. Now, it was literally a track through virgin undergrowth. Flowers bloomed everywhere and humming birds clustered around them. There were far more than in the future and with the sun streaming through the trees it was utterly enchanting. There were even his favourite Jacaranda trees starting to come out in full bloom. He pointed these out to Melissa, saying they must be a good omen. As the sun started to sink and the light started to fade, they knew they were getting close to their destination. They caught a glimpse of the roof of the house and called a halt, finally dismounting much to Jack's relief.

'Right,' ordered Charles. 'We leave the horses here. We can hobble them and tie them to those trees over yonder. Mr Bevan, your job is to keep an eye on the horses but also the house. We are going to try and sneak in, find Emma and bring her out. No fuss and no one else the wiser until we are long gone. But if there is any altercation you two are to assess the situation and either attempt to come to our aid or if it looks hopeless, return to Andromeda and warn the First Lieutenant, is that clear?'

Mr Bevan nodded.

Jack broke in. 'Yes but we should give Paul the chance to come with us.'

Melissa looked at him as if he were mad. 'You what? He tried to kill us and then stole your girlfriend and your yacht and you want to help him?'

'Whatever Paul did, he was my friend for years. He was clearly under a load of pressure at home and the trip here wasn't exactly untraumatic. Yes, I am prepared to give him a chance. In all honour, I can't just dump him here without giving him the option to return.'

Charles looked at Jack with some approval. 'That's very noble of you Jack and I do understand your motives but any sign of betrayal and he will have me to deal with. I am not and have never been his friend. If it's too difficult to get to him, we come out without him.'

Jack was about to say something but then just nodded in agreement.

'Let's get to it.'

The gates to the plantation were just around the bend and there was no one in sight as they slowly crept through them and across the lawn to the side of the house. There was light in windows on both floors and voices drifted across the still night air. All the sounds seemed to be coming from the first floor rooms where people had their veranda doors open to catch the evening breeze.

'All the guests will be getting changed for dinner in their bedrooms this time of evening,' whispered Charles. 'Let's move slowly around and try to hear Emma or Paul's voice.'

It wasn't long before they hit pay dirt. Going around the corner to the side of the house, Jack immediately heard Emma. The thrill of hearing her almost made him cry with joy but he stifled the urge. It was coloured by a spasm of anger as he then heard Paul reply.

'What were you discussing with Jean this afternoon after your little demonstration Paul?'

'Oh this and that,' came Paul's reply. 'If you really want to know, I was warning Jean about the French revolution.'

Jack hissed and Melissa looked angry, Charles simply looked puzzled.

Emma sounded annoyed. 'Paul you really are a prick. How much history do you want to change?'

'Look, we have to keep in Jean's good books as you well know. It was obvious he was going to ask about future events at some stage. Frankly, I'm amazed it took him so long. Anyway, I am dressed and I know how long you women take, so I am going down. See you in the drawing room.' And there was the sound of a door closing.

'Perfect timing,' whispered Jack. 'Now, how the hell do we get up there?'

Charles grinned and pointed. 'If you have climbed as many masts as I have Jack, getting up that support column is not exactly a problem, especially with that vine around it. Just follow me'

So saying, he grasped the vine that was twined around the column that held up the veranda at the corner of the house. A soon as he was up, he looked about but there was only one room with light coming out of it. He turned, lay down and stretched out his hand and soon his two friends joined him. They slowly crept towards the light. Looking through the open veranda doors, Jack saw Emma sitting in front of a dressing table doing something to her hair. She was dressed in a cream gown and in the soft candle light looked absolutely stunning.

In a soft voice he called out. 'Emma, don't make a noise. It's me Jack. We've been searching for you.'

She turned and her eyes flew open in astonishment. Without knowing how they had moved, they were in each other's arms.

'Oh God, it is you,' she cried, hugging him with all her strength just to prove he was real and with tears pouring down her eyes. 'Paul said you were dead but I never really believed him. What happened?' And then her eyes flew open even further as she saw Charles and Melissa slip into the room.

Reluctant to let go of Jack, she managed to give the other two a hug all at the same time.

Melissa looked at her friend with tears of joy in her eyes. 'We're a lot harder to kill than Paul can imagine.'

'What? He said you were blown up when you went to try and rescue the crew of the helicopter that crashed.'

At that point any thought of including Paul in any rescue fled Jack's mind. Fuck him, he had engineered this, let him stew.

Jack laughed, 'I wondered what cock and bull story he would come up with. I must admit I didn't think of that one. No Emma, he forced us off at gun point but look we can tell it all when there's time. We need to get you out of here. Do you have any other clothes? Anything suitable for riding?'

She thought for a second. 'I've only got some of these old fashioned dresses now but if Melissa helps me we can cut something down.'

Just then a much louder rumbling and groaning was heard from behind the house.

Jack looked worried. 'Damn I wish I had the pilot book from Jacaranda. It has a historical note in it about that bloody volcano.'

Emma looked surprised. 'I had that thought too and got it off the boat when I was down there two days ago. Dammit, I forgot all about it. You just get used to the noise after a while, hang on.' And she rummaged around in a bag by the bed. 'Here it is, you have a look while we try and find something suitable to wear.'

Jack grabbed the book and turned to the section on Martinique. He quickly read the section on Mount Pelee as he discovered it was called. His blood ran cold when he saw the date. 'Shit, shit, shit,' he exclaimed and showed the relevant section to Charles and then to Emma and Melissa as they were rummaging through the wardrobe.

'Well, that puts a different slant on things,' said Charles. 'Guess we'd better get a move on then.'

'Oh really and why would that be then?' Came an all too familiar voice from the door.

They all spun around and there in the door cradling the shotgun was Paul.

'Jesus, just how hard is it to get rid of you three,' he smiled.

Chapter 28

Paul had gone down to the drawing room to meet the others and found he was almost the last to arrive. He apologised for Emma, jokingly saying that now she had her cosmetics from the boat they all would have to allow an extra hour for her to get ready. Madam le Clerc's ears pricked up at the word 'cosmetics' and she asked Paul if he would go up and ask Emma to bring some down to show them all. Dutifully, he returned upstairs but as he approached the room, he could hear voices. Knowing that everyone else was already downstairs, he crept to the door of his room and listened. Cold water ran down his spine as he recognised Jack's voice. So he had survived! And even worse he had managed to find him and Emma. He made a quick decision. At the end of the corridor was Jean's study. He went there as fast and quietly as he could. Sure enough, lying behind the desk were the two guns. He grabbed the shotgun and checked it was loaded and then made his way back to the room. They were all still chatting away and although he could recognise voices, Melissa's as well now, he couldn't make out any distinct words. Nothing for it, he pushed the door open and made his entrance.

They all looked quite shocked at his opening words. It would have been quite funny if it hadn't been so bloody tragic.

'Well, whatever you were discussing, you can forget it. I think you all need to meet my new boss,' and he called out over his shoulder at the top of his voice. 'Jean, anybody, we have intruders.'

There was the sound of feet on the stairs but Emma ignored them, looking straight at Paul she spat in his face. 'I have total contempt for you now you piece of crap, you had better be ever so careful what you say and do now because if you give me one inch, I'll have your balls.'

Paul grinned a sickly grin as he wiped his face on his sleeve, while carefully keeping the gun trained on them all.

'What is going on?' Came a voice from behind and Paul moved to one side to let Jean into the room.

'We have some uninvited guests Jean I'm afraid and I am pretty sure they are well armed. Would you please do the honours of checking them while I keep them covered.'

Jean was not all sure what was really happening but he was certain that he didn't want people that Paul obviously knew carrying weapons in his house. He carefully went to each of them and relieved them of pistols and knives. When he was sure they were disarmed, he turned to one of the strange men. 'I don't know who you are. I am sure Paul will tell me soon anyway but anyone who sneaks into my house carrying so many weapons is no friend of mine, is that clear?'

Charles nodded and looking Jean straight in the eye said, 'monsieur for that I apologise but if you really knew that snake over there holding the shot gun, you would understand why we felt it prudent to come here armed.'

Jean nodded back. 'I think we will all go into my study and continue this conversation in a controlled manner.' He picked up two of the pistols he had just taken from them and along with Paul motioned them down the corridor.

When Emma started to go with them he looked confused. 'Madam please, you're not with them surely?'

Emma looked back at Paul. 'No matter what Paul has told you, much of it is lies and the first one is that I am his wife.' and pointing to Jack. 'He is my husband and Jacaranda is his yacht. Paul deceived me into thinking Jack was dead after he stole the boat. As far as I am concerned, these people are my real friends and I stay with them.'

Jean was getting even more confused and worried. His other guests were holding back at the end of the corridor. He called to them. 'One of you, go and get my overseer please and the rest of you go downstairs. I need to talk to these people in private,' and he ushered them through the study door. Seeing the rifle lying by the desk, he grabbed it with one hand and chambered a round putting the two pistols on the desk top.

'I see it hasn't taken you long to teach the locals bad habits,' Jack said to Paul.

'Just keep your gob shut or I'll shut it for you,' hissed Paul.

'That's enough,' said Jean in a firm voice. 'I want you all to sit down over there,' and he motioned to some chairs along the back wall of the room.

Just then, a very large man in a scruffy shirt and trousers came in.

'Ah, Michel, we seem to have some unwelcome guests. Please go and get four sets of slave manacles and some locks as fast as you can.'

The overseer nodded and hastily shot out of the door.

'We wait for my overseer to return and no one speaks until then.'

The uneasy silence did not last long. The overseer was soon back with four sets of iron wrist manacles. Jean motioned to the four seated individuals and he fitted them to their wrists.

'Normally we would rivet those in place. You are lucky there is not time, so we will have to make do with padlocks.'

When the overseer came to Emma, Jean started to look concerned. 'Madam you are a guest here, this is not right.'

Emma looked quite determined. 'Jean, these are my friends. If you see fit to treat them like this, then you must do the same to me.'

'Very well madam, it is your choice.'

When the four of them were secured to his satisfaction, he told the overseer to wait outside and close the door.

'Some explanations please.'

Paul started to speak but Jean cut him off. 'Paul, I have heard your story or at least the one you have seen fit to tell me. I would like to hear what these people have to say. Firstly who are you?'

Jack answered for them all. 'My name is Jack Vincent. I am the Master of the Sailing Vessel Jacaranda which is anchored near here. This lady is my wife, who you already know,' and he indicated Emma. Then pointing to Melissa, he continued. 'This lady is Melissa Morgan she is a close friend and is also one of my crew.' He realised there was no point in trying to conceal Charles's identity as Paul already knew who he was. Turning to Charles he said, 'Charles, I think you had better introduce yourself.'

Charles looked the Mayor haughtily in the eye. 'I Sir, am Charles Lonfort, Fifth Earl of Hinchfield and Master and Commander of Her Majesty's Brig Sloop Andromeda which is also moored here and I might add the only warship in the bay.'

Jean looked thoroughly taken aback. What on earth were these people doing with so influential an aristocrat and the Commander of a Royal Naval warship as well? The whole situation was escalating out of control.

'I take it you know who these people are and where they have come from?' Jean asked looking directly at Charles.

'Indeed I do Sir and in fact I probably know more about them and their secrets than you do. The first thing you need to know is that man is a pirate and murderer.' He glowered pointing at Paul.

'That's as maybe but he is the one with genuine papers of ownership of that boat. I should know, I supplied them for him and I might add that your presence here constitutes a major diplomatic incident, one might even say an act of war!'

'You may be technically correct Sir but if it came out you were harbouring such a fugitive and had molested an English aristocrat and naval Captain at the same time, I don't think you would fair too well. Bear in mind that my crew know where I am and will come looking for me if I don't return.'

Jean knew that Charles had a point there. The local militia would outnumber any landing party a brig could put ashore but they would be trained fighting men. The militia mainly consisted of farmers led by spoiled aristocrats. He would not want to bet on the outcome of any confrontation. But would they really risk such a dangerous act? Surely, that would exceed any orders he may have been given. Oh God, what a mess. He needed time to think.

'Ladies and gentlemen, this is an impossible situation. Frankly, I am at a loss over what to do. However, what I do know is that you entered my house under arms when you could have walked up to the front door and behaved like civilised people.'

Charles interrupted. 'We have tried to explain why.'

Jean shouted him down. 'How am I to know the truth in this matter? You devils come here with your wild tales and machines. I think it would be better if all of you just disappeared.' And he realised that would be the simple answer if it wasn't for the complication of a senior English aristocrat in their midst who just happened to have a warship parked in his bay. Maybe this could be the key to sorting out this mess.

Looking at Charles he asked. 'Sir, would you be prepared to offer your parole for yourself and these people? And then maybe we can work something out.'

All this time Paul had been getting more and more worried. His hold over Jean was based on his monopoly of ideas and information. With the arrival of the others and the testimony that was starting to come out, things could go very wrong, very quickly. He could see how Jean's manner had changed when he discovered that Charles was a senior aristocrat. If it came to his word against Charles's, he was pretty sure who would be believed and it wasn't going to be him.

Time to go.

As Jean was speaking, he slowly moved to get closer. Suddenly he reversed the shotgun and clubbed Jean on the back of the head with the butt.

Before anyone could cry out he hissed. 'Silence everyone. I will get us out of this mess.' Hoping this little bit of misdirection would keep them thinking for a few seconds he called out for the overseer who flew into the room. As he looked down in surprise at this master lying out cold on the floor, he received the same treatment from Paul who had moved to be behind him as he entered.

'My God, I'm really getting quite good at this,' he smiled at the seated four. 'And before you get any ideas, please stay quiet and seated.' And he pointed the gun at them.

'You utter shit,' said Jack. 'Just for a second there I thought you might have turned back into a human being.'

'Sorry mate, far too late for that. I've got kosher contemporary ownership papers for Jacky now. I can sail off into the sunset. The question is how do I stop you bloody lot from following again?'

Jack looked behind Paul as the door slowly opened. Paul caught his eyes and laughed. 'Jesus Jack, not that old bloody 'behind you' pantomime joke.' He suddenly stiffened as there was the unmistakable sound of a flintlock pistol being cocked at the same time as a cold steel barrel pushed into the back of his neck.

'Sorry monsieur, we may not have fantastic guns like yours but this pistol is quite capable of blowing your head off. Now give me that weapon.'

Paul slowly dropped the shotgun to the floor. He recognised Monsieur Bouchier's voice and knew the gunsmith would be quite determined, especially having seen the state of his host laid out on the floor with blood over the back of his head. Suddenly, the overseer started to groan and sat up looking around in some confusion. Seeing the gunsmith holding the pistol to Paul's head, he quickly worked out what had happened. He stood groggily but was quickly regaining his senses. Monsieur Bouchier spoke to him while keeping the pistol held into the back of Paul's neck.

'Quick, check Monsieur Le Clerc. Is he alive?'

Michel knelt down and examined the body of his master. 'Yes Monsieur, he is breathing but he is unconscious.'

Charles started to talk but the gunsmith stopped him. 'I've no idea what was going on in here and until Jean regains his senses I do not wish to know. As far as I am concerned you are all dangerous people and I don't want to take any risks with any of you. Michel, go and get another set of manacles for this one and take them out to the distillery where we were this morning. We must chain them up securely until Jean is in a fit state to talk.'

So saying, the overseer went out and returned with another set of cuffs for Paul. They were then all marched out of the house past the surprised guests. They gasped when they saw Emma and Paul were included but whatever they had been told they asked no questions as the group were herded past under the watchful eyes of the two men. On reaching the distillery, they were made to sit around the central pillar in the main hall. A chain was linked through all the manacles and they were left to sit uncomfortably in wan moonlight to contemplate the morning.

Surprisingly, they were left alone. Jack suspected it was because they were so used to treating slaves this way they didn't consider the need to supervise them once the chains were in place.

'Paul not only are you a bastard, you are also a complete twat,' spat an angry Jack.

'Before you start shouting at me, I know a way to get us out of here. Do you want to hear it or just spend the night abusing me?' responded Paul with a slightly smug air, despite their predicament.

'Go on but don't try another bloody trick. There are four of us and one of you. I wouldn't fancy your chances.' There were murmured words of agreement from the others and one extremely inventive threat from Melissa.

'My dear even if that were physically possible you are just not strong enough. Now everyone, shuffle towards that table over there. Let me see if I can reach it.'

With them all moved in the same direction, Paul was just able to get his manacled hands onto the table top. With the utmost care, he reached for some of the fulminate of mercury crystals that they had left drying in a bowl from the afternoon's experiments. Lying next to the bowl was a small spoon and very carefully he poured some into the crude but strong padlock that secured his wrist cuffs. When he was satisfied the lock was full, he got to them all to move back and then with a muttered prayer swung the lock at the edge of the table.

There was a loud crack and a puff of smoke and the lock flew apart. 'Phew, didn't blow my bollocks off,' he grinned at the others. 'That's always a good thing. Oh shit, where did you get that from? Damn, I knew I should have searched you myself.'

Jack was pointing his nine millimetre pistol at him. Up until then, he hadn't had the opportunity to get hold of it but while Paul was concentrating on his chemicals, he had managed to get Charles to reach behind him and pull it out of his waistband.

Jack smiled at Paul. 'For some reason, I didn't want you to release yourself and then just sod off, now did I? Believe me, you have given me every reason to use this, so don't push your luck. Just do the same for all of us please? In fact, you can use that stuff on the chain not the locks, then we can be free to move first.'

Paul eyed the gun. It never wavered in his direction. He thought he knew Jack pretty well and that he would probably not use it but there again, he did sound pretty pissed off. No, he'd better comply at least for the moment. He looped part of the chain over the edge of the table and heaped some explosive over it. Taking a mallet, he smacked it down and the chain cracked in half. They all pulled the chain through the manacles and were half way there.

Paul motioned to Emma and he used the same method on her lock. As she shook the manacles off, he suddenly grabbed her and spun her around, his arm around her neck.

'Sorry Jack but I don't think you will fire and risk hitting Emma.' He pulled the struggling girl with him as he backed towards the door.

Jack aimed the gun at them but Paul was right, there was just too much risk of shooting the wrong person even though he was mad enough now to try a shot given half a chance. Paul reached the door and pulled it open behind him and then with a sudden shove pushed Emma stumbling forward and disappeared into the night.

Jack rushed forward, torn between chasing Paul and helping Emma. In the end he, stopped at her and made sure she was unhurt and then looked out into the darkness but Paul had gone.

'Jack,' called out Charles. 'We may have cut the chain but there is no more of that explosive left. We are still shackled. What do we do?'

Chapter 29

Paul was thinking and running fast. There was no time to go back into the house and retrieve anything. He doubted anyone had heard any sounds, as the water wheel would drown out all but the loudest sound from the distillery. The stables were in the opposite direction and anyway he didn't have a clue how to saddle a horse. No, it was going to be shank's pony whatever happened. He only had one option now and that was to get back to Jacaranda. Luckily, they knew him down at the fort, so he should be able to blag a boat to get out to her. It was just over five miles and all downhill. It all rather depended on how long it took Jack and company to get out and after him or the locals to find out and give chase or both. He made towards the gates skirting around the house where some lights were still on. As he jogged through the gates, he heard the distinct sound of Jack's pistol and had a shrewd idea of what he was doing with it. However, hopefully it would alert that bloody great overseer and that should delay them at the least. Nothing to do now but fly down the track and get to the sea.

Mr Bevan also heard the shots, just as a few seconds later they heard running footsteps and an unidentified man shot past their hiding place heading towards the town. Thinking quickly, he instructed Cummins to take a horse and try to catch the man while he went to help his friends in the estate.

Jack and the others were talking urgently. 'We can run after him but we really need to get these manacles off first. Now this looks easy in the movies but could be bloody dangerous, so let's be careful.'
He got Charles to hold his wrists high up and slightly forward so the padlock was dangling free, then stood next to Charles and put the barrel of the pistol on the lock.

'Girls, hide behind the pillar please, health and safety you know. Bits could fly anywhere.' When they were safely clear he fired the pistol.

'Well what do you know? It worked.' He exclaimed in satisfaction as the lock flew apart.

As quickly as he could, he freed them all using the same method. Unfortunately, the shots must have alerted the staff because the door flew open and there stood Michel the overseer, backed up by two more of the staff with lanterns. They were all carrying pistols.

'Michel stop there,' yelled Jack pointing the pistol at them. 'You must know we have special weapons. Those pistols of yours will be of no use.' This was of course at least partial bluff but Jack had no other cards to play. Just to make his point he fired four rounds in quick succession into the air. The look of stunned disbelief on the faces at the door was similar to those on the natives back in St Vincent but Jack wasn't really in the mood to appreciate it just then. However, the overseer was made of sterner stuff.

'Monsieur, you may have a gun that fires quickly but I and my men have three pistols and the men from the main house will be here soon. You cannot get away.'

'No monsieur, you're wrong, there are also two pistols behind you, so please drop your weapons now.' The voice came from behind them and they looked around to see a young lad with two large flintlocks pointed steadily at their backs.

'Now, go into the barn please,' and he indicated them to move in. 'And place your pistols on the floor.'

Michel realised he had little choice and indicated to his men to do as instructed.

'Well done Mr Bevan,' called Charles. 'An excellent job but where is the Coxswain?'

'Sent him after the man we saw running down the hill Sir. I hope that was the right thing to do.'

'You, my lad have just earned field promotion to Lieutenant but there is no time to waste. We must secure these men and deal with anyone coming from the house.'

While Jack kept the overseer and his men covered with the pistol, which they looked at in fearful wonder, Emma and Melissa demonstrated their rope skills using some they had found at the back of the barn.

Just as they were trussed securely to the central pillar, Charles called for them to be quiet and to douse the lights. The gunsmith and doctor had crept up to the door but as soon as Charles and the Midshipman pointed their pistols at them they quickly surrendered. The girls made quick work of tying them to the other men.

'My God girls, I'll bet the Royal Yachting Association never envisaged using the knots and splices syllabus in quite that way,' Jack said, smiling and then turning to the bound men. 'Look you may not believe this but all we want to do is get back to our boats and leave here. We mean you no harm. It shouldn't be long before someone comes and sets you free. Good luck and give our regards to the Mayor.'

With Mr Bevan in the lead, they ran straight to the gates and retrieved the horses.

Charles looked at Jack. 'There's only one place Paul can go and that's Jacaranda. If he can get to her, he can get away and we won't be able to stop him. Andromeda might be a match if I could get close enough but she's just too fast.'

Jack nodded. 'We could just leave him to it but I dread to think what other damage he could do. No, I'm not prepared to let him get away and I want my boat back.' He looked around at his friends who all nodded in agreement and he then looked behind them. 'And remember that's not the only deadline we're working to.'

They mounted up and sped off down the road. Jack saw that Emma was also quite comfortable in the saddle. 'Of course, I know that your daddy bought you riding lessons when you were a little girl, well it's up to you and Melissa to stop me falling of this bloody thing.'

She grinned excitedly back, the hair whipping back from her head. 'Just lean forward and hug its neck if it all gets too much. Just don't fall off.'

'Surprisingly, that is exactly what I am trying not to do.' he said through gritted teeth.

But within a few minutes they had to stop as they came across a figure staggering up the lane towards them. John Cummins was more embarrassed than hurt, despite the blood that was pouring down his face from a cut to his forehead.

'Sorry Sirs, I thought I was still following the man but he must have heard me and hidden in the bank. The next thing I know is this bloody great branch hits me on the head. He took the horse but he's not that far ahead.'

They gave him one of the spare horses and sped off in pursuit.

Jack remembered that ride for the rest of his life. The moon gave them adequate visibility as they thundered downhill. The others may have felt in control but it was all he could do to keep seated and cling to the horse's neck. Even so, after a few minutes, he started to gain some measure of confidence. Looking around, he saw Charles and the Midshipman leading with Emma ahead of him and presumably Melissa and the Coxswain behind. There was the wonderful night smell of the islands, mixed in the warm wind as it whipped past his head. It became wild and exhilarating, rather like flying a helicopter at extreme low level or when he had tried ski racing for the first time. The horses seemed to sense the urgency and responded to whoops and calls of their riders. They tore through the night like a bunch of idiots. At some of the turns, it was all he could do to cling onto the mane of the horse and not fly off. On the straights, he was able to sit up more and enjoy the ride. But all the time, a knot of burning anger spurred him on. On more than one occasion, if wasn't for the rage inside him, he would probably have gone sprawling into the undergrowth but there was no way he was going to fail now.

It was almost five miles down to the town but it seemed to be only minutes before the leading riders were pulling up and Jack could see the glint of the sea in the moonlight. The buildings of the town were dead ahead.

Somehow, Jack also managed to get his bloody nag to stop with the rest. Charles called over. 'I think we must split up here. Mr Bevan you and the Coxswain are to take the ladies to the town and get back on board. Jack and I will go after Paul. Mr Bevan, as soon as you are on board, instruct the First Lieutenant to weigh anchor and proceed towards the fort. If Jacaranda is trying to flee, you must do everything you can to stop her, understand?'

Mr Bevan and Jack nodded in agreement but he could see the girls weren't happy. 'Before you two start to argue, you can't help us physically but you will be invaluable in advising Tom on what to do if we are unsuccessful and that includes pulling us out of the sea if necessary, right?'

Emma rode her horse next to Jack and reached over and hugged him. Jack hugged her back. No mean feat given his level of horsemanship but at this moment he couldn't care less. There were tears in her eyes. 'Don't you dare do anything stupid you hear me? If you have to, let him have the bloody yacht. We can always get home another way.'

He kissed her hard and long. 'Yes my love but this has got to be settled once and for all and there is something in Jacky that will be of great help in getting us home as you well know. Now go, before you completely destroy my resolve.'

They parted there above the town. Charles and Jack rode down the left hand path towards the fort and it wasn't long before they could see Jacaranda's tall mast picked out by the first rays of the sun towering above the battlements. They stopped well clear and dismounted leaving the horses to graze at the roadside. Dawn was just starting to cast a shadow as they walked on carefully. They soon had the little jetty in front of the fort and the yacht in sight.

'Oh shit,' murmured Jack as he caught sight of a small tender tied to Jacaranda's stern. 'He's already on board.'

'Then why is he still there?' queried Charles.

Jack grinned. 'I'll bet he left the keys back there, up the hill. He knows I have a spare set on the boat somewhere but not exactly where. Without them, he will never be able to get the electrics on line, so he won't be able to get the anchor up or start the engines. Come on there's still time.'

They stripped down. Jack had retained modern underwear much to Charles's amusement who removed all his clothes.

'Now look, I'm probably the better swimmer.' Jack said staring seawards. 'I will go past her to seaward and try and get on board midships where her freeboard is least. It's hard but I've done it before. Charles, you go to the stern and use that tender to climb on board. Hopefully, we can come at him from two directions, OK?'

Charles grinned back. 'OK.'

They slipped carefully into the warm water and swam out to the yacht, trying to make as little noise and splash as possible. Charles looked towards the fort and as expected no one was looking their way. Even if they had looked, they would be almost impossible to see silhouetted against a dark background with the sun rising behind them and the island.

Paul was getting angry. Getting that idiot's horse had been easy and the fort's duty officer recognised him immediately. He had made no objection to lending him a dinghy despite the odd time of the day. So here he was, a hair's breadth from getting away and he couldn't find Jack's spare bloody keys. Jack had explained to him the security arrangements and he knew there had to be spares somewhere. Without them he was bollocksed. He wouldn't even be able to get the sails up as the winches locked solid unless power was available. *Stop panicking and think like Jack. Where would be put them?* he thought savagely. He had already tried the obvious places most yachtsmen the world over used, including under the gas bottles and in the cockpit lockers. But the key he needed was separate from the one that unlocked the hatch, so Jack must have hidden it below somewhere. Luckily, Emma hadn't locked the main hatch when she left in such a state two days ago.

What would that idiot have done with them? And then he had a brainwave. He shot into the galley and grabbed each cuddly shark in turn. Sure enough, the third one he felt, a rather stupid looking great white, had something hard inside. Wasting no time he grabbed a kitchen knife and cut the sodding thing open and there it was, his ticket to freedom. He shot back to the master electrical panel and inserted the key. Everything lit up. Suddenly there was a muffled thud from the upper deck. He froze. Someone must have just climbed on board. Creeping back to the galley, he grabbed the biggest kitchen knife he could find and waited to one side of the saloon steps.

Jack made it to the side of his boat in good time. He ducked underwater and then swam up as hard as he could, reaching for one of the wire shrouds that held the mast up. It would have been much easier if they had left the guard rails there but they had been removed before they came for authenticity. He missed. Ducking down he tried again with all his strength and this time his fingers closed around the base of the shroud. With his arm shrieking in agony, he managed to pull himself waist high and get his other hand on the shroud as well. He waited a second while getting his breath back and listening for any sign that he had been discovered. All appeared well. Slowly, he pulled himself up until he was able to roll sideways onto the deck.

There was no sign of Charles but he couldn't afford to wait. Actually, he didn't want to wait. What he really wanted to do was to beat the shit out of Paul on his own. As he approached the cockpit, he reached out and pulled a large winch handle out of the pocket next to the winch. The handle was about eighteen inches long and made of solid steel. '*It would look really good wrapped around Paul's head,*' he thought.

There was no sign of anyone on deck, so he peered cautiously down the ladder into the main saloon. There was no one in sight but the main panel lights were all lit up, so Paul must have found the key and must be down there somewhere. The time for subtlety was over. He called out.

'Paul you big fucking shit it's time to show your face. You're not leaving here if I have anything to do with it.'

Silence, no response.

Jack knew he should wait for Charles, knew that Paul was trapped below but all his frustration, all his rage over his former friend's betrayal was bubbling sourly in the back of his throat. Without thinking, he started slowly down the saloon steps. He had almost reached the bottom, when a flash of silver caught his eye out to the left. He spun around but was too slow and the large kitchen knife slashed his upper arm. Roaring in anger, he swung the winch handle towards where the knife had come from. There was a satisfying thud and the knife flew across the saloon.

Paul launched himself at Jack, reaching for his throat. Jack swung the winch handle again but missed and it shot out of his hand as it came into contact with the steps. The two men fell to the deck as they grappled together. This was not Hollywood fighting. This was two men fighting desperately anyway they could. One full of anger and rage, the other fighting for his life. They kicked, gouged and bit. Paul managed to get a good fist into Jack's gut which made him whoop out all his air but at the same time Jack slammed his knee up into Paul's groin. They fell apart for a second. Then ignoring the pain in his balls, Paul lurched for Jack. Jack saw him coming and suddenly remembered a lesson in self defence from his Dartmouth days. 'Real fighters don't use their fists, they use their elbows.' As Paul came closer, Jack swung his right elbow as hard as he could into Paul's face. The blow was the culmination of everything that had built up over the last weeks. The sense of betrayal, the anger at the loss of Emma, the sheer bloody rage he felt against someone he thought was his friend. The pain was excruciating but the blow was effective. Paul's head flew back in a spray of blood and teeth and his head hit the same saloon table that had caused Emma's injuries all those days ago. He slumped to the floor unmoving.

Charles pulled himself over the stern of Jacaranda from the little wooden dingy. He could hear fighting down below. But when he got there all he could do was grab his friend who was sitting astride his assailant.

'Jack stop now, stop, he's not going anywhere.'

Chapter 30

Gasping and sweating, Jack allowed Charles to pull him back of Paul's prone body. Charles leant over and found that Paul was still breathing but he was going to have to see a dentist fairly soon.

Jack sat back on saloon chair panting. 'Well, I finally sorted out that son of a bitch. Charles, can you look in the little locker above the galley. There's a bottle of whiskey there.'

As Charles went to the galley, Jack went to the first aid kit. Luckily, most of it was still there. He found some pads and bandages. The wound on his arm really ought to be stitched but there was neither the time nor the expertise for that right now. He applied some antiseptic to a pad and pressed it on the wound. When Charles returned, he helped him apply a tight bandage. That would just have to do for now. Jack poured two generous slugs of malt with slightly shaking hands and downed his in one gulp. As the spirit hit his stomach and the warmth spread through him, he started to think more clearly.

'We need to sneak away from that fort as soon as we can and Charles you need some clothes.' So saying, he went to his cabin in the forepeak and found a pair of shorts and with amusement a T shirt emblazoned with the logo 'Sail fast, Live slow' that should look good on the quarterdeck of HMS Andromeda. Returning to the saloon, he talked while Charles dressed.

'If we try to pull up the anchor, the fort will hear it as it clanks up and it could take some time. So, we will have to get rid of it. It will still make some noise but will be a lot quicker.' Looking up the hatch, he realised it was almost full daylight now, so any movement on deck would be seen. He looked down at Paul who was still wearing period clothes. With Charles's help, they managed to get the shirt and breeches off him and Jack dressed in them. Hopefully, it would help confuse those ashore a bit longer. At the same time, they took the precaution of tying Paul's hands behind him with some cable ties from the tool box and anchoring his legs to the saloon table leg.

'Last time I dealt with an unconscious person, we put him in the recovery position and then did first aid ABCs,' remarked Jack.

'I'm sure that all made sense to you,' responded Charles smiling. 'But once again, I'm afraid I didn't understand a word.'

'Oh yes, sorry, modern medicine stuff. Anyway, time to go. You know how to start the engines don't you?'

'Yes, you showed me that back in your time.'

' So, you stand in the ladder, just below the level of the cockpit. I'll go and release the anchor. As soon as you hear it run out, get to the engine controls and fire them up.'

'More modern idioms Jack but I know what you mean, let's go.'

Jack rummaged around in the chart table and found his sailing multi tool. It had a special saw blade for quickly cutting through strong line which he pulled out. He then nonchalantly walked up into the cockpit and forward to the bow of the boat. He forced himself not to look at the fort, although he was pretty sure there would several pairs of eyes trained on him by now. Reaching the anchor windlass, he noticed that a snubber rope had been attached as he had hoped. It was nice to see good seamanship even if it was probably that shit Paul who had fitted it. Before he got rid of it, he knelt down and opened the chain locker. He was looking for a loop of the nylon line that was spliced to the end of the anchor chain. It was not normally used but allowed the anchor to be let out a long way should really bad weather require it. Rummaging with his fingers, he found some nylon and pulled a loop up and quickly cut through it with his saw blade. He then took a small winch handle from its stowage and released the clutch on the anchor windlass. All the time he felt a crawling sensation between his shoulder blades and expected a cry or even a shot from the fort but nothing happened. His last task was to cut the snubber line. This was also made of nylon and acted as shock absorber for the heavy anchor chain. Unfortunately, even with the gentle breeze that was blowing, the whole weight of Jacaranda was being held on that one line. He took the saw again and carefully cut as close to the cleat that secured the line as he could.

With a sudden crack, the line parted and the anchor chain started to fly out through the windlass, making a hell of a racket in the process. Charles was already in the cockpit as Jack checked to make sure it was all running freely and then ran down the boat to join him. Before he got to the cockpit, there was the comforting growling sound of two marine diesels starting up. The last of the chain and nylon flew over the bow roller just as Jack reached the throttle levers.

There was a shout from the fort and Jack looked that way for the first time. They must be pretty confused he realised. They could see two people on board when there should have only been one and they had released the anchor without putting up the sails first. Well, hopefully they would be even more confused in a second.

He put both engine levers in reverse at maximum throttle. Jacaranda started to accelerate backwards and there was even more confused shouting from ashore. Jack thanked God for Jacaranda's modern underwater design. Her two spade rudders made her incredibly easy to steer when going astern. He kept her going parallel to the front of the fort, aiming to get clear of their field of fire as soon as he could. He needn't have worried. They could clearly see the soldiers on the battlements standing stationary and gazing in awe at the impossibility that was taking place before their eyes. He realised it was the same as when he had reversed away from that pirate ship all those months ago. He started to giggle, which soon turned into a belly laugh of pure joy. They were free and Emma was free and soon they could go home. Charles slapped him on the back as they cleared the edge of the fort and joined in the laughter.

Their course had taken them back into the main bay which was fine. The fort was designed to defend against ships approaching from the south. They could easily exit by sailing straight out the middle when the time came. But now they had a rendezvous to make.

Andromeda had just weighed her anchor and was about a mile away slowly coming towards them on the early morning breeze.

Jack put the engines in neutral and with Charles' help, hoisted the mainsail. It was one thing to astound some French soldiers ashore. Jack didn't want to do the same to the professional seamen on the warship. Charles would have too many impossible questions to answer.

Ten minutes later, the two vessels were alongside one another. Rows of curious eyes looked down on Jacaranda including a smiling Lieutenant Bevan.

The two girls climbed down Andromeda's side and Emma made straight for Jack.

'Careful girl, I have a few bruises you know,' cried Jack as Emma hugged him.

'My God, your arm, are you alright?'

'You should see the other fellow,' he grinned back.

Charles looked at the two of them. 'What are we going to do with that knave down below?'

Melissa had already gone down to the saloon when she saw Paul down there lying on the deck.

'Well, someone sure rearranged his face,' she said looking at Jack in admiration. 'But he's awake now and apart from the damage to his jaw he seems fine.'

Jack snorted. 'He might have some sore wedding tackle as well but we better decide what to do about him. I suppose we can release him now.'

He knelt down and cut his restraints with his sailing knife and escorted Paul as he hobbled up into the daylight. He looked at them all sadly and spoke through the side of his bruised jaw. 'I don't suppose you are going to accept an apology are you?'

Four stony faces stared back.

'Look, I didn't actually murder anyone. You're all here safe and sound.'

Melissa got in first. 'My God, you've got a nerve. How about stranding us in the tender and then shooting out the engine? What would you call that you utter bastard?'

'Oh come on, you would have rigged up something, oars or a sail and in the end I'm guessing you had a spare outboard didn't you?'

'Yes but you didn't know that you pig,' retorted Melissa.

'I suppose you're going to take Jacaranda back to our time aren't you Jack? You know how to do it, just happened to forget to tell me what the trick was right?'

Jack merely nodded.

Paul thought for a second. 'If you are returning, I would appreciate it if you left me here. Life could be very difficult for me for many reasons back at home. How about it?'

Emma was about to say something but Jack stopped her and he also looked meaningfully at the others at the same time.

'If that's what you want Paul but you get no technology, no books, just the clothes on your back. Think about it.'

They were interrupted by a shout from Andromeda. The guard ship was approaching with an irate Harbour Master in the bows. They hooked on alongside Jacaranda with the Harbour Master demanding to know what was going on and saying that he had instructions from Monsieur Le Clerc to arrest everyone in sight.

'At least the Mayor has woken up,' muttered Charles and then turning to the red faced man in the boat. 'Sorry monsieur but no one is being arrested. Both ships are leaving now and before you protest, please remember I have an armed crew and twenty four pound carronades. You don't.'

'Hang on,' said Jack. 'Did the Mayor mention anyone in particular?'

'He did say he would really like to speak to the man who sailed this boat in last week, monsieur Smythe.'

Jack looked at Paul. 'If you want to stay, this is your ticket off but you'll have to make your peace with Jean le Clerc.'

Emma tried to interrupt again but Jack just whispered at her. 'I know what I am doing, trust me.'

While Paul thought, Jack went below and slipped into some shorts and came back up giving Paul his clothes back. That seemed to help him make up his mind. What did he have to lose? Going back to the twenty first century held absolutely no appeal and he was pretty sure that Jean needed him as much as he needed Jean. Yes, staying here was a gamble but at least he could start afresh with incredible advantages.

'Thank you Jack. I don't deserve any mercy I know that. Look for me in the history books.' And he clambered painfully over the side, into the waiting guard boat.

'Where will you put him monsieur?' Jack called down to the departing boat. The Harbour Master called back. 'In the town jail monsieur, where else? Until the Mayor returns in a few days.'

Jack smiled and waved at Paul as they rowed to shore but he didn't look back. He just stared ahead at the town.

Just then the volcano growled and belched grey smoke from a vent in one side.

'Right everyone, we really need to get away. Charles my friend, it would be nice to make proper farewells but as you know we need to get out of here.'

Melissa looked at her friends. 'Sorry Emma and Paul but I'm staying too.'

They both looked at her with astonishment but Emma quickly put two and two together. She stepped forward and gave Melissa a hug. 'I hope you'll be really happy together, you're really sure?'

Melissa nodded with tears on her cheeks. She looked at Charles with love in her eyes. 'We've spoken about this a great deal.' And then with an impish grin, 'how could I give up the chance of being a real Countess?'

The penny finally also dropped with Jack. 'Sorry to be so slow. Well done Charles,' and he shook his hand warmly. 'Best of luck. She'll be quite a handful you know.'

'Oh yes, I realise that but I wouldn't have it any other way. Now look, I'm sorry but we really must depart.'

'Yes, you get on board but one more minute,' and he shot below. In the storage locker he found several suitcases and into these started to dump anything he could find, all the first aid equipment and medicines, the few books still on board and all the remaining cosmetics. He rummaged in the galley and found the coffee that Charles had bought from the supermarket as well as loads of tins and sauces. Struggling up the ladder with the two cases, he called for a line and they were soon being hauled on board Andromeda where Charles and Melissa were looking down.

The two vessels parted company in the bay. Jack headed south west. They had time to get clear and that would put them in the best position to find the gate home. Andromeda sailed north, a course more suited to a square rigged sailing ship to make good speed in the south easterly breeze. Jack knew this meant they would both be well clear when the time arrived. The last sight Jack and Emma had of their two friends was of them standing waving from Andromeda's taffrail. Melissa was holding onto Charles tightly and he was standing proudly on the quarterdeck of his own ship once again.

'*Shame about that T shirt*' thought Jack.

Jack and Emma sailed in silence knowing they needed to get well clear of St Pierre. Neither spoke much, the trauma of the last two days and the sadness of losing their two close friends weighing on their minds. As soon as the sails were set, Jack went below and made them both the first decent cup of coffee they'd had for weeks.

'I see you didn't give it all away then,' said Emma, taking the cup appreciatively.

'No, I didn't but I do hope Charles and Melissa appreciate what they have.'

Do you mean the coffee or something else?' she replied smiling sadly.

'Both, I hope they're happy. They certainly seem made for each other. I guess we can look it up when we get home.'

Emma sighed and leaned against her man. 'Now are you going to explain why you were so keen to get Paul off the boat. You know what's about to happen. I know you and I can't believe you are that callous. So what do you know that I don't?'

'Hang on a second,' and he went below and found an out of date copy of the pilot book that he kept as a spare. Returning to the cockpit he passed it to Emma who read the indicated paragraph.

She frowned and then smiled and then started to laugh. 'Oh yes, you clever sod, well done, yes well done.'

Two hours later St Pierre and Mount Pelee were distant on the horizon. Jack looked at his watch and as the time ticked down they both looked back. Suddenly, the whole top of the mountain simply lifted into the air. Millions of tons of rock flew upwards followed by an enormous dirty grey pillar of smoke, rock and ash and it all happened in eerie silence. It was several minutes later before an angry violent rumbling reached them.

'Oh lord, all those poor people, why didn't they leave? It was obvious it was going to happen sometime.'

'Human nature I guess, no one wants to believe it will happen to them. When Montserrat exploded, they'd been given ten years notice but still did nothing and that was in an age of science and understanding. It was the same here I suppose. At least all that modern technology we left behind has been destroyed, so hopefully our history will be unaffected. Let's go home.'

Jack sailed a little further then turned the boat eastwards. As soon as she was steady on course and approaching the right longitude he went down to the galley and looked his shark in the eye. '*Come on you little bugger, do your stuff,*' he thought anxiously. The sun glinted in the emerald eyes and Jacaranda gave a lurch and a shudder. Emma cried out from the cockpit.

Jack shot back up. Emma was staring at Martinique, which was now at peace. Mount Pelee was green and dormant. Jack looked up and saw the contrails of a 747 taking holiday makers to their five star hotels. His satnav was locked on again. They were home. He hugged Emma with joy and she watched as a small white bone shark was flung into Jacaranda's foaming wake.

Later, as they sailed home Emma looked concernedly over at Jack. What are we going to say to the navy when we arrive? They're not going to be too happy.

'No, they're not but I think we made just a little too much publicity last time for them to try anything else.'

She chuckled and gave him a hug. 'And what about us? We kept telling all those French Aristos that we were man and wife you know.'

He turned and looked at her. 'I can take a hint and I'm not risking losing you again. Let's get married.'

She smiled, said nothing but gave him an even harder hug. Sometimes words were not necessary.

Postscript

Excerpt from the Caribbean pilot about the island of Martinique:

....the eruption caused devastation. St Pierre was totally destroyed along with many outlying towns and villages. In all, it is estimated that over 30,000 people perished. Only two people were known to have survived. One was on the periphery of the town, who was badly burned. The other was the sole occupant of the town jail, who was protected by its thick walls and poor ventilation.

Excerpt from the family history of the Hinchfield dynasty:

Charles, the Fifth Earl of Hinchfield returned from the Caribbean in the summer of 1785. He resigned his commission in the Royal Navy to take up the duties of the Earl after the death of his father and older brother....

During this time he married Melissa, a lady he met on the island of Antigua. Little is known of her before this time but as Countess she became well known as a philanthropist and sponsor of medical science. She died at the age of eighty three leaving four children.

Author's notes

My wife and I spent several happy years sailing our boat in this area and so hopefully I've got the geography right. For instance Marigot Bay was one of our favourite anchorages and is exactly as described, in the modern day at least. The story about hiding ships inside with palm fronds on their masts is well known amongst the locals.

The eruption of Mount Pelle happened but about a hundred years later and all but two people perished. The cover of the book shows the volcano today.

The final location of the Mayor's house is as exact as I can recall from my visit there. It is now a working rum distillery and museum. Mind you, my comments about how the French make rum are true and 'rum Agricole' as they call it, is not my favourite. No, let's be honest, its best use is for killing fish!

The historical element of the story is accurate. The Navigation Acts and Nelson's part in them all happened. He did end up being prosecuted but in the end he got off. He also met his wife there, unfortunately history tends to ignore her after a certain Mrs Hamilton appears on the scene. If you are ever in St Kitts a visit to Fort Brimstone is a must. It has been remarkably well restored.

Nelson's dockyard is a fascinating place and it was there that I got the idea for this book. It is so well preserved that one can easily imagine it in Nelson's time. One day, after a few beers, I was contemplating the view and wondered what would happen if a modern super yacht, like one of those currently moored there, went back in time. The seed was sown.

The Guadeloupe Guillotine

Jacaranda may have returned safely but questions are now going to be asked. In the sequel, they have to return and arrive just as the French Revolution arrives in the Islands:

Chapter 1

He sat on the stone bench with his head in his hands staring at the rough stone floor. He should have been worrying about the pain in his jaw and groin; about the loss of his friends and his real life. Maybe he should also be worrying about what would happen when the Mayor caught up with him. Hitting him over the head with the butt of a shotgun was probably not the best thing to have done bearing in mind he was the only benefactor he had. It didn't help that this prison cell belonged to the Mayor in the first place. All this was enough to burden a man down with worry, yet it was the least of his concerns.

No, what was scaring the daylights out of him now was the noise and vibration. Over recent weeks he had become so used to the monster grumbling in the mountain behind the town that it barely affected his consciousness. Over the last few hours it had steadily grown worse. So much so, that plaster was starting to rain down from the ceiling and he could feel shocks through the soles of his feet to accompany the increasingly loud and frequent explosions. He had tried to attract the attention of the guard, to ask to what was going on and beg to be let out but no one answered when he hammered at the heavy wooden door. For all he knew, everyone had already fled and he was alone in this tiny enclosed space, surrounded by emptiness.

He cursed the old friend who had put him here. He now understood why he had asked where he would be held. He clearly wanted rid of him and it was looking increasingly certain that he would be successful. However. it didn't look like revenge would be on the agenda.

Suddenly there was a crack so loud it hurt his ears. even inside his stone tomb. A second later a continuous rumbling sound was felt as much as heard and he knew that the top of the mountain must have finally blown out. No expert on volcanoes, he nevertheless knew what was likely to happen now. There had been enough television documentaries about the Pompeii eruption to inform the people of his time. The vast explosion would be accompanied by the ejection of superheated gasses and these would be forced down and out along the face of the mountain, right where the town was built. The Pyroclastic surge would generate temperatures of over a thousand degrees which would incinerate everything in its path.

He never espoused to believe in the Almighty, so he was surprised to find himself kneeling on the floor in terrified contrition, knowing what was about to hit him was compounded by his isolation both in time and space from his home. The last thing he held in his mind was a picture of Emma, the girl he was never able to obtain and that bastard Jack who had got him into this place to die. Another violent shock and the world went black.

Pain and light. Pain in his legs and back but light seeping through gummed up eyelids. Then noise, he couldn't understand it at first then he realised it was voices, human voices calling out. He tried to call back but could only manage a croak. With returning consciousness, he was able to make more sense of his surroundings. He could see a portion of sky above him where the ceiling had been and something was lying over his legs. He screamed in agony as he tried to move and realised his left arm was broken. Panting in reaction, he lay back again and almost passed out from the pain. Someone had heard his cry and there was renewed shouting somewhere in the distance. Suddenly, a face appeared above him.

'Hey, there is someone here! Someone alive, come and help,' the man called to others nearby. Suddenly he was surrounded by smiling faces and he felt the weight taken off his legs. The agony of returning circulation was nevertheless a relief, at least he could feel his legs.

'Alright monsieur, we have come to rescue you,' said the stranger. 'We will get you to help. You have been very lucky. We have found no other survivors.'

He smiled up at his rescuer, 'where am I, what happened?'

'St Pierre monsieur and the volcano finally erupted but surely you remember this?'

He smiled back suddenly realising how little he knew. 'No, I don't remember, everything is a blank.'

Just before he slipped back into unconsciousness, he realised he didn't even remember his name.

Printed in Great Britain
by Amazon